A SCENT OF SAGE

A Scent of Sage

by Linda Kavelin-Popov

A Scent of Sage

by Linda Kavelin-Popov

Publisher: Create Space, www.amazon.com

Cover photo: by author

Cover and book design: Dan Popov

LIBRARY OF CONGRESS CATALOGING-IN-PUBLICATION DATA

Popov, Linda Kavelin; Kavelin-Popov, Linda; romance; spirituality; wilderness; Hawaii; First Nations; virtues; Canadian Indians; residential schools.

ISBN-13: 978-1533313027

ISBN-10: 1533313024

Published in the United States

Dedication

This novel is dedicated to First Nations residential school survivors of Canada, who have taught me much about soul retrieval after generations of trauma, and the deep need to honor culture and tradition.

The indigenous world view of the oneness, harmony, and interconnectedness of all living things – people, plants, water, mountains, animals, sky and earth -- is reflected in the First Nations version of amen -- "all my relations."

Call to me and I will answer you and show you great and mighty things that you do not know. Jeremiah 33:3

I am going to venture that the man who sat on the ground in his tepee meditating on life and its meaning, accepting the kinship of all creatures, and acknowledging unity with the universe of things was infusing into his being the true essence of civilization. Luther Standing Bear

Kate leaned against the granite counter, gazing out the kitchen window as a rose-tinted dawn slowly illuminated the tiny back garden. White, yellow and wine-colored chrysanthemums, scarlet cyclamens, and blue hydrangeas, still buxom in early September, sparkled with dew. She sipped from a steaming mug of rich, dark Sumatra coffee, savoring the aroma and the heat.

Today's broadcast in less than two hours would be a turning point in Kate's career. She had endured long bone-chilling months of rain and snow living on the streets and hidden recesses of underground Toronto, her life in constant jeopardy as an undercover investigative journalist for CBC.

Convincing Stanley Levinson, her top boss at the network, to even allow her near this story was a feat in itself, much less to take the lead. And now, for the first time, she would appear live on The Fifth Estate, an award winning Canadian news magazine program known for its fearless investigations. The name of the show played on the fact that the media was often referred to as the Fourth Estate. The name highlighted a determination to go beyond everyday news into journalism with meaning and social impact. It was this very aspect of the corporate mission that allowed Kate to break the gender and age barriers by the youthful age of twenty-six. As a First Nations woman, she fit the profile of cutting edge journalistic practice, in which diversity was the new mantra.

To reach this spectacular move in her career, Kate had to overcome another obstacle – the intense degree of danger to which she would be exposed. She had to sign a pile of legal documents waiving liability on the part of Canadian Broadcasting Corporation in order to pursue the elusive Anthony Sabatano, one of Toronto's most notorious Mafioso. Today would be her crowning moment. She was about to debut on air as a journalist, presenting irrefutable evidence against Sabatano, who would be brought up on charges of dealing in drugs and prostitution.

The heart of the exposé was the trafficking of children. Kate had videos of young victims (their faces blanked out) tearfully recounting horrific stories, as well as countless audio clips, and incriminating documents gathered during the undercover operation.

Sabatano had a reputation as "the Teflon Don", with a battery of lawyers enabling him to slip through one loophole after another. Past attempts to prosecute him had failed. Despite being in protective custody, witnesses kept disappearing. Kate persuaded Stan and Artie Goldberg, director of the show, that going underground was the only way to collect hard evidence against Sabatano. Her most convincing argument was that she could use the racist assumptions about urban Natives to her advantage, posing as an addict. She lost weight, letting her luxuriant hair go un-brushed and stringy, and had needle marks hygienically inserted by a police surgeon. She didn't bathe for a week before she disappeared underground. The worst part of the ordeal for Kate was the cold. She had always hated cold.

As she sipped her morning coffee, scenes of the fourteen month ordeal rose in her mind -- hiding in squats in crumbling, unheated, boarded-up buildings, meeting homeless kids as young as nine recruited by Sabatano's organization to sell drugs, then hooking them on meth and cocaine, leading them into prostitution to support their addiction. While she had to turn a blind eye to what was going on for the bigger goal she was struggling for, she connected deeply with a couple of the kids. It broke her heart not to rescue them and literally take them home with her. She kept focusing on letting go of what was important in order to do what was most important. She had given more than a year of her life to the project, and it took every ounce of her self-discipline to keep going.

Under the pseudonym, Jane Charlie, she moved from addict to distributor to a position close to Sabatano. A tall, barrel-chested Native man named Bear, one of Sabatano's minions, took an interest in her and believed he was helping her to become sober.

He often said, "Janie you're better than this. You need to get clean and make some real dough." He made sure she ate well and put her up in a small apartment with central heating owned by the syndicate. The gloss returned to her hair and the coppery glow to her skin. He began to prep her to work directly with Sabatano, believing that to be worthy of the potential he saw in her. When she first met the Don, he said, "You clean up real good. Wanna work for me?" She had returned home to her row house just three days before, and spent long hours making a back-up plan for escape, then poring over her notes and recordings. She had no desire to be a martyr, and if anything should go wrong, she was ready to flee, although she had a fierce desire to stop Sabatano.

Kate pulled her thoughts away from memories of the children's suffering to focus on the fact that this show would move her from the research and writer's cubicle to her own office as an investigative journalist. She could finally fulfill her dream to make a difference to children who were helpless and hurt. It was her passion and her purpose.

Kate remembered her grandmother's advice to "call on Creator before you start anything important". She didn't have to be in the studio for several hours, so to quell her excitement laced with anxiety, she decided to spend a few moments in prayer. She smiled, thinking, *Gran would approve.* Memories of her Tlingit grandmother -- her life-saver -- always calmed her.

She took a basket and a long deerskin bundle from the pantry shelf, wrapped her thick plush robe tighter, and drew the old woven prayer shawl around her shoulders. Slipping into garden clogs placed neatly by the back door, she stepped out onto a winding slate path interspersed with pale moss and took a deep breath of the cool autumn air. She stood before a simple wooden table and laid out her sacred bundle -- a small jar of sage and a box of matches, a long, eagle wing feather, its shaft encased with tiny beads of red, white, yellow, and black, and an abalone shell in rainbow colors into which she poured a few pinches of sage, preparing to do a "smudge", a sacred purification and protection practice of her people, in which they cleansed spiritually by lighting the sage, then wafting its sweet smoke around their bodies by fanning the ember with the eagle feather.

Before she lit the sage and began chanting a prayer, she smiled as a familiar thought of gratitude arose. How blessed she was to have found this bower of quiet on the outskirts of bustling Toronto. In the tiny, remote village of Telegraph Creek, British Columbia, where she lived as a child, she could never have imagined this life as a television journalist and owner of a bay and gable row house on a fashionable, tree-lined street in North York. She raised her voice in an ancient song of protection, intoned by her people in northern British Columbia for 10,000 years. At that moment she had no idea how desperately she would need it.

Thirty minutes later, after a hot shower, Kate stood in her walk-in closet, scanning neat rows of black, grey and blue suits, and blouses in rich colors that complemented her violet eyes. She chose a dove gray suit with a pencil skirt, and a soft cobalt blue jersey blouse with graceful folds draped just below the neck, simple silver earrings and necklace and dark gray Manolo heels. She arranged her long, shining blue-black hair into a French twist. She preferred to do her own hair as she didn't trust the studio make-up artist to know what to do with it. He had run into her in the hall recently and touched her hair, saying, "Too thick, too silky." Then he added, "But such cheekbones! And your color is just divine. I'm only going to highlight you a little. With you, Bella, less is more."

Kate stood for a moment checking herself in the mirror. Her slim waist and ample curves were accented well by this outfit, yet it felt subdued and professional enough to legitimize the dramatic presentation she was about to make. Kate's thoughts kept returning to the months she had spent in the underworld of Toronto. She shuddered, uttering a quick prayer of gratitude to Creator for helping her to survive. She took a deep breath and left the house, a pearl gray London Fog raincoat over her arm, and slim briefcase with the notes she had studied the night before.

"You'll do just fine, Kate Mackenzie. Be yourself. Just be yourself. Don't try to be more than you are," she murmured, repeating the words she had so often heard Gran say. Yet, she had a feeling she had forgotten something important.

As she walked toward the silver Porsche Cayenne in her driveway, she pulled out her keys. An urgent thought came into her mind in Gran's voice, *Careful! Watch out!* She frowned and clicked the

6

keyless fob. She climbed into the driver's seat and hesitated a moment, wondering what she had forgotten and what exactly she should watch out for. It suddenly dawned on her she had left the protective bracelet Gran had given her on her vanity table. She had promised to wear it always. Not wanting to ignore her promise and Gran's warning, she stepped out of the car. A moment later, an ear-splitting explosion blew her sideways, and she landed hard on her side on the front lawn ten feet from the car which was now engulfed in black smoke and flames. Then she saw nothing.

2

Little Kate curled into a tight ball in the corner of her hiding place, shivering uncontrollably. She moaned at the pain in her side from Mama's kick. The shed was frigid, autumn temperatures in the Yukon already plunging with the threat of early snow. A cold wind blew across the surface of Teslin Lake, already beginning to form a coating of ice along the shore, a few feet from the sagging two-room log cabin where she and her mother, Charlene, lived. She could hear Mama stumbling around inside, howling curses at the empty bottle. Kate wore only a threadbare T-shirt and the soft fleece pajama bottom her grandmother had brought last Christmas.

Ma had wrapped her spare bottle in the pajama top to keep it from freezing and told Kate not to wear it anymore. "It's not all about you!" she screamed.

At age four, Kate knew she had to stay safe, but she couldn't think of anything but hiding. She prayed as her grandmother, Elvira, had taught her, that one of the village aunties would stop by for a visit as they often did, bringing food or a warm blanket.

Kate could hear a keening sound, getting louder and louder. She wondered if she was making that sound herself, and suddenly, she was no longer a child huddled in a small wooden out-building as in her memory dream, but in present time, lying in a yard beside the burning car, with a sharp pain in her side and blood seeping into the lawn. She could hear sirens in the distance. *Now is the time. Run!* she heard, in Gran's soft but urgent voice. She pushed through the pain to make her way around to a side door leading to the laundry room, fished for the small pouch holding her spare key buried in the soil under a juniper bush and made her way into the house.

She grabbed a clean facecloth folded on a shelf to staunch the blood. Not wanting to leave a trail, she stripped and put her clothes into a green garbage bag. She then looked at the wound now oozing blood and saw a small piece of shrapnel sticking out just below her ribcage. She pulled it out, pressed the cloth firmly, and then quickly cleaned the wound with peroxide. Her adrenaline was pumping so hard, she barely felt the sting. She covered it with a piece of gauze and a clean, folded towel, taping it on with duct tape from her backpack. She wiped up the blood with the used towel, stuffed it into the bag with her clothes, and placed the bag by the door. She quickly changed into the getaway clothes always hung by the door -- slim sweat pants, a dark blue turtle neck and black sweat shirt, light all-weather jacket, socks and running shoes, a battered baseball cap and dark glasses, and ran upstairs to grab her bracelet. She checked the makeshift bandage, and it wasn't wet. The bleeding seemed to have slowed.

She went into a small freezer and dug out a wad of cash wrapped in a deerskin cloth and plastic baggie, beneath packages of fish and frozen vegetables. She shoved the cash down into an inner zippered pouch of the backpack, which she had carefully packed with everything she would need for her planned escape. She swallowed three Tylenol tablets scooping water from the tap, not wanting to open the bottled water in her backpack. She checked for the cheap prepaid cell phone in her jacket pocket. In less than seven minutes, she was ready. She grabbed the garbage bag with her soiled clothes, locked the side door and limped into the back garden. She slipped through the shrubbery bordering a neighboring yard and made her way to the street behind hers moments before the fire truck and police cars screeched to a halt in front of her house.

She walked as swiftly and normally as she could toward the park, first veering into an alley beside a cafe. As she lifted her arm to toss the garbage bag into the dumpster, she winced with the pain, realizing she may have some broken ribs. She strolled into the park, trying not to limp, and called a taxi on her new cell phone. Then she rang her assistant at the television station. "Maggie, listen carefully. Please let Stan and Artie know I can't come in to do the interview today. I've been in an accident." "Oh, no, Kate! Are you okay? You've worked so hard. What…?" Before Maggie could ask the question, Kate hung up.

3

Kate leaned back in the taxi and pulled a folded sheaf of paper from the outer pocket of her back pack. There were three escape routes plotted by Google -- by plane, bus, or train to her destination of Squamish, a small west coast town just north of Vancouver, her first stop to safety, on the far side of Canada. Because of her injury, she chose to fly. But first she had to make her way to an airport in the States.

Within the hour, she was on a bus heading south to Buffalo International Airport in New York State. While waiting for the bus, she arranged flights to SeaTac in Seattle via O'Hare in Chicago. That evening, she was dozing on a train from Seattle to Vancouver. In the small toilet on board, she made another call.

"Yup?" answered a familiar, gravelly voice.

"Uncle Willy?"

"Katy, is that you?"

"Yes, uncle, and I need your help."

Kate nodded off on the forty-five minute drive north in Willy's comfortable vintage Lincoln Continental. She woke as they came to a stop, when his garage door clanged shut behind them. "Sorry, Uncle, it's been a rough day."

Willy patted her knee, "No worries, little one. I'm patient. Tomorrow, I want the whole story. Tonight, we'll just have a visit with Doris Brokenleg."

"How did you...?"

"You keep leaning to the right, taking pressure off of whatever is troubling your side. And I noticed the sideways hug you gave instead of our usual bear hug."

"Brokenleg is a healer? You're kidding."

"No word of a lie. She gets a lot of flak for that."

Doris came within minutes of Willy ringing her, carrying a large backpack full of her "potions". She wore clean jeans and a ribbon shirt over them, a long braid hanging down her back. "Girl, you are blessed to be alive," Doris said. "If that piece of metal had gone any deeper, it would have pierced your liver. The wound is shallow and the hurt you feel is from bruising. You may have a cracked rib or two but they will mend. Now, before I start, let's give thanks to Creator."

Kate was tucked up into a luxuriantly plump bed, covered with old quilts and soon slid deep into sleep. Remembering little Kate's trauma with her mother when she was a small girl, living in that freezing shack at the lake, Willy shook his head. He knew how she hated to be cold. She awoke to the aroma of Uncle's strong "camp coffee" and heard bacon and eggs sizzling in a pan. She stretched and moaned, feeling the herb-soaked moss taped to her side and the bandage wrapped tightly around her ribs. She put two of Doris's homeopathic Arnica tablets underneath her tongue and immediately noticed the pain easing.

She looked small in Willy's old Indian blanket robe which he had laid out for her across the foot of the bed. It was soft and smelled of Tide and wood smoke. As she gingerly sat down at the Formica kitchen table, Kate suddenly realized she was famished. After saying Grace, Willy ate quietly, waiting for her to speak. "You look good, Uncle. So, how is it being chief of the Squamish Nation?"

"Well, I tell ya, girlie, there's a target on my back, and arrows sticking out of it. That's how I know my people are behind me." She laughed and gasped. Not smart until her ribs healed a bit more. "Enough about me. When you finish, come on into the front room and sit in my resting chair," he said. He perched on the couch, elbows on his thighs, sipping from his mug. "I'm listenin'."

Kate told him of the months of undercover work tracking the labyrinth of connections in the Toronto drug underworld. She told him how she ate practically nothing to lose fifteen pounds, posed as a disheveled heroin addict, then became a dealer and gradually regained her looks in order to join the inner circle of assistants to Sabatano. She used a micro-camera and other tiny high tech tools to gather incriminating evidence from his computer and from porn films she had discovered in his office.

The tears Kate had been holding back seeped down her cheeks. "I worked so hard for it, Uncle. The whole time I was at UVic and Harvard, this was my dream. I wanted to do something to make a difference. I wanted to be a journalist who told the hard truths, to stop the bad guys from hurting innocent kids. And all those months of living on the street, watching those kids get so sick and abused…" Kate finally let the sobs come. Willy listened and moved beside her, placing his hand gently on her back.

"It will come right," he said when she finished. He raised his cup. "Here's to you, Cridhe, woman of courage. You have a strong heart." Kate smiled at the Gaelic nickname her Scottish father, Hiram Mackenzie had given her, pronounced with Willy's Tahltan accent.

Kate was one of the first students in the Indigenous Studies program at the University of Victoria in British Columbia, entering First Nations House at eighteen. She was then selected for Harvard's one year graduate Justice Institute. Being an advocate for justice was her legacy -- a passion which came out of the painful effect on her and her family of the residential school experiences of her grandmother Elvira Johns and her mother Charlene. A multi-million dollar trust was set up for her by her father's Scottish family, who owned a large Orkney Island conglomerate that had partnered with McCain's, the frozen food magnates in Canada. One of the conditions was that until she was twenty-one, she had the freedom to spend to the max on education alone. Her living allowance was modest but adequate. Now twenty-six, she had much greater access to the trust fund. Her investment in the row house in an exclusive neighborhood in North York met with enthusiastic approval by the lawyers administering her trust.

"Now we have to keep you safe," said Uncle Willy. "Those drug lords are smart. Don't tell me your plan, but please let me know how you are when you get there. What do you need?"

"For starters, I need 'Beater'."

The battered old vehicle was legendary within the family. Willy kept the engine of the aging brown Ford pick-up in immaculate and souped-up shape, but the exterior was all "dust and rust", the perfect vehicle for someone who wanted to disappear.

By noon, Kate was wending her way north on Highway 99, past Whistler through Pemberton and Lillooet. She breathed in the sweet air and felt her heart open to the familiar beauty. Lush ferns and small waterfalls gushed from the hills hugging the road, and sudden vistas of pine forest and snow-capped mountains opened out to the east, with crystalline, shimmering lakes to the west, the amethyst stalks of late blooming fireweed along the verge. She found herself humming and then singing out loud to the Bonnie Raitt CD she found in the plastic box behind the seat. "I can't make you love me if you don't…just hold me close, don't patronize…" *Why the heck am I feeling happy*? she wondered. *Oh. Going home.* She and Willy always liked the same music -- an eclectic blend of Robby Robertson, Shania Twain, Hank Williams, Willy Nelson, Nelly Furtado, KD Lang, Johnny Cash, Quincy Jones, the smooth jazz of Vancouver's own diva, Diana Krall and crooner, Michael Bublé.

Kate's ambitious goals required her to live in a city, but spiritually, she felt suffocated by the noise, the dirt, the crowds, and the hurry. It was the beauty of "supernatural BC" with its vast forests and soaring, snow-capped mountains that fed her soul. She stopped at one of the sparkling sun-lit lakes below the road, in which a perfect mirror-like image of mountains rising straight up from the shore glistened in the water. The quaking aspens were already beginning to turn gold, bright threads amongst the deep green firs and pines. She breathed in the heady scent of lake water and sun-sweetened pine.

Kate had three days of driving ahead of her, maybe four, to get to her grandmother Elvira's remote cabin on Atlin Lake in Northern British Columbia, where she had spent the happy – and safe -- summers of her childhood since Gran had taken her in as a bruised, malnourished five year old. Gran always insisted that Kate keep the details secret of where she had been raised, including the tiny village of Telegraph Creek, as much to protect its small population of elders and young families as for some mysterious reason Gran would never tell her. "One day you'll understand," she had said.

Kate obeyed, trusting her grandmother's wisdom. In the information she provided for university and job applications, she gave Chemainus on Vancouver Island as her home town, which had been true for a brief while, when she had to stay with Aunt Esther to heal from injuries her mother had inflicted during one of her drunken tirades. It was the last time her mother had ever hurt her, the last time she had hurt anyone but herself.

Kate took more Arnica, and drank some of the special bittersweet juice Doris Brokenleg had prepared for her. Fresh lemon and pineapple juice laced with willow bark for pain and inflammation. *Vitamin C and Indian medicine,* she thought, smiling, grateful to have had some time with her people. As the truck took her further toward the Cassiar Highway, now re-named Dease Lake Road, she looked for the deep red Indian Paint Brush and white Shasta daisies that usually grew in profusion along the highway, but few still bloomed as summer weather shifted to Fall.

She wondered whether the lake would be too windy and wild to make the one hour trip in Gran's "scow" as she called the Lund outboard she kept moored at the Atlin dock. She wondered how the weather would be at the isolated cabin at this time of year, when she and Gran usually packed up to winter back in Telegraph Creek, returning to Atlin Lake each spring.

Kate often remembered the trip she and Gran made to the cabin each year, gliding over the emerald water that lightened to turquoise closer to the glaciers. She always searched the peaks of Theresa and

17

Atlin Mountain for tiny white dots. Gran had taught her that if there was no movement, they were probably bits of snow. If Kate noticed any motion, she raised her arm, pointing, and Gran would wink, their sign for spotting a family of shaggy, snow-white mountain sheep.

She remembered the first time Gran decided she was old enough to climb, at the age of ten, when they were making their way up to a high cliff above the Yukon River rushing and tumbling far below, where Gran said they could view the Llewellyn glacier. Kate's heart was pounding, and as they neared the top, she was afraid, but she didn't want to stop. At one point when they had almost made it to the place Gran had described, Kate halted suddenly, unable to see a way up. A huge granite out-cropping loomed in her way.

"Pray, Kate," Gran had yelled from below, "Trust!"

Kate closed her eyes and asked Creator for trust. Suddenly, she just darted forward, finding a narrow path to the side of the boulder. When she scrambled to the top, she froze and Gran stopped just behind her. A stately grandfather mountain sheep stood completely still on a ledge, gazing out, wind ruffling his long white coat and beard, his short pointed horns gleaming in the sun. They stared into each other's eyes for a long moment before he turned and leapt effortlessly onto the crags above.

"Gran, did you see?" she asked, her cheeks flushed, as Gran came up behind her.

"Aren't we lucky?" Gran said. After making their way back to the camp they had set up that morning near the lakeshore, they sat by a small driftwood fire, roasting fresh-caught grayling on pointed sticks Kate had cleaned and sharpened with her knife. After dinner, the night sky darkened enough to see the stars. Kate felt awe deep in her belly as she lay mesmerized beneath the blanket of sparkling, winking diamonds, clustering in dense layers along the Milky Way.

Suddenly, Gran broke their long, companionable silence. "Remember the sacred moment you had today, Kate. Creator gave you a gift."

"What does it mean, Gran?"

Gran was silent for a few moments. Then she said, "What does your heart tell you, Katy?"

Kate took a deep breath, "To stand strong."

Gran just smiled and stroked Kate's hair. Kate looked up through the pines at the mass of stars. *I will never forget this day*, she thought to herself.

4

Kate veered off at the Dease Lake junction and parked in front of the Do Drop Inn, which had a small restaurant, six cabins and a small, long-standing bakery. *That's the fifth name I know of*, she thought to herself, The Snack Shack and Roadkill Café, among them. For more than twenty years, the place was beloved by locals for Charlie Charlie's and his wife Ethel's excellent bakery, which still had its dilapidated old sign out front, "Get your buns in here or we'll both starve." Kate sat down to a bowl of hearty mulligatawny soup, a huge fluffy yeast roll, and a cup of strong coffee. She took several of Ethel's moist brownies to go as a gift for her next stop.

Feeling restored, she continued on the unpaved dirt and gravel Dease Lake Road toward Telegraph Creek. Suddenly, a red fox with a long, silver-tipped tail, rushed out of the bush, and stared into her eyes. Although the truck kept moving, time seemed suspended. Gran taught her that animal "visits" brought special messages, and Kate took in the moment deeply. *Another gift*, she thought, promising herself to pray its meaning later. The old truck efficiently maneuvered the steep hairpin turns down into the valley, a sheer black rock cliff rising high above the bubbling rapids of the Stikene

River on the far side of the canyon below. She had called Auntie Rose from Willy's.

"You're always welcome, Katy girl. Do you even need to ask?"

She arrived to find a circle of elders sipping her Aunt's signature rose hip tea, and grinning up at her. "Welcome home, honey. How long you stayin'?"

"Just a day this time," Kate said as she removed her down jacket and back pack. She dutifully kissed each soft, wrinkled cheek and then went to the kitchen to plate up the brownies. She sat, gratefully sipping from a steaming cup.

Auntie Rose then announced, "Okay ladies, thanks for helping me welcome Katy home. Now it's time to skedaddle. Katy has something she has to do."

Knowing looks passed among them and gradually they filed out. "You take care now, dearie."

Kate looked quizzically toward her aunt.

"You'll see. Go freshen up and then go out to the fishing cabin. Someone is waiting for you. And thanks for the Death by Chocolate brownies, honey. They're the best. We'll have some after supper later. Now scoot."

Kate's adrenalin took a sudden spike. "What? Who, Auntie? Do you know them?" The memory of the explosion pierced her awareness, eroding the soothing effect of the long drive to familiar ground.

"Have faith, Katy," said her aunt. "I do know him. He's here to help."

Kate had learned early to abide by the elders' decisions, sensing that whatever they arranged was for her benefit. As her heart rate began to calm, she still felt some trepidation, not knowing who or what was waiting for her.

5

Kate noticed the salmon drying on racks outside the fishing cabin and a late model Nissan truck parked beside it. She called out, "Hello, the cabin." A deep voice called back, "Come." The cabin was dim, except for the glow of the crackling fire in the wood stove. She stood just inside the door waiting for her vision to adjust. A tall, broad-shouldered man about her age stood up to greet her. He wore slim jeans and a cable knit sweater. He had high cheekbones, full lips, and his eyes were dark chocolate pools. His long black hair was held back by a deerskin thong. He looked remotely familiar.

Kate felt herself trembling. He held out his hand and Kate hesitated, then took it. It was like touching an electric fence. "Jason Red Deer," he said.

"Pardon?"

"My name. And you are Kate Mackenzie," as if she didn't know. She felt oddly offended. "Have a seat. I'll get you some tea." She sat gingerly on the bench across from his mug at a small rough wooden table covered by yellow oil cloth.

"Do I know you?" she asked. He didn't answer, but came back with a cup of Willow Bark tea, laced with honey. "How did you know?" she asked.

"You know the speed of the Tahltan tom-tom system," he said. "So, how are you feeling? Any remaining soreness? I'd like to have a look if you…"

Kate cut him off, "What are you, a doctor?"

He smiled. "Well, they call me a healer."

"No thanks. I'm fine," she said, wondering what in the world her aunt was thinking when she sent her out to this arrogant fellow.

"Fair enough," Jason said. "What I would like to offer is a listening ear. Sometimes, when we are going through a challenging time…"

"No thanks, I *said* I'm fine. I just need to get going." She took a sip of her tea and started to get up.

"There is one thing I ask of you," he said in a commanding tone. "Are you willing to take a few hours for a Vision Quest…to guide you?"

Kate sat back down. "Well, that *is* why I came here. How did you…?"

The memory hit her suddenly – a waking dream during her prayer time when she found herself flashing through space, and had stood beside him on the high black cliffs gazing down at the Stikine River.

The experience had been incredibly vivid. He was chanting and held a stick of smoking sage. "You were in my vision," she said.

"Yes, Kate, you were with me. That's why you needed to come here physically. There's something for you here."

Although her thoughts were swirling, she agreed to go to that spot with him to seek Creator's help. Lord knows she had little idea of what she was doing other than fleeing to safety much farther north at Gran's Atlin Lake cabin.

"Now you need to sleep. We'll go at dawn."

Kate felt the stiffness in her sore body and knew sleep was her only choice, but her stomach was achingly empty.

"Have some of Auntie's moose stew, and you'll sleep well." Again, she was disconcerted by how he seemed to read her thoughts almost before they formed. "Come to the cabin about five, we'll have breakfast, then we'll go." She didn't argue, but wondered to herself, *who died and made* you *king?*

She walked stiffly back to the house, feeling disoriented. This was all going too fast. She found Aunt Rose in the kitchen, humming to herself and stirring a fragrant stew. "There's fresh bannock, honey. Help yourself."

Kate bit into the tender, chewy bread and moaned blissfully. "Auntie, who *is* that man? *What* is he? Why…"

25

"Katy girl, some things you just have to let go and trust. You know that is one of your life lessons, for good reason. And he is one you can trust, believe me. Just be grateful he came all this way to help you."

"Hrrrmph." Kate murmured.

"You sound just like your daddy when you make that Scottish sound," Aunt Rose said, laughing.

The next morning, Kate's footsteps crunched through the crisp, frozen grass as she made her way to the small cabin. The cold air was laced with delicious aromas of bacon and coffee. *I could eat a horse,* she thought. There were two steaming cups at her place, one of healing tea and the other of coffee, rich with cream. He stood at the stove, preparing pancakes, bacon and fried eggs, his hair a shining mane down his back. He flicked it once as a strand crept over his shoulder, light from the fire glinting over it -- so black it was almost blue, like Kate's. She felt a quiver deep in her body and realized she was powerfully drawn to him. *Hol-ee,* she thought to herself, pronouncing the word in her mind like Gran did. *Get a hold of yourself. You're running for your life, not looking for a date!*

His voice startled her. "A Vision quest is deep work. You need some calories." He shoveled the hot, fragrant food onto her plate and sat down across from her. He smiled a slow, full smile, like light coming out from behind a cloud, and for the first time, she returned it.

As they sat eating, he said, "I have a few sacred things I'll be bringing. Is there anything you want to have with you?" Kate had slipped her prayer shawl into her backpack before leaving Toronto. She nodded.

"This is really good. Thanks," she said. He gave that slow smile again, looking into her eyes as if he could read her thoughts. *God forbid*, she thought. She had to stare at her food to keep from gazing back, to resist the pull of those dark, thick-lashed eyes.

She followed him in Unc's truck across a small wooden bridge spanning the roiling river, to the base of the sheer black cliff. They wound upward on a hard-packed dirt road and parked beside the plateau at the top. Kate climbed out and they walked to the edge. "Oh, my God," she said. "We *were* here… together."

"Yes, Kate, that's why I knew I had to come down from Whitehorse to be here when you arrived."

"You're from Whitehorse?" she asked.

"Never mind that now. I'll set things up. Please stand over here, and let the quiet come. Then we'll see what Creator has to say to you."

She watched in silence as he spread a faded cloth in muted blues and reds on a large flat rock. He laid out an eagle feather, a shell, a long bundle of sage wrapped in red string, and matches. Then, slowly and gently he lifted from his basket a well-wrapped object large enough that he had to use both hands.

27

"I only bring this out when great power is needed. It has been with me a long time," he said softly. It was as if the wind had whispered. Fold by fold, he unwrapped the eagle's egg and nested it reverently in its wrappings. The egg was cream colored and slightly mottled. Perfect and whole. He lit the sage stick and began to chant, circling Kate slowly, smudging her. She raised her arms and closed her eyes, giving herself up to the rhythmic sound and to the pungent aroma enveloping her. Then Jason stood still and began to pray, at first in Tlingit, then a different language she had never heard before, all vowels. Then silently. Time felt suspended. After what seemed like only a few minutes, she felt the throbbing soreness leave her body and opened her eyes. He was standing quietly watching her.

"I...I don't hurt anymore," she said. "Was there a message...when you prayed?"

"Creator has a sense of humor with you," he laughed. "Just one phrase, and I don't know what it means – 'Catch the rabbit.' You'll need to pray on that one."

It was Kate's turn to laugh, which surprised both of them. "Oh, I know something about it," she said, remembering her fox of the night before.

"Now you need to be alone, Kate, to meditate. Take a few hours. As you know, most vision quests are over a period of days, but you don't have the time for that. This will be enough for now. You'll get away at the right time. Notice the animals, as they are often the messengers. There is a grandfather eagle around here. Watch for him. Listen with your heart, and open to what comes. Be still if you feel you need to be still, and move if your body wants to move. If you want, I can come back."

"No, I'll just go afterwards," she said. "But, thank you for all this. You've been very kind." She felt a wrenching melancholy about leaving him. *I don't even know him*, she thought.

"I'll see you again, Lady Kate," he said, using the nickname her father had given her.

She was thrown back in time to memories of her tall, handsome Scottish father, Hiram Mackenzie, who would swing her around whenever he visited. The visits stopped when she was nine. She learned from Gran that he had been killed by an out of control semi on an icy prairie highway on his way back to New Brunswick, a maritime province in Eastern Canada.

Hiram had traveled to British Columbia as a representative of McCains, the Canadian partner to Mackenzie Enterprises in Scotland. They had lured him to Canada with a position in their company and the freedom from his father's restrictions he had always craved.

When Hiram was negotiating in Vancouver with the BC First Nations Fisheries Council for the purchase of salmon, the chairman invited him to a pot latch in Squamish. "Come see how the other half lives," he joked. It was there that Hiram met Kate's mother

Charlene. She was the most beautiful woman he had ever seen. Having had a bit to drink, she was very flirtatious, and he found her irresistible. A few months later, he flew back to BC from New Brunswick, and they were married.

Kate could barely remember the times they spent together as a family. Her memories were segmented into the lonely, scary times with her mother when her Dad was on the road, and the special times when they would go to a pot latch or visit her Gran together. Her mother was always quiet and jittery. Kate could tell she was suffering in her temporary sobriety. When she was four, her mother spirited her away to Teslin, 170 kilometers and about two hours south of Whitehorse, Yukon on the Alaska Highway. They stayed in a shabby cabin where her worst nightmares began. Her father finally found them and moved her to Aunt Esther's in Chemainus, south near Victoria. Five years later, he was killed.

"How did you...?" By the time she surfaced from the memory, Jason had packed up his things, and his truck was gone.

6

Kate stood silently for a moment, looking down at the bubbling creek, its water high at this time of year with the summer glacial melt. She knew that she needed to go to the water as the first step of her quest. She climbed back into the old Ford and bumped her way slowly down into the valley below. She parked behind a stand of pines, now instinctively seeking to hide, she realized. A long meadow stretched out between the high winding road down from Telegraph Creek Road on one side and the sheer black cliffs on the other, with the water flowing just below them.

She had memorized words on mindfulness from Vietnamese Zen Master Thich Nhat Hanh, whose writings had been central to her masters' thesis at Harvard on "Spirituality and Indigenous Rights."

"When we walk like we are running, we print anxiety and sorrow on the earth. We have to walk in a way that we only print peace and serenity on the earth...

"Be aware of the contact between your feet and the earth. Walk as if you are kissing the earth with your feet."

These words echoed the reminder Gran repeated each time they set out from the Atlin Lake cabin on one of their adventures, to *"walk* gently upon the breast of Mother Earth. It is a privilege and a blessing."

As she entered walking meditation, she slowly, carefully, placed one foot in front of the other, feeling the ground through her moccasins. She breathed deeply in and out, three breaths for every step, feeling the full length of each foot as it touched the earth. She felt a tenderness rising through the soles of her feet. As she made her way toward the water, she was conscious of the sound of it bubbling over stones as it rushed onward. She knew what she had to do.

Kate slowly stripped and laid her clothes neatly on the grass. The early autumn sun warmed her skin. She looked for five stones and placed the largest one in the center with the rest in a circle. Raising her arms to the sky, she felt the medicine wheel around her, and stood beside the stone in the center, representing Wakan-Tanka, the Creator of all life. She reflected on its Butterfly totem bringing transformation. She prayed as she turned to face each of the four directions, focusing on the totem her people believed to represent each direction: east, Eagle, west, Bear, south, Coyote, and north, Wolf. She invited each to send her their special powers: spiritual wisdom and awareness of Eagle, solitude and protection of Bear, Coyote for humor and humility, and Wolf for feminine moon energy and unity with one's familiars.

Then she walked to the edge of the water for the purification ritual an elder had taught her during her first vision quest. She entered the icy water, which was waste high, and pushed toward a large rock

32

jutting from the center of the stream. She climbed up swiftly, and sat for a moment holding her knees, took a deep breath, and slid into the frigid water, immersing completely. She emerged shivering, water streaming from her body. Standing firm with her legs wide, she recited the prayer Gran had taught her as a child, the one she said every night. "Creator, guide me, protect me, purify my heart. Teach me the way that is straight. Make safe the path, that I may always walk in Your ways. All my relations."

When Gran first brought her to the remote cabin on Atlin Lake, at age six, this nightly prayer was the only thing that calmed her terrors, and finally banished the nightmares from which she awoke screaming for many nights. In those dark dreams, she felt her mother's blows and kicks, her feet bleeding from broken glass as she tried to run. And the cold, the icy cold that sliced into her bones and shook her mercilessly. It was months before she could stand to be touched. If Gran casually reached out a hand to smooth her hair out of her eyes, Kate flinched, putting her thin little arms up over her face for protection. Gran just gently shook her head and whispered, "Poor child".

One day Kate climbed into her grandmother's lap and began to cry. Gran rocked her and murmured, "Yes, you cry those healing tears, little one. It's time."

Kate waded back to the grassy bank and lay down, pulling her fleece over her body, gradually feeling the gentle lift of beaded water evaporating in the warmth of the sun. She lay there for a while listening to the river burble. She dressed and stood, looking around, preparing herself for the next step.

Now it's time for my spirit walk, she thought. She recounted the order of virtues in the vision quest: purity through immersion in water, discernment by opening to meditation, courage to face life's challenges, and certitude – a sense of certainty about the path ahead.

She entered the meditation of the spirit walk by letting her mind become open and relaxed, yet alert for an animal or plant, a cloud, whatever drew her attention. In her mind she held the question lightly, "with open palms", Thich Nhat Han would say. "What now, Creator?" She walked slowly, mindfully, toward the hillside on the other side of the valley, and nestled herself into a shallow hollow. She leaned back as if resting on the breast of Mother Earth. She became very still, emptying her mind of thought, opening to discernment.

Fear began to bubble up. Scenes of violence including the explosion in Toronto, rose up in her mind. She remembered to let an unwanted thought come and then let it go, like a leaf passing by on a stream, releasing it to Creator. Suddenly she heard the sound of powerful wings whipping the air as a large eagle came to land on a branch jutting out from the cliff across from her. She felt as if he was training his power toward her. Somehow she knew that he was one of her spirit guides, sent to watch over her. She waited with her question.

She recalled Jason's words "Catch the rabbit" and instantly the fox she had encountered the afternoon before came into her mind, as clearly as if it stood before her. Again its piercing eyes looked into hers as if to say, "Watch this."

Aloud Kate said, "What is your message for me?"

In her mind's eye, the fox turned, swishing its luxuriant tail, and slowly moved into high grasses where it crouched and remained quiet. She noticed how its soft russet colors blended with the meadow. *Disguise yourself,* were the first words of the message. She noticed the fox's patient stillness, and at the same time, its acute alertness. It was on the hunt, yet it didn't run around wildly searching for prey – the thought came, *Remain focused.* Then in her vision, a rabbit hopped out of the bush. The fox waited, waited, until the rabbit came nearer, and suddenly leapt high in the air and pounced. It looked once more into her eyes and the words, *contemplative vigilance* came to her. *What a good description of discernment*, she thought.

A great calm settled over her and she looked up to see the eagle lift off. She then opened herself to the message about courage. The words of the Prophet Isaiah came to her: *Those who trust in the LORD shall renew their strength. They shall mount up on wings as eagles; they shall run and not grow weary, they shall walk and not faint.* She reflected that trust was the portal to courage for her -- trust in Creator to guide her and protect her.

35

She asked her final question – *What path do I take? Where do you want me to be?* Had she made a wise choice? Was she truly meant to disappear in the wilds of Atlin Lake? Certitude came swiftly as the tiny cabin appeared in her mind with startling clarity.

7

Kate was grateful to be driving Unc's old truck rather than her Porsch as the vehicle lumbered its way over yet another pot hole on the Alaska Highway. As she neared the site of the residential school where her mother, Charlene, had felt imprisoned, she surrounded herself with protective light as Gran had taught her. She felt a stirring of compassion for her mother, who had been kidnapped and forced to live in the residential school as a child, while dulling the stories and memories of Charlene's abuses toward her, keeping them at a distance within herself for fear that she would be swept back into the pain of the past.

She slowed the truck and pulled to the side of the road across from the crumbling brick hulk – the government funded, Catholic residential school where the roots of family pain and grief had begun -- the site of the "lost generation". A memory surfaced of her beautiful mother, now hazy with the passing years, in one of her rare forays into sobriety. Charlene Johns had talked about the cruelties and the fear, the other children weeping in their beds. She had often recounted her courageous trek through the snow, back to Telegraph Creek.

Charlene was taken off to Mother of Mercy Residential School at age five. She was ripped out of her mother Elvira's arms and thrown into the bed of a truck. As she screamed, cried and held her arms out to her mother, she saw her own terror mirrored on Elvira's face.

The truck bumpily wound its way up the Alaska Highway to the school, stopping once more at another village to corral other children. When the rag tag group arrived at the stark brick building, exhausted from being jostled in the truck bed, they were herded into a small building with concrete floors and a huge drain in the center of the room.

They ordered the children to strip naked, and lined them up. This was the first humiliation for Charlene, who was very modest and always dressed and undressed behind a hanging blanket at home. They roughly chopped off her waist-length hair into a blunt bowl shape, and sprayed her and the others down with cold water and something that smelled harshly chemical.

A nun dressed in a scary black cassock, standing over the group said, "That should help get rid of your nastiness."

Charlene cried bitterly and asked over and over, "What did I do?" in her Tlingit language.

"Stop that caterwauling!" shouted a short, plump nun, her jowls pressed by the sides of her wimple. "Speak English, you little savage." Charlene could barely understand her strange words and kept crying. Then the nun slapped her and hissed, "Shh!" She stopped and didn't say another word for many days.

Charlene learned that complaining was forbidden. When she told about the weevils in her porridge, even very politely, she was made to kneel for hours on salt spread on the stone floor of the chapel. She learned early that the only way to avoid the wrath of the nuns was to become invisible, to keep quiet, not to stand out in class, to act like a "dumb Indian". When she heard another child crying in the frigid, cavernous dormitory in which they all slept, she would climb into her bed to rock and shush her. Silence was their only protection.

She didn't see her parents again for five years, until the children were granted a summer leave at home with their families. By then, she had become a silent, rail thin, suspicious ten year old. Once back in her home village of Telegraph Creek, it took two weeks for her to feel comfortable when her parents touched her. Little by little, she began to feel at home, as she swam in the river with her cousins, sat around the campfire listening to stories of the "old days" her grandfather told, and blueberry-picking with the large, extended family of aunties, uncles and cousins.

When the truck came for her in late August, Elvira's tears blended with Charlene's. She never forgot the wrenching ache at once again being torn from her mother's arms. It was three years until she saw her mother's face again.

At fifteen, Charlene sensed she was a beauty. The priest in charge of Mother of Mercy often told her so. More and more often, he invited her into his private office, asking her to read aloud to him from one of the catechism books. He would pace around, coming up close behind her, stroking her head or putting a hand on her shoulder. One day, he said, "You're my little beauty," reaching out his hand. The other hand was fiddling with something beneath his robe. His breath had quickened, and beads of perspiration appeared on his forehead.

Charlene quickly stood and said, "Father, may I please go to the washroom?"

"You can wait," he growled, frowning.

She whispered, "It's my curse time."

"Oh, go then."

That night, Charlene made her decision. She crept into the linen closet and took a sheet, wrapping it in a small, torn blanket used for polishing floors. She knew they would never expect her to try leaving at this time of year. Snow was thick, and temperatures were below zero. She crept to the cloak room at two AM, holding her bundle like a baby, grabbed some boots and a thick cape worn by one of the nuns, and slipped out into the darkness.

Fortunately, she found a pair of wool gloves in the pocket. She made her way down the long driveway, and squeezed through an opening in the fence she and others had made earlier. She had to plow through crusted snow up to her thighs to reach the highway and began walking south on the smooth, ploughed snow-packed road. As a light snow began to swirl around her, she started to shiver. She kept her head lowered over her bundle.

Charlene knew her mother's village of Telegraph Creek, some seventy kilometers away, was much too far for her to walk, but desperately hoped a semi would be going that way. She listened for them every night for the past month, and noticed they often rumbled by in the early morning hours.

She figured that no one would allow a helpless mother holding a baby to continue walking in the cold. It was an unspoken law in winter always to stop for someone who was walking. Within an hour, she was numb and shaking uncontrollably. Her feet were damp and freezing despite the long socks she wore and the nun's boots, which barely fit her.

Suddenly, the high beams of a transport truck glared behind her. She turned and faced the truck, waving one arm. The driver slowly applied the screeching air brakes, not wanting to slide on the hard, compacted snow of the plowed road. She hoped it was far enough from the school that no one would hear. The driver opened the passenger door and held out a hand. Charlene climbed into the warm cab.

"What are you doing out here at this time of night, little lady?" the burly driver asked her.

"My baby is sick and I have to get him home."

"Where you from?" She told him that the doctor in Telegraph Creek knew her son's condition and would be there to help.

"I'm driving right by the Dease Lake crossroads but I have to let you off there. There's no way this rig will make it down the hairpin turns to your village. And I have a deadline to meet, too." She nodded and thanked him. He poured her a cup of sweet, milky coffee laced with bourbon. "This'll warm your bones." Nothing had ever tasted so good.

After the semi driver dropped her off at the Roadkill Café, she knocked on the manager's door. A man disheveled from sleep finally opened the door, yelling, "Hold yer horses! What in God's name? Who? Come in. Come in."

Charlene explained to Pete, the owner, that she had escaped from Mother of Mercy school, needed to get home, but couldn't make it at night. He took pity on her, knowing she had no money, and allowed her to stay the night in one of the guest cabins. She shook and shivered, as much from fear as cold, and he immediately chucked some logs into the wood stove and had a fire going within a few minutes. She thanked him shyly, and he brought her some toast with peanut butter and a cup of sweet tea.

He told her, "Don't worry, girl, I'll take you back to your mama in the morning." Peter was a good Catholic, ashamed of what was happening to the children from the villages but felt helpless to change it. This kindness to Charlene was the least, and the most, he could do.

Charlene knew that her mother, Elvira, had had a very different experience in the residential school on Vancouver Island. A kindly young nun had taken an interest in the bright six year old and had privately educated her in the evenings, preparing her for a university education.

Sister Mary Joseph managed to find grants and scholarships to send Elvira to McGill for a degree in social work. Elvira was committed to using her advantages to serve her people. She returned to her village in Telegraph Creek, and set up a women's healing circle as well as an Alcoholics Anonymous program. She went off to Whitehorse for a while to expand the programs there under the Yukon Territorial Government, and met a recovering alcoholic named Jedediah Johns, a handsome Tlingit man with chiseled features and penetrating hazel eyes.

Elvira and Jed first met at a pow-wow in Whitehorse attended by members of her village. Elly noticed the good looking Indian around the drum with the other men and could decipher his high wailing chant from the other voices. She closed her eyes and felt a tremor through her core. It felt as if her heart was expanding to fill her chest. The thought came unbidden, *this is the man I will marry*.

She had been so purposefully focused at university and then back in the village, she hardly had time to think about a personal relationship. When the prayer was over, Jed raised his head and his eyes met hers. He nodded toward the door and she headed for it, wondering at his boldness and her own. She was twenty-three, and he was twenty-five.

A year later, they were settled in a small, neat house in Telegraph Creek. He was a band counselor, and Elvira had her own little women's healing center funded by the Aboriginal Healing Foundation. She gave birth to Charlene, and they had a good life as a family until the day Charlene was taken off by the church.

A few days after Charlene returned that wintry day at the age of fifteen, a van from the school came and parked in their yard. "Where's the girl?" the driver asked.

Elly and Jed took a stand, refusing to allow the school to take her again. "Not this time. You can't have her. Or we'll report you for abuse and kidnapping." Rumors of government intervention in some of the residential schools had begun, since allegations of abuse were mounting. Because Charlene was a few years shy of eighteen – the time of her release from the institution -- and even more significantly, the head priest had a growing fear of exposure -- the school didn't fight it.

Charlene spent nearly a year at home in Telegraph Creek, attending the one room village school house, assisting the teacher with the younger students. When she was sixteen, she agreed to attend her last years of high school at the public school in Whitehorse, Yukon, which had just begun to accept Indian students. Charlene dutifully wrote home from her little attic room under the eaves of her Aunt Doris's house. And then the letters stopped.

Elvira called Aunt Doris, who said, "I think you'd better come up here. Charlene's in trouble." Elvira drove up to Whitehorse the next weekend.

When she arrived at Doris's, they sat over coffee. Doris said, "I'm afraid she's getting lost, like so many of our kids, to that demon alcohol. She's stopped going to school, and she's drinking in her room all afternoon. Then she disappears every evening. I don't know where she's getting the money. No matter what I say, she won't stop."

Elvira sighed. *Why*, she thought, *can I help others, but not my own child?*

"She hasn't stirred yet today" said Doris, "and it's already past eleven."

Elvira climbed the creaking stairs to the attic. She knocked, and there was no answer. She pushed in the door and nearly gagged from the stale odors of alcohol, sweat, and unwashed clothes. "Get up, my girl. Right now!" She pulled the covers off of Charlene who moaned and turned over. She was still wearing jeans and a stained t-shirt.

Twenty minutes after Elly shoved Charlene into the shower and found some relatively clean clothes for her to change into, they were seated at the Tamarind Café over breakfast. Charlene claimed she couldn't stomach anything but coffee, but Elly noticed she was stuffing her mouth with the biscuits, gravy and sausage she had ordered for her.

"Charlene, what's happening? Tell me," she said gently.

Charlene's eyes filled with tears, "I can't be like you, Ma. I can't do it. I get the shakes in class. I just can't go to that school anymore." Elly slowly drew out of her that the racism and resentment of the white students had gotten to Charlene, that they called her "dirty savage" and "Injun whore." She had dropped out of school and gotten a job at a local bar, taking much of her pay out in cheap alcohol, and drinking herself into oblivion most nights.

Elvira felt a familiar shiver of guilt, regretting that she had been unable to rescue her girl from the residential school where her trauma had begun. "Charlene, what do you want to do with your life?" she asked.

"I don't know, Ma. I liked teaching the children back home, I guess."

"Okay, here's what we're going to do. You're coming home with me today after you clean up your room at Doris's; and I mean spic and span clean! You're going to sober up. Then, we'll figure it all out with your father." For the second time in her life, Charlene was at a crossroads, with a choice that could change the course of her life.

8

Kate sat in the truck with the window open, breathing in the piney air tinged with the earthy scent of dry leaves. She took a long swallow from her water bottle, which she had filled from a pure spring by the creek, and ate a handful from the large bag of homemade granola Aunt Rose had given her just before she left Telegraph Creek that morning.

She recalled a course at the University of Victoria given by Dr. Teaukura Matatui, a Maori from New Zealand, who was seconded to meet the university requirement of cross-cultural exchange between First Nations. That first morning, the class filed in and waited, chatting quietly. Suddenly, the professor leapt into the room, with a loud shout. Kate felt shock erupting through her body.

He stood before the astonished class covered more by tattoos than by the loin cloth he wore, barefoot, holding a spear. He glared ferociously at them, stuck his tongue way out toward his chin, slapped his chest and grunted loudly, beginning a Haka dance. She recognized the challenge ritual from watching the All Blacks rugby game on APTN, the Aboriginal Peoples' Television Network. When he finished, he straightened up, said in a calm voice, "Excuse me a moment," and went into the hall washroom to change into jeans and a sweater. As he stood leaning against his desk, his first words to the class were, "Who are you?" She recalled the silence as she sat, rapt by his exotic facial tattoos, with no idea how to answer the question.

One student lifted his hand gingerly, and said, "I am a Cree from Flin Flon, Manitoba."

"A good start," said professor Matatui, his fierce expression softening in a smile. "Anyone else?"

A young woman with a braid all the way down her back said, "I am a Tsawateinuk woman. My people are from Kingcome Inlet on the Pacific Ocean, and my mountain is Mount Waddington."

"Excellent!" Matatui said. "To know who you are, you must know five things: Who are your people? What is your land? Where is your water? What is your mountain? And what is your song?" He went on, "What is the song that you were created to sing in this world? What is your calling? Brueckner, the Quaker mystic said, 'Our calling is where our deepest gladness and the world's hunger meet.' Unless you find your path of creativity and service, you will be lost. You may live a comfortable life, but you will never be fully alive."

Kate winced at the memory of the professor's words, wondering if the explosion had ended her career. Would she ever have the chance to sing her song? With her background in indigenous studies, justice

48

and spirituality, she had dreams of bringing a new dimension to investigative journalism. To have been selected for the internship at CBC was nothing short of a miracle. *Have I lost my miracle?* she wondered. A tear slid down her cheek. *Stop it, Kate*, she said to herself. *Time for tears later. Stay on the path. You know what you have to do now. Follow your vision quest.*

She thought of the Fox's message: *Contemplative vigilance*, and it calmed her. She knew she could ill afford the distraction of grief. She needed to stay alert and mindful. As she drove north toward the Yukon, the miles went by in a blur, with Kate occasionally pulling over to gaze up at the majestic snow-capped, granite mountains lining the Alaska Highway and the emerald green lakes, like jewels strewn casually across the valleys. Finally, she pulled into Jake's Corners for gas, coffee and a delicious bowl of pea soup loaded with carrots, onions and ham. She mopped up the soup with bannock, baked just as she liked it, crispy outside and fluffy inside.

Kate braced herself for the last three hours of driving as she made the turn south to Atlin and put on some rocking Waylon Jennings to keep her awake. Her heart swelled as always, when Atlin Mountain loomed ahead of her, its rounded green piney curves reminding her of a voluptuous woman lying on her side.

She drove through the tiny town to an empty wooden house two streets up from the lake shore belonging to her family, where she planned to spend the night before making the trip to Gran's cabin. She parked the truck in the huge wooden shed out back and swung the door closed. She went in through the back door and found the place cleaner than she expected. *Auntie Rose must have called a neighbor,* she thought, realizing she must have guessed where Kate had decided to go. She went into the small bedroom to find it tidy, the double bed made up with fresh sheets and two quilts. She quickly pulled off her mocassins, jeans and sweatshirt and slipped beneath the covers. As soon as she closed her eyes, she fell into a deep sleep.

9

Kate awoke the next morning to birdsong. The Black-billed
Magpies trilled cheerfully, and when the big tousle-headed gray
"Camp Robber" Jays began calling raucously in the tree outside her
window, she got up. She showered, put on clean clothes and washed
out her travel clothes in the deep laundry sink beside the back door.

She made a pot of camp coffee, and sat on the back deck steps,
gazing out over the lake in the distance, sipping and listening,
relaxing into the familiar sense of home and safety. She stood on the
grass barefoot for morning prayers, taking deep breaths of the cool,
sweet air, facing the four directions, smiling as she moved and
chanted in the old way. She gave thanks for the calmness of the
lake, and prayed it would last until she arrived at the cabin, an hour's
trip across the lake through Torres Channel. She knew the wind
could rise suddenly, creating waves that could swamp a small craft,
and decided to dry her clothes later and get underway.

She went inside and made a list of supplies she would need to take to
the cabin. *Disguise yourself*, she thought -- Fox's first instruction,
remembering how it had camouflaged itself in the grass. Pulling her
baseball cap down over her eyebrows, she walked into James's

Grocery Emporium, hoping no one would recognize her, especially after being away for the past seven years.

She filled her basket with cans of corned beef, stewed tomatoes, bags of rice, beans, potatoes, carrots and onions, wheat and rye flour, some packets of Ramen which she and Gran had happily lived on at times, adding whatever vegetables grew in Gran's summer garden. She added fresh things such as celery and two dozen eggs, which she knew could last a while without a fridge.

Gran had never put in a fridge, though she took pride in her propane stove. "No room in this place to swing a cat much less put in a fridge," she would say. Kate bought cooking oil, toiletries, climbing rope, more duct tape, nails, a tarp, a container of propane for the stove, a new flashlight, batteries and a broom.

"Want some help with all this?" said James as he toted up her purchases. "No thanks," Kate said in a deep voice.

"Hey, aren't you…?" he started to say.

Kate shook her head, looked around and whispered. "You don't know me. You haven't seen me." James nodded, understanding that trouble was likely following her.

Kate parked the truck by Gran's boat, and unloaded everything, dividing it between the blue rubber bins in the bow, transom, and stern as Gran had taught her. "When the water is rough, you need ballast and balance. Just like life, you need common sense as well as faith. Trust in God and tie up your boat." Kate always laughed knowing Gran would add, "No camels 'round here."

Once the boat was ship-shape, and Kate had checked the gas line, she drove the truck back to the house and parked it in the shed, shutting the door. She walked to a pay phone and called Uncle Willy collect. "I'm okay, Unc. You won't hear from me for a while. And 'Beater' is safe and stored."

"Be real careful, Katy. Don't try to take care of it all on your lonesome," he said.

If you only knew…Kate thought.

As she sat in the boat, idling the engine, she took a moment to breathe, to offer up a prayer of gratitude, and looked up at Theresa and Atlin Mountain hugging Torres Channel, like giant, curvy Brunhildas -- sentinels guarding the portal. Kate felt the same childlike awe that always filled her at the sheer beauty of this place -- her holy ground. As she gently steered out into the bay, she imagined the water protectively closing over the traces of her wake.

Kate kept the boat at a steady pace for the hour it took to get to the tiny bay where Gran's cabin sat, thirty feet from shore, largely hidden by pines and firs. Floating skirts of pine needles fanned out from the lakeshore. Russets, reds and the gold of aspens wove through the varied shades of green on the mountains. She peered up above the tree line to the high granite crags, searching as always for the snow white dots of mountain goats. She could picture Gran's deep grin and wink whenever the goats appeared. "This is God's special gift, Katy, like wee white pearls. They're so precious and free."

When the point came into view, she throttled down, her heart opening to the familiar sense of homecoming. Not until she was parallel to the shore could she spot the green tin of the cabin roof, surrounded by scrub pines. She pulled up and tied the boat securely to a strong limb.

Kate opened one of the bins in the boat, pulled out the cleaning supplies, and grabbed the new broom, leaving everything else secured. As she walked gently up the path, tears filled her eyes, and she missed Gran more at this moment than ever before. As a wise friend of hers had said of her grief after Gran had died, "It's like an amputation. You never get over it. You just get used to it."

She stepped up onto the miniature deck, pulled the wooden peg attached by a piece of doeskin out of the latch on the door, which opened with a gentle push. *So neat and yar*, she thought. Like everything Gran fashioned, the door was simple in design -- trim and responsive. She caught a whiff of mouse droppings and dust as she stepped into the room, which looked smaller than in her memory.

She cleaned for two hours, taking breaks only to fetch water in a pail and to transfer well-seasoned firewood from the neat stack under the eaves on the leeward side of the cabin. She placed it under the storage shelf created for that purpose beside the wood burning stove.

54

She cleaned the Plexiglas windows with white vinegar and newsprint, then opened them to air out the cabin. She pulled the storage boxes out from under the window seat by their twisted rope handles, and cleaned the space behind them. She used Gran's aging bottle of Old English polishing oil, smoothing it over the built-in varnished, wide-planked wooden table until it shone.

She climbed up the ladder to the loft, where she had slept each night as a child, cushioned by old quilted moving pads as the mattress for her down sleeping bag. She pulled the pads out for a good airing and bent to sweep the corners under the peaked roof with a whisk broom.

The little window beside her sleeping place still had its screen in place, easily removed to take out the plywood piece that protected it over the winter. Then she replaced the screen, to keep out the mosquitoes that sometimes swarmed on summer evenings. When she was satisfied that every surface and space in the cabin was as clean and neat as she could make it, she brought up the rest of the supplies and placed them in their proper boxes before sliding them back in.

Gran always kept one for miscellany: coils of rope, recycled jars of nails and screws of different sizes, a hammer and other tools, balls of string, bundles of little wire ties of green and red which Gran insisted on saving, and remnants of Gran's beloved duct tape, to which Kate added a fresh supply. She then went up the path through the bush a few feet to the door-less outhouse that just needed a bit of cobweb removal. Its Styrofoam seat was still in good shape. There was never a need for a door, because there wasn't another house for fifty kilometers around. The air kept it smelling clean, and Gran always dumped the ashes from the stove into the pit, keeping it fresh.

The cabin looked just as it always had -- scrubbed down, with the small, four-burner white enamel stove gleaming, and the table "clean as a whistle", as Gran would say. Kate wiped her brow and decided to take a dip in the lake.

She walked down the gravel beach to the shallow end of the bay, where the water was warmer. Suddenly, she glimpsed movement in the corner of her eye. She quickly crouched down behind a low bush and froze, her heart pounding.

A fat porcupine lumbered out onto the sand flat by the end of the bay. Kate took a breath of relief and slipped up behind the porky. It was "one of God's dumbest creatures", Gran always said. She taught Kate that you could follow it quite closely. It would occasionally look around, one paw lifted, and if you stood very still, it would not see you as anything but a tree. She tracked the porky for a few minutes, stopping when it stopped. Sure enough, each time it stopped, it raised a paw, looked around, then moved on. Then, it took a drink from the lake and waddled off again into the bush.

Kate reached the shallowest place at the north end of the bay, and breathed in the boggy smell of wet sand and clay. She shed her clothes, folding them neatly, so she could dress quickly if need be, and placed them on the rough sedge grass beneath a willow bush.

The water was cool here but not cold, still warmed by the early autumn sun shining in a cloudless blue sky.

Kate recalled at the age of eight leaping from Gran's boat and diving head first into the frigid glacial lake, shocked by the icy cold and shaking uncontrollably within moments. She could hear Gran chuckling. She had never attempted it since.

She waded out into the bay up to her waist and slowly immersed. The water felt like cool silk as it rinsed away the dust and sweat from her body. She lay down on the narrow shore to dry off, her tension melting into patient sand. It felt as if the warm, lake-raked gravel remembered her, molding gently to her body. She dozed lightly, unaware that she was being watched.

10

Kate contemplated getting up, although she felt finally, utterly relaxed lying in the warmth. She heard a mournful chorus of honks high above, and looked up to see the ragged V of Canada Geese calling out as they made their annual migration south. She knew that they continually changed leaders so as not to tire one, and if any goose was in trouble and fell, others would swiftly rush to help. She remembered the devoted pair Gran had called Troilus and Cressida, who spent long summer days floating in their bay. They mated for life, as all geese do. One spring day, Troilus arrived alone without his beloved mate. It was as if he had come one last time to bring the sad news. He never returned again.

Kate startled at a rustling in the thicket of pines and brush a few feet from the narrow shore where she lay. She quickly stood, put on her clothes and looked around. The noise had stopped. Slowly she crept, "Indian footed" toward the path to the cabin, her steps nearly silent. The rustling increased, and she turned as a moose and her calf burst out of the bush on their long, spindly legs and leapt into the water. As they swam across the lake, leaving a wide, rippling wake, Kate remained hidden behind a cedar with a flaring skirt, and watched for half an hour as the pair receded toward the opposite shore.

She recalled a painful lesson during her sixth summer, the first time Gran had brought her to the cabin. One afternoon, Gran went very still as she stood looking out the front window with an expansive view of the lake. In a low voice, she told Kate, "There's a Caribou doe and her fawn swimming across the lake. Do you want to watch?"

Before Gran could instruct her, Kate bolted from the cabin and ran as fast as she could to the water's edge, her feet tripping over stones and small branches in her path. The doe pricked up her ears, and sensing Kate with her sharp hearing, made a wide U-turn, and started swimming back the way she had come, followed by the tiny fawn. They had already reached mid-way across the lake, heading toward the bush near the cabin. Kate realized that the racket she made had frightened them. She felt searing guilt tightening in her chest, knowing she had forced the pair to abandon their journey.

She returned to the cabin, head hanging, wondering if this time, Gran would lose her temper as Mama always did, and finally give her the hiding she still expected. She was afraid to look up, remembering Charlene's hard slaps whenever she began to cry. "I can't stand your fucking Bambi eyes!" she'd shout. Katy never understood what she meant. But she kept her eyes down awaiting Gran's anger.

Gran lifted Katy's chin in her soft hand and said, "Kate, what is your teachable moment?"

"Not to run around animals?" she answered, tears coursing down her cheeks.

"Well, yes, and why is that?"

"I need to respect them and think before I act?"

"Yes, dear one. You didn't intend to disturb them, yet you acted without thinking. Be thoughtful, and then you will enjoy whatever Creator sends you."

Kate asked Gran for a pinch of tobacco and went back to the shore to offer her apology to the Creator and the caribou for wasting the gift she had been offered and interfering in their swim.

Gran smiled at her tenderly that evening during their dinner of bannock, beans and rice and said, "That was the honorable thing to do, Kate. A good day for a good lesson." That night Kate smiled as she snuggled down into her sleeping bag and drifted off into a peaceful sleep.

Memories of Gran were like a cherished, well-worn quilt in soft, faded colors that Kate could wrap around herself for comfort. She decided to make bread, as Gran had taught her, adding sunflower and pumpkin seeds to a mixture of rye, white, and whole wheat flour. As she stood at the table kneading the dough, leaning into her hands, her peace was disturbed by a clear thought, *Danger!*

60

She couldn't imagine that the Toronto mob had any idea of where she was, so she figured it was nerves. She knew it would take time for her mind to shed the terror of the explosion and to recover from the flood of adrenaline that buoyed her for the escape.

Gran had often quoted Peace Pilgrim, an elderly woman who walked across the United States for the sake of peace with nothing but her travel apron and good shoes. "If we knew how powerful our thoughts are, we would never have another negative thought."

I just need to calm my thoughts, Kate said to herself. She recalled Gran's water trick where she demonstrated how negative thoughts and emotions such as fear, anxiety and anger could be replaced with the redemptive virtues of courage, peace or justice. With a large bowl for catchment, a small, clear juice glass, a large pitcher full of water, and a little bottle of blue food coloring on the table, Gran would pour water into the small glass.

"When we are born, our soul is clear and pure, like this water. Then sometimes bad things happen, like being hit or called names, or doing things we regret like lying or stealing." Kate would blush remembering how her mother had made her steal things from shops.

"And sometimes, our ego gets the better of us, and we are filled with fear or greed or we become unkind and cruel, even to people we love." Gran added some of the blue dye, clouding the water. She then pretended to try pulling out the blue dye.

"If we want to get rid of these bad things -- and we have all done them – we cannot go back and change the past." She then picked up the pitcher full of clear water, and as she spoke, kept pouring water into the small glass.

"But there is a magic we all have that Creator gave us – the power of our virtues. If we have been cruel, we can choose to be kind. If we have stolen, we can choose to be honest and generous. If we have failed at something, we can replace the fear of trying again with courage."

As she went on pouring, slowly the water cleared, the blue completely flushed out, until the glass once again held pure water.

"So our purity as newborn babies comes from innocence, but the purity of our lives as we get older comes from choice -- choosing to practice the virtues."

Kate loved the magic water demonstration and asked Gran to do it for her repeatedly, until she learned to do it herself. It became a weekly ritual for the two of them, which they shared with occasional visitors.

Kate had come to her grandmother a tense, jumpy, fearful child, from years of unpredictable abuse followed by guilty affection and indulgence from her mother, Charlene. She never knew from one day or moment to the next what to expect, and it took several months of living with Gran for Kate to relax her hyper-vigilance. Gradually she learned what to expect, and Gran's constancy was a healing balm to her.

Gran told her what the house boundaries were and kept them consistently. Kate loved following the simple daily routine of washing up in the small basin on a bench outside, sitting together for a breakfast of oatmeal with raisins, or eggs and canned ham, or some of Gran's seedy bread spread with peanut butter and jam. There was always ample food. After a few weeks, she stopped sneaking food and hiding it under her sleeping bag. Gran had known, but believed Kate would stop when she felt safe enough. She chuckled to herself thinking the mice must have thought they'd hit the jackpot for a while.

Right after breakfast, they took time for a Bible reading and some prayers, then did their chores. Gran had a rule about keeping everything in its place in the cabin, putting things back "where they live".

Every morning, Kate fetched clean water from the lake, remembering to clear away any debris on the surface before submerging the grey metal bucket, then slogging back to the cabin and pouring it into the big bucket standing on the hearth by the wood-burning stove. When it wasn't raining, she would air out her sleeping bag for an hour or two, then smooth it out neatly in her sleeping place. Every other day, she swept out the cabin the way Gran taught her, by sprinkling water on the wide pine planks so the dust would settle as she swept.

Gran's daily routine was always the same – chores in the morning, then something creative like making bread or jam, or sketching the lake, then lunch, and a nap for both of them. In the afternoon, there would be an adventure unless Gran could feel the rain coming "in my bones".

On fair days, they would set out in the boat for a fishing expedition at the falls that splashed into the far side of the lake where the grayling and sometimes lake trout would gather. Kate loved watching the fish circle around her hook as she stood in the boat gazing down into the crystal clear water. She and Gran often went into the bush to pick berries, Gran showing her to look under the leaves for the shy low-bush cranberries. Sometimes they foraged for kinnick kinnick -- "bear berries". When they got back to the cabin, Gran gave Kate a towel and showed her how to roll the berries over it to pick out the leaves and other debris, which would stick to the cloth.

Sometimes they walked along the shore, collecting stones and driftwood with interesting shapes. In the evening, they would have a tasty supper of fresh-caught fish, or corned beef with potatoes and onions, or Gran's beloved Ramen with vegies followed by a chunk of sweetened baking chocolate for dessert.

After they did the dishes together and put them away, they sang Tahltan songs and Gran would teach her a new word or two in their language. Then Gran read to Kate from a carefully kept box of special books – a well-thumbed copy of the hard cover *A Child's*

Treasury of Nursery Rhymes with its colorful old-fashioned pictures, Maurice Sendak's *Where the Wild Things Are*, *Green Eggs and Ham* by Dr. Seuss, which Kate quickly memorized, or Kate's favorite, *Wind in the Willows*. When her eyes became too heavy to hold open any longer, Gran would give her a gentle kiss on the cheek, and Kate groggily climbed the ladder to the sleeping loft and fell into a deep sleep.

Sundays were their day of rest. "Even the Lord rested on the seventh day," Gran would say. They would read a scripture from the family Bible, which Gran always had with her, and then talk about what it meant. Sometimes Gran would read a Bible story to Kate out of a children's book. Then, they would spend the day lying around reading, or Kate would draw and color.

As she got older she began to write her own stories. Gran encouraged her, saying, "Katy, you have a gift – a way with words." On Sundays, they also ate yummy leftovers. Each year, from early June when school let out to the first week in September was the same.

As the years went by, Kate's memory of pain dimmed and faded, and no longer had the power to frighten her. She grew "like a spring colt" as Gran said, eyes sparkling, ebony hair thick and glistening, with long legs and a slender build. "Must be your Dad's side," Gran would say, her ample tummy shaking with laughter. Gran wasn't fat. She had strong arms and legs from tending the garden and hiking, but her middle bits were round and soft. "Good for

65

cuddling", as Kate learned once she finally allowed herself to nestle in Gran's arms.

That night, Kate looked over her bountiful supply of foodstuffs and decided to make one of her favorites -- corned beef hash with potatoes and onions, pouring in a bit of canned milk to crisp it up, a salad of celery, carrot and tomato, and chocolate for dessert. *Tomorrow I'll take a real look around,* she thought.

Images of Jason Red Deer floated into her awareness throughout the day and now seemed to crowd out her plans for tomorrow. When she lay down to sleep, she tried to shake off the clear memory of the acute bodily response she had when he casually touched her, but it persisted, and sleep eluded her.

Kate preferred to sleep in her loft rather than to take Gran's place on the window seat which ran the width of the cabin. She lay there, arms behind her head, and turned toward the screened window. Stars, like tiny brilliant gems, appeared in the darkling blue-black sky. Suddenly a brilliant swath of green undulated across her field of vision. She raced down the ladder, unlocked the cabin door and went out to view the Aurora Borealis, which danced and soared in shades of green, then purple and white. *Oh, Gran, I wish you were here to share this with me*, she thought. She heard Gran's chuckle and the words, *my dear one, I am.*

Kate awoke to the sound of a raven trilling and to a simple wish – to breathe easy today, to put crisis behind her. She decided to explore the changes brought by autumn, when normally she and Gran had already departed back to Telegraph Creek. She was keen to see what birds were here now; to watch for the changing colors of mosses, bushes, trees and flowers; to search for autumn berries.

After breakfast, she locked the cabin, and, hefting her backpack, followed an animal trail up into the forest. She headed for her sacred spot, the little medicine wheel she had made years before in a small clearing a mile or so into deep woods. The first thing she noticed as she hiked, taking deep breaths, was the change of scents – the earthy aroma of leaf mold and the peppery perfume of pine and fir. She noticed claw marks scored on larger trees and rabbit fur on the path, telling her that the black bears were feeding in preparation for their long hibernation.

As she approached her special spot, she had to pull hard at the low branches that shielded it from view on the path. She did so carefully so as not to disturb the natural camouflage or harm the trees. She stepped through into the small clearing which was lit with the sun's mid-morning rays.

There were the small white stones she had gathered to make the medicine wheel, the center filled with mosses and their tiny miniature flowers, now in russet and gold she had not seen before. There beside the circle was her special round, smooth, glacier-hollowed stone -- perfect for a sage ceremony. She pulled out her deerskin medicine bundle and unwrapped her sacred things. She cleaned out the soil and leaves that had drifted into the stone bowl, and replaced them with dry sage. She lit it and fanned the embers with the eagle feather. After smudging, Kate chanted the protection prayer Gran had taught her, "Almighty Lord, protect me with Your power from what is behind me, before me, on my right, on my left, above me and below me, on all sides to which I am exposed."

When the prayer was finished, she sank into the silence, listening for guidance. Gran had taught her that chanting is the speaking part of prayer, and meditation is the listening part. "Unless we listen, how do we know what Creator's answer is? It's like calling someone on the phone and hanging up before they answer," Gran said.

The word *Danger*! came again, but like a loud alarm in her mind this time. She sighed deeply, realizing it was not just her imagination, knowing that she had to leave the shelter of the cabin, which was just starting to work its magic on her mind and body. Tonight she would prepare, and at first light, she would take the boat and move deeper into the wilderness of Atlin Provincial Park.

When she returned to the cabin, after making it clean and tidy, Kate put a note in the guest log book Gran always kept in plain view on the table, saying she was leaving Atlin Lake and returning to southern BC, to mislead anyone who might be following her.

She had left a store of canned goods in a rubber bin in the boat to which she added fresh supplies, including climbing equipment and fishing gear, and eased into the lake. She took in the unbelievable beauty of the aqua glacial water, deepening to turquoise as she neared the glacial mountains. The jagged snow-capped peaks of Cathedral Mountain loomed in the distance with its waterfalls cascading like sheer veils down its granite sides.

The constant sound of the motor was soothing, and as she neared the inlet where she would climb to higher ground, she turned off the motor and used the oars, the exertion helping to release her nervous tension. She was grateful she had stayed fit by working out several times a week at a Toronto gym and thought to herself, *this is better – "earth gym"*, remembering Gran's expression.

She pulled into shore at a beach which fanned out from a sharp vertical cliff leading to a high plateau, where she and Gran used to climb with ropes and repel down, laughing the whole way. Gran made sure that Kate had good hiking shoes, but wore only her old lace-less sneakers, patched with duct tape, even when climbing. "Still got a lot of life in them, and they know what to do. Got me this far," she would say.

As Kate made her way up to the first flat recess of the cliff, the back of her neck prickled as if someone was behind her. She scrambled up and crouched beneath a rock overhang, looking around. She was laden down with a large back pack and camping supplies and had to climb carefully. As she made her way up the second rock face, she prayed she would make it to the plateau and disappear into one of the large caves before…what, she didn't know, just that she trusted her inner voice and knew in her gut that trouble was not far behind.

11

"If you don't find her, you're dead. You'll bloody well find a way," said Anthony Sabatano to his three top men. Standing ramrod straight, they paled, taking him at his word, knowing he wouldn't hesitate to eliminate one or all of them if they failed. Through their Vancouver connections, they hired a Native man who was known only as "Hunter". He was familiar with the tribes throughout British Columbia and the Yukon. He garnered outrageous sums for his work and had never failed to turn in evidence of his victims' deaths.

Using the latest internet technology, he began the search for Kate in Chemainus, a seventy-five minute drive north of Victoria on Vancouver Island. By checking school records, he saw that she had not attended that school past the age of six. He knew the Native bands in that area and where their relatives lived in northern British Columbia. One of his best sources of information came from pubs where he could spot Natives in their cups and lure them into the garbage area behind the bar before they could get too drunk. He would terrorize them with his sharp stiletto. All it took was the loss of a finger or two, and they would quickly spill whatever they knew.

He sat in the smoke-hazed bar, nursing a ginger ale, watching carefully for two hours. He struck up a conversation with a man nicknamed Elvis, who had a huge greasy pompadour. Elvis was well on his way to inebriation, and Hunter shouted him a fourth whiskey. "I'm back here to trace my roots," Hunter said. "I need to know my family." The man nodded. "Family's everything," he replied. "Who are your people?" The hunter named a few of the relatives he had unearthed in his internet search on Kate. "Oh, I know them," he said. "There's a branch up Telegraph Creek way." *Man, this is simple*, thought Hunter.

He made his way north in a four wheel drive SUV, and stopped at the Dease Lake crossroads restaurant as Kate had, for food and coffee. He asked directions to the village of Telegraph Creek. As he sat at the table, the waitress made a call. "There's a stranger here asking about your village. I thought you should know."

Aunt Rose thanked her and immediately called Jason Red Deer on his cell phone. "I'll call you again when he gets here," she said.

Jason had moved on to White Horse, Yukon, where he had set up a mobile holistic health clinic in a large motor home, combining First Nations medicine and modern technology. He asked Rose, "Where is Kate likely to hide?"

Rose said, "Well, she and her grandmother Elvira always spent their summers in a small cabin Elly built up on Atlin Lake. There's nothing else around there, no other cabins, so my guess is that's where she's headed."

Jason immediately made a decision to move the mobile clinic to Atlin, where Rose had revealed to him what she knew about Kate and Gran's summer getaways.

Hunter knew he would have to be much more subtle and clever at this stage of the chase, since Kate's community would protect her with their lives. *Their loss*, he thought. He waited until evening to make his way down the switchbacks to the valley of the Stikine River where the tiny village of Telegraph Creek was situated. Once he arrived, following the sound of clinking bottles, he located the local watering hole, which was no more than a shack with three picnic tables and a makeshift plywood bar.

The tom-tom telegraph had preceded him. As soon as he walked in, all talking stopped. The five men there looked down at their drinks. The bartender looked none too friendly either. He leaned on his knuckles over the bar and stared. Hunter narrowed his eyes and looked around. He selected the most disreputable looking of the men, and stood over him, asking in a frighteningly polite voice, "Would you mind coming outside to give me a direction?" The man just shook his head. Hunter grabbed him by his collar and dragged him outside, the others looking on nervously.

"Where is Kate Mackenzie's aunt?" he asked, shaking the man. He kept shaking his head and wouldn't speak until Hunter pulled out his knife. "You *will* tell me," he said thrusting the razor sharp point of the stiletto into the folds of the old man's neck and giving a flick. Blood started seeping from the flesh wound. The man whimpered and pointed at a house down the dirt road, then crumpled to the ground, holding his bleeding neck.

Hunter raced to the darkened house and knocked. There was no answer. Rose had shut down the house and left for a neighbor's house, first wracking her brain and scanning the house to see if Kate had left anything behind that would hint at the fact that she was moving on to Atlin, more than seven hundred kilometers north of Telegraph Creek. Kate hadn't told Rose this but she thought, "Where else would she go?"

Hunter took out a tool he carried and jimmied the lock open. He entered the house quietly and scanned each room for sounds of breathing. It was empty. In the kitchen, he opened the fridge and found leftovers in Tupperware, and a carton of milk. He sniffed at each item and didn't detect any spoilage, which told him the house hadn't long been vacant. Using a small pen light, his next search was for a desk. He found one in the corner of a bedroom beside a neatly made bed. He pulled out all the drawers carefully, and started rummaging through them. One drawer seemed stuck. He yanked hard and discovered a bunch of old letters, which he quickly scanned for addresses, finding none. Then he felt around where the drawer had been stuck, and sure enough, there was a crumpled, yellowed envelope stuck behind it, with a faint Atlin postal stamp. Hunter was nothing, if not thorough.

He was known for making snap intuitive decisions that more often than not, led him to his prey. He decided to immediately drive north. While several men in the bar were discussing what to do about the stranger who had poked Willy with a knife, Hunter peeled out and drove away. Several hours later, he pulled off at a boarded up motel, parked behind it and got some sleep. The next morning he drove toward Atlin.

Once he arrived in the small lakeside village of Atlin, Hunter booked a room over the local pub and spent the evening trolling for information. He struck up a conversation with a toothless old man, asking him how long he had lived in Atlin.

"All my life, fella. I'm tenth generation Tlingit First Nation," he said proudly.

"It's a good thing to know your roots so well," Hunter said. "My people left me in a foster home down south in Vancouver and I have very little info about them. That's why I'm looking for them now."

The old man shook his head in sympathy.

"I think they may have a place out on the lake somewhere."

"Only a couple of places I can think of. Peggy's Cove and then there's the little cabin Elvira Johns built some years ago. But there's no one there now. They just used it in summers."

"I was thinking while I'm here I'd get to know the land, do some fishing, maybe hunting."

"Not the best time of year for hunting, I can tell you. The animals have skedaddled for the winter by now. Fishing's good all year though."

The next morning, Hunter hired a private float plane, in the guise of fishing and hunting moose. He told the pilot, "Just keep flying around until I tell you to let me off." He had a SOCOM M24 sniper rifle, night goggles, binoculars and a collapsible rubber boat.

"You sure you have enough equipment there?" joked Fran Eliot, the pilot.

Hunter cracked a thin-lipped smile. "I'll ring you on my satellite phone in a day or two once I land something."

"Pretty optimistic there, Mister. Ya know, it's pretty rare to find a moose until next month, the rutting season, especially without a guide. Want me to...?"

Hunter cut her off in mid-sentence. "I don't use guides. I'm usually pretty lucky," he said. "Can you arrange for a boat to pick me up?"

"Sure," Fran said. "Archie Turner runs a charter fishing boat that has room for game," thinking, *you cocky son of a gun.*

Hunter had watched for the cabin as the plane circled and indicated to Fran to land a couple of miles past it. Several minutes after the plane took off for the return to Atlin, he stowed most of his equipment, except for the gun, and trekked back until he had the cabin in his sites across the lake. Then, he waited.

He watched Kate swimming and napping, splendidly naked. For one brief moment, he contemplated having some fun before he killed her, but quickly nixed the idea, returning to his relentless discipline. He decided to bide his time, in case she should leave the cabin. He preferred to get her in a less obvious place. Soon, his patience was rewarded.

12

Midway through her climb to the cave area, despite her building sense of urgency, Kate began to tire. She stopped at a narrow outcropping to rest. Suddenly a bullet zinged past her ear. She flattened herself on the rock shelf. Another bullet pierced her side, reopening the wound that had just begun to heal properly. As blood began to gush from her side, Kate's last thought before she passed out was, *how did they find me?*

Through his miniature, high powered binoculars, Hunter watched the inert body and saw the flow of blood. He knew that soon the raptors in the area – ospreys, eagles or owls – would take care of the remains. He watched until he saw a large bald eagle circling, and then land beside her. He took a photo with a high powered miniature camera zooming in to capture the scene. Two hours later he had hiked around a point to a different bay and shot a large male caribou that had come to the lake to drink. He called Fran that afternoon to send the boat for him, his gear and his trophy.

Jason Red Deer trundled down the Atlin Road from Jakes' Corners as fast as his mobile clinic could go, trailing a long plume of dust. He thought of renting a car but knew he might need the supplies in the motor home once he found Kate. He prayed for guidance, "Help me to find her first, Creator. Guide me to her."

He felt a powerful connection to beautiful, frightened Kate and could sense that she was in deep trouble. After parking the motor home, Jason quickly packed emergency medical supplies, food and water. Shouldering his rifle, he raced to the end of the dock. He saw that a man in a yellow Anorak was revving the engines of a sturdy fishing boat.

"Hey there, can I hitch a ride?" he asked.

"Well, sure. I'm off to Desolation Cove to pick up a hunter, but you're welcome to come."

"That'd be fine," he said.

"What are you after?" the captain asked.

"I hope to bag a moose."

"Not the greatest part of the season, but at least there aren't many guys out this time of the week," said the Captain. "Say, aren't you that nature somethin' doctor that was here two summers ago? Milton's cousin?"

"Yes," he said. "I'm just taking a break."

They headed off through the channel. "Never known anyone go out without a guide like you two," Archie muttered.

"What did you say?"

"You and some other Indian guy I'm s'posed to pick up now. Apparently he got lucky and bagged a caribou."

As the boat made its way through the emerald green water, Jason barely took in the beauty as it faded to pale turquoise with a vista of jagged, snow-capped Cathedral Mountain in the distance. He closed his eyes as if resting and leaned back against the rail, moving deep into meditation, silently chanting.

When they slowed to a stop to pick up the hunter, Jason felt an electric charge. *He's the one*, he thought, knowing that the killer would not be returning to Atlin unless he had found and disposed of Kate.

When the boat turned into shore, Hunter was surprised to see a tall Native man on board with the Captain. "Where you headed?" he asked.

"Wherever I can find a moose," Jason said. Hunter tensed, but then, realizing the man would be going deeper into the bush for game instead of climbing, he relaxed. Besides, he had no boat. The body was on a ledge several miles south on the opposite shore.

She's still alive. I can feel her, thought Jason. He watched the boat heading back toward Atlin until it was a good distance away. He moved into a grove of Aspen and made a call on his satellite phone, which had been tucked down into his large backpack. "Cousin", he said, "I need a canoe and rescue gear, and the medical supplies by the door of the mobile clinic. Can you bring a stretcher from the motor home as well and get it all in your boat?"

"Sure thing, coz. Right now?"

"Yes, as soon as you can."

"So I take it you're not after moose."

"There's someone stranded out here, Milton. Just keep it between us, okay? That's super important."

"Gotcha. I won't even tell Mable."

Jason added, "And wear climbing gear," then gave him his coordinates and settled against a tree to wait. He knew it was the most efficient way, so calmed himself to wait for Milton to arrive.

Once the boat pulled up, Jason tossed in his gear, jumped onto the boat, and stood at the prow looking up. *She would have tried to make it to the caves,* he thought. As they moved deeper into the Provincial Park, he looked up and noticed a large eagle take off from a ledge. It found a current and circled the spot several times without flapping, as if signaling to Jason. "There," he told Milton. "Cross to that cove, let me out, then stand by with the stretcher, will you?" As he climbed, he prayed. When he came to the ledge where Kate lay in a pool of blood, he signaled for Milton to come up.

He put his ear against her back and felt a slight rise and fall. Her breathing was shallow. He saw that the blood on her side was clotting -- a good sign. He gently turned her over, careful of her wound, and bandaged it quickly. He covered her with a thermal sheet from his back-pack and tried to give her some water, but she just moaned and couldn't seem to swallow.

"You're okay. You're fine. Just breathe, Lady Kate. I'm here," he murmured.

They managed to pulley the stretcher up, buckled Kate in, and slowly lowered it to the ground. Carefully, they moved her to the boat. The evening wind over the lake had risen, and white caps were forming. "We'll never get her over the open water to town in this condition. It's too rough, and she's in severe shock," said Jason. "Take us to Elvira's old cabin."

When they arrived, the waves were cresting. "Want to spend the night here?" asked Jason.

"Naw. I'll make it back okay. Mabel will have my head if I don't show up for supper." After they brought the stretcher up to the cabin, Jason opened the door and was amazed to see it pristine and tidy, with logs stacked neatly beside the wood-burning stove. He found a fire already laid and lit it, warmth quickly suffusing the small cabin.

Milton waited until Jason had made a bed for Kate on the floor with half the long cushions from the window seat and clean sheets, and they gently transferred her to the bedding. She began to moan. "Remember, man, not a word," said Jason.

"I hear you. Let me know if you need anything. I'll just tell everyone I'm after caribou myself if you need me to make a trip out." With that, Milton left them alone.

Kate was deathly pale beneath the livid flush on her cheeks, and hot to the touch. Her breathing was still shallow. Jason rigged up a saline drip, took Type 0 plasma out of the ice chest Martin had picked up, and set up a transfusion. Kate had lost a lot of blood. Then he removed the dressing, cleaned out the wound and applied a fresh bandage.

He thanked God the bullet had gone through instead of lodging in her flesh. The biggest danger was sepsis, so he added an antibiotic to the drip. Before she could gain consciousness, he cut away Kate's soiled, bloody clothes, and washed her gently. He put a soft flannel over her and tucked it around her.

As he ministered to her, he chanted softly and reassured her that she was strong, alive, and healing. He recited a healing prayer, which he believed had great power: "Creator help her, heal her wounds, and bring her back to health. Bless your daughter with your ever-abiding tender mercy, oh great physician. Amen."

After a sandwich and some camp coffee, he lay down on a sleeping bag on the window seat beside her. He woke through the night to check her temperature and to chant softly. Kate moaned often as she started to sweat and shake. He bathed her forehead with cool lake water, and added pain killer to the drip, as she still could take nothing orally.

"That's right, sweat it out," he whispered. "C'mon Katy girl, you can do this."

13

After two days of barely coming to and then drifting down into sleep, Kate's eyes fluttered open. She felt disoriented and woozy. She saw the backs of Jason's legs as he stirred something on the stove. He was humming. In a soft voice, she asked, "What are you doing here?"

"Good morning, Miss Kate, how do you feel?"

"Like a truck ran over me."

"Close enough. Are you hungry?" Kate felt her stomach roil and realized she was ravenous.

"I have some good Indian broth here for you."

"What is it? Actually I don't care."

Jason spooned up some of the Ramen cut into small bites with onions, leeks, carrots, and tiny bits of dried moose meat which were now tender and plump. He handed her a baked bannock, not as good and greasy as she liked, but filling. He also gave her a weak cup of coffee to help with the headache he knew she would have after her body had battled the infection.

He helped her to slip on a flannel nightgown he had found, respecting her need for privacy by turning away as she gingerly put her arms through it, while covered by a quilt. He lifted her to the built-in window seat and put her down gently on a cushion. Though her hand shook, she managed to spoon up the soup as rapidly as she could.

"Slow down, Kate. You don't want to lose it as soon as you've gotten it down."

"Thanks for the lovely image," she said, willing herself to slow down. When she was finished she leaned back, and found more cushions piled behind her.

"I know you have a lot of questions, Kate, but today you need to rest, get some fresh air, and stay quiet. You may want to thank Creator you're still with us."

"Who died and made you king?" she said irritably. Jason knew this was a good sign she was recovering and stifled his grin.

"Well, I am your doctor. You know how we like to play God."

It was her turn to suppress a smile. "So, now you're a doctor, not a medicine man?"

"Later," he said, and went out the door. "I'm going to chop some kindling. I'll be right outside." Leaning back, feeling deeply sated, she was asleep before he even picked up the axe.

Jason made corned beef hash for dinner with a side of cucumber, celery, and fresh wild herbs from Gran's garden, and once again, Kate ate heartily. "Tomorrow we'll try for a fish. I didn't want to leave you until you were stronger," he said.

"Why are you doing all this for me?" she asked.

He laughed, "That's your first question? Don't you want to know what happened to you?"

"Well, yes," she stammered. "But that *is* my first question. I want to know who you are. What's your story?"

"Ever the journalist," he said, laughing. And then he began.

14

"I was born on a Cree reserve on the prairies of Saskatchewan. We lived simply in a tepee, and life was good; we never went hungry. The men of our lodge hunted moose, fished in the lakes, even in winter, and the women picked berries and dried the meat. Our band moved around following the food sources, and our family was always together. During the long winters, we hunkered down in buffalo robes and always had a warm fire going in our tepee. There was always something good, like moose stew, simmering on the fire.

"In many ways we were rich. My parents were devoted to each other and to me, my sisters and my grandfather. We laughed. We loved each other. We worked together trapping, hunting, and fishing. Summers were wonderful. We had bonfires under the stars with our Aunties and their families. We watched the kîwetinohk kacakastek – the northern lights. In our language it means 'ghosts dancing'. Grandfather told us stories of the souls who had gone on, dancing with their colorful robes to let us know they watch over us. He was a medicine man. They called him doctor or healer – onanatawihowew. I followed him around from the time I could walk. I wanted to be like him, to help people.

When I was six, the white men came and grabbed me and my sisters and took us off to a school. I was hurting so much, I cried every night for the first week. Then I got angry. And that became my fuel. I decided to be their best student, to be beyond reproach. I was tall, and the priest left me alone. I knew he was interfering with some of the younger boys.

When my manhood started, I noticed I had special abilities, like traveling through time and space. The first time it happened, I was scared senseless. Then I realized, this could take me home. I started to visit my Granddad. He told me to be careful with the power, not to let anyone know. The only reason I'm telling you, Kate, is because you have it too. That's how we first met."

Jason paused and took a long drink of water.

Katy said, "How did you…?"

He noticed Kate fighting fatigue as her lids grew heavy. "Enough," he said.

"I want to hear more," she said.

"Later, Kate; rest now." He carried her out to the outhouse and left her, then came back for her and laid her in her bed. He went outside to breathe as Kate slid into sleep. Talking of his past stirred up harsh memories, and he turned to meditation to recover his peace. He relaxed his abdomen, and breathed in four beats, holding for six, breathing out for seven, his tongue curled against his teeth, his palms turned upward. With each in-breath, he thought "peace". With each out-breath, he pictured tension leaving his body like a soft wind over water.

The next morning, Jason was surprised to see Kate slip out the door, a shawl around her shoulders. When she came back in, he had heated some water and placed it in a tin basin painted with roses for her to wash. She smiled gratefully as he left her alone in the cabin. When he returned, she had coffee brewing in Gran's old blue enamel pot and eggs sizzling in a pan.

"Are you sure you're up to this?" he asked.

"Believe me, after breakfast, I'm taking a nap," she said. He brought the coffee and plates of eggs and bannock to the table and waited for her to start eating.

"Let's pray first," she said. "Gran always did." She murmured a prayer in Tlingit. They ate in companionable silence, and Jason noticed that Kate's face was once again a rosy copper color.

"You're amazing," he said.

"What do you mean?"

"First of all, your body is incredibly resilient, and even more, your spirit. You've been through so much, yet the first thing that comes to you is curiosity, not fear."

She smiled and took in his acknowledgement. "I think it comes from being a tough little kid. I had to be."

"Will you tell me your story, Kate?"

"Later," she said. "First, I want to hear more of yours and then, what *did* happen to me?"

"Oh, now you're making *me* wait," he laughed. "Fair enough. Where was I? The school was a cold, unhappy place, but I found that if I could help the other boys, I developed a kind of contentment."

"How did you help them?" Kate asked.

"When they cried at night in the dorm, I would go to them and touch them – placing my hand on their shoulder, or their forehead, and I rocked the little ones. I chanted as my grandfather did when someone was ill or grieving. I told them they were good boys no matter what anyone did to them. It calmed them, so I learned that touch and prayer can be healing."

Kate thought to herself, *He must be using healing touch on me. He's the first person other than Gran to touch me without bringing on the panic. I feel so peaceful around him, so...at home.* She recognized there were other feelings for him as well, that were anything but peaceful, rising up in her belly like a swarm of butterflies. She blushed and hoped he wouldn't notice.

"When I was thirteen," Jason went on, "the schools started closing, and we were allowed to go home to our villages. It took me weeks to find out where my family had gone because the Cree territory is huge in Saskatchewan. I got really hungry. An old woman took pity on me, fed me and helped me search. Finally, we found them camped beside the Pipestone river. My mother took one look at me and burst into tears.

"My father lay dying inside the tepee and my grandfather was still there, his hand on Dad's forehead. I will always remember seeing Granddad's beautiful face, a tear slowly moving down his wrinkled cheek. My mother didn't know where my sisters were, since they had been taken to a different school, an Anglican one. I spent the next three weeks hunting for them with my new adopted auntie, who was an excellent trapper.

"We found them half-starved and passed out, twenty miles away. We set up camp and nursed them back to health so that they could walk the rest of the way home to our parents. That's when I knew I wanted to be a doctor.

"I wanted to continue my education, so I found a family of farmers in Saskatoon who gave me room and board and a small salary in exchange for work, and started high school. Again, I studied all hours when I wasn't mucking out the barn or repairing fences. I was six foot two when I was fourteen, and none of the white kids messed with me. I got a scholarship to McGill and went to Montreal. After that I got into Johns Hopkins medical school and went into medicine. I'm a holistic physician you might say."

Kate was entranced by his story. She had so many questions, but once again she began to drift into fatigue and slept the rest of the morning while he quietly swept out the cabin and put away the breakfast things. He hunted for a pole in the shed beside the cabin and found one already set up with a lure. He went to the edge of the lake, where mist was rising in the morning sunlight, and cast out into the shimmering turquoise water. He came back with two fat trout and cleaned them while Kate slept on. *She avoids touching me*, he thought. *Probably all for the best. I don't need to complicate her life further. And I'm afraid of what could happen if she did. She feels so...as if she's mine. And I've waited so long... STOP*, he told himself. *Enough! Just do what you came here to do.*

Many women had made it clear to Jason that it wouldn't take more than a word or a look, and they would fall into his arms, but he resisted. Although, he harbored a dim but relentless hope that one day, there would be someone who could share his bizarre life of going wherever Creator guided him, he had deep reservations about attachment to a woman for fear that the "mana" he relied on for his service would be destroyed. Mere attraction or even love was not enough. He had a calling, and he would remain faithful to it. He also had strong ethics about keeping boundaries clear between a physician and a patient. As unfamiliar yearnings for Kate arose, he decided to take a plunge into the icy lake. It sobered him quickly, and he shook off the water like a dog.

He dried off in the sun, then pulled the two trout out of the water where they had remained cold, and headed back to the cabin. Kate was awake and dressed, toweling her long dark hair, still wet from

92

the solar shower bag Gran had rigged up beside the cabin. Jason cleared his throat and thought of going back for another polar bear swim. She smiled and said, "Have a nice swim?"

"Er, sure," he said. "Cold, though."

Kate laughed. "The only bearable water is in the shallows at the east end of the bay."

Jason changed the subject. "Kate, how is your pain level now, from 1 to 10? Do you need any meds today?"

"I'm achy but okay, about a 3. I'd rather not get hooked on them. They make me sleepy."

"Okay, but let me know. Now that you know I *am* your doctor."

"Okay, God," she said, her eyes twinkling.

Suddenly, Jason went still as he spotted something moving into the water. "What the...?" he said.

Kate turned around and said, "Oh, that's Ballerina Bear. She lives on that little island across the bay and likes to swim over here for berries. Gran and I used to love sitting on the beach watching her cross."

"Shall we do that?" Jason asked.

They quietly left the cabin and sat together on the gravel beach, several feet down from where the brown bear was swimming across, holding its snout just above the water. Their arms were touching, and Kate couldn't help noticing that same electric response in her body. She cleared her throat and moved slightly away.

Jason whispered, "Why do you call her Ballerina Bear?"

"Watch this!" she whispered back, a smile lighting her face. As the small brown bear came out of the water, she pointed each paw daintily and shook it, shedding droplets of water. Then she gracefully trotted off into the bush.

"Did you see why we call her that?" Kate said.

"This place is incredible," Jason said.

"I know," she answered.

"Kate, you've asked about my story, I'd really like to hear yours."

"But I have so many questions," she said.

He smiled at her. "We have plenty of time. I'm not going to leave you…until you're really better," he said, as if correcting himself.

"Okay. Where do I begin?" she said.

15

Kate chose to ignore her curiosity about how she had been injured, yet again. She wanted to bask in this unaccustomed sense of safety she felt with Jason, something deeper and more pleasurable than she had experienced in a very long time. In response to Jason' request, she began her story. She closed her eyes and took a deep breath. Breaking through a long-standing protective wall, she tapped into her earliest memories, which felt like re-entering an old recurring nightmare.

She talked about the cold as a painful, invasive presence that overwhelmed her as a tiny, malnourished four-year-old, shivering in her thin t-shirt. She was cold all the time in the dilapidated cabin in Teslin where her mother was hiding her. The cabin smelled of dust, urine, cigarettes, stale beer and whiskey. Some days, Charlene would be so drunk she'd forget to light the stove. One frigid morning, Kate unrolled from her musty blanket, and padded over to her mother, who had fallen asleep in a chair with her head on the table beside an empty bottle and an ashtray stuffed with cigarette butts. "Mama, it's cold. Please light the fire."

Her mother's arm swung out and knocked Kate to the floor. "Getoutahere, you fuckin' little half breed!" she yelled.

"But Mama…" Kate dodged a fist and ran back to her mattress on the floor. Her breath came out in frosty puffs. She decided she had to do something or they'd both freeze. She had overheard one of the aunties telling Charlene about Billy's dad who left an all-night drinking party, staggered out to use the out-house, and fell into a snow bank. By the time Billy found him, he had frozen to death. People never thought little kids understood what they were talking about, but Kate was always listening. She was curious about everything. She often heard visitors whispering to Charlene about her drinking as they washed the pile of encrusted dishes and tried to set the cabin to rights.

She crept out of her nest again, pulling her blanket around her and found a pair of filthy socks to put on. She dragged a log over, climbed onto it and stood on tip toe by the pot-bellied woodstove. As quietly as she could, she pried up the lid up with a stick. There was nothing but ashes in the bottom. She knew she had to find more wood to burn. There were a few sticks of kindling and an old Yukon News in the corner. She wadded up some of the paper, and threw it into the stove, then tossed in some kindling.

She couldn't reach down far enough to arrange it like a tepee the way her Dad had showed her once, telling her she needed to know how to make a fire. She was able to do it on flat ground, but the stove was too deep. She hoped she could light the jumble of paper and sticks. She looked around for the box of matches, and finally spotted it beside her mother's outstretched arm. As stealthily as she

96

could, she reached out to move it to the edge of the table, but grazed her mother's arm. Charlene moaned but didn't waken. As Katy stood on tiptoe again to light the match, the log rolled slightly and she lost her balance and toppled to the floor.

This time, Charlene roared and grabbed her, flinging her out into the snow and slamming the door. Katy moved through the drifts to the shed and pulled the thin plywood door with all her might, opening it wide enough to slide through, and wrapped herself in the blanket she had stowed there. She wondered if she would die, and thought maybe that wouldn't be so bad. Two hours later, a police officer from the reserve who had heard about Katy and her mother, came by to check on them. Following Katy's footprints, he found her blue and unconscious in the corner of the shed. "Oh, God in Heaven." He scooped her up and drove her to the little health clinic next to the band office.

Kate described to Jason how Charlene would often cuddle her and pet her, apologizing for being a "mean mama." Then unpredictably, she would fly into rages and blame Katy for her miserable life. She remembered a day when her mother had coaxed her close and then slapped her hard. That day, Katy decided, no more tears. Whenever she cried or begged her mother to stop, it only fueled Charlene's rage.

"She was sick," Kate said. "My father had to travel back to New Brunswick, where his business was located, and he was on the road for work most of the time. For a while, he couldn't find us after my mom left the last place he had visited us. I prayed and prayed for him to come and get me."

"Kate, how did you live through it? What gave you the strength?"

"I've never told anyone this before, but I discovered a way to disappear, inside myself. It was a beautiful place of warm colors – pink and orange, like a garden in the sun. I felt safe and…loved. And I just kept thinking of my Da and calling to him. I knew he would come one day.

"When he finally found us, he saw the bruises on my body and took me away. He had my mother placed in a residential rehab program in Vancouver, and told her she would never see me again. I think he did something through the courts too, like a restraining order.

"He was always driving from one province to another for his work, and didn't think I should have to travel with him, so he brought me to my Aunt Esther for a while in Chemainus, near Victoria. Then, I ended up with my Gran, Elvira, in Telegraph Creek. After that, everything was better. We spent every summer here at the cabin. I adored my grandmother, and gradually, she taught me to trust. My Da came whenever he could. And as I told you, he died when I was still quite young."

"Who was your father?"

"He was from the Mackenzie clan in Scotland; they're partnered with McCains."

"You mean the big frozen vegie company?"

She laughed. "They make a lot more than vegetables, but yes."

He whistled. "So you're actually a little rich girl."

"Well, my father made sure I would be very well provided for, and the family set up a trust for me, with certain conditions. I came into my inheritance at eighteen, with the provision that I could have an unlimited advance from the trust for my education. I'm grateful for that, because I was able to be part of a First Nations leadership program at the University of Victoria here in British Columbia, and then was selected to attend a new post-graduate program at Harvard which was keen on recruiting minorities. I studied everything that I had become curious about – from geopolitics to journalism. I did very well there and as a result, had no problem applying for an internship with CBC Television in Toronto. These days it's the thing to do to bring in a bit of 'red power.'"

Jason was mesmerized by her story. *This woman is absolutely awesome*, he thought.

Kate went on, "I became an intern in investigative journalism. I worked hard, and they liked what I did, so I was given the undercover assignment that led to this." She pointed to her wounded side.

Jason could see that she was tiring, so he said, "Let's go have some lunch and we'll carry on later".

Why, Kate thought, *am I spilling my guts to this man? Why am I so open with him? And why am I reading hidden meanings into everything he says?! Get a grip, girl! He doesn't mean anything by it.*

Jason was thinking, *Why did I say 'carry on'? I've got to get a grip!*

After a lunch of salad greens and lentil soup, fragrant with ginger and basil, Kate fell into a deep sleep. Jason sat and read. Suddenly he heard her whimpering, "No, Mama, don't!"

He realized that talking about her past had dredged up painful memories. It was all he could do to resist holding and rocking her. *Me and my damn scruples,* he thought. Instead he waited for her to wake on her own and tell him of the nightmare if she chose to.

While she slept on, he went for another dip down toward the shallow end of the bay, and found the water a bit more temperate this time. He realized he was dangerously close to losing his boundaries around doctor/patient relations and knew himself well enough that he would not trust Kate's understandable transference for love. And he had too much respect for her, respect that was growing as he got to know her. He didn't want to complicate her life when it was already chaotic, and once again she was facing issues of safety. He sighed deeply, realizing how much his self-restraint was costing him.

When Kate woke again, they decided to take a short walk on the forest path near Gran's cabin. Jason insisted on supporting her, and she was amazed at what holding his well-muscled arm did to her.

100

He was acutely sensitive to her slender hand in the crook of his arm. They both breathed deeply as they walked slowly along the trail, which had nothing to do with the exertions of their gentle pace. They noticed scratches in the larger tree trunks, and bear scat with rabbit fur on the trail as well as moose droppings.

"I hope we see Mama Moose," Kate said, "but we can't get too close. They're fierce when they have babies to protect. They attack more people every year than bears do, and they're especially aggressive when defending a calf. More people are killed by moose than by Grizzlies, did you know that?"

"You learned a lot from your Gran, didn't you?" Jason suggested they turn around and head back, "That's enough exercise for your first walk," he said.

"Yes, doc," Kate answered, turning her violet eyes up to his. After a long rest in her gravel nest beside the lake, warmed by the sun, this time fully clothed, Kate offered to make dinner. She prepared the trout as Gran had showed her, stuffing it and wrapping it in foil. While it baked for about forty-five minutes, she fried up some of the cooked lentils with onions and leeks she found in Gran's overgrown garden. *When I get better*, she thought, *I need to clean up the garden, maybe put in some more potatoes for next spring."* It suddenly hit her that she had no idea what was coming next. They couldn't stay here over the winter, but where would she go? Where was Jason going? Where did he live? How could she avoid another attempt on her life? She was dizzy with questions and sat down suddenly.

Jason, who had been cleaning Gran's rifle, noticed. "What is it, Kate?"

"I'll tell you over dinner. I think it's ready."

"This lake trout is delicious, Kate! How did you season it?" Jason said as they tucked into their meal.

"Gran's secret recipe, but I'll tell you – just bread crumbs sautéed in butter with onions, garlic, a bit of lemon pepper and a pinch of sage."

Jason smiled and continued eating with obvious pleasure. Kate nearly blushed. He waited patiently until she was ready to talk. "Jason, I have so many questions, but now that I'm really awake, I need to know what happened to me and figure out what's next -- what the danger is now. I don't want to involve you in this."

He stifled a laugh and thought, *a bit late for that!* "Well, as far as I can figure, it was a tall Indian who went hunting for you. Archie picked him up when he brought me out before my cousin and I found you."

"How did you know where I was?"

"Grandfather Eagle led me to you. He circled until I arrived."

"Actually, I believe you," she said. "What about the hunter?"

"He won't be coming after you again."

"What? How do you know?"

"As far as he knows, he killed you, and I assume he reported that to his clients so he would get paid."

"But how does he know for sure?"

"Well, my cousin and I got you down from the cliff and brought you here in his boat. Then I sent him back with instructions to hold a small funeral service for you in Atlin after about ten days, under the pretense of having come across your body. He'll also put an obituary in the paper."

"But what about Aunt Rose...?"

"She knows you're all right."

"Lord, Jason, you've thought of everything. I still don't understand why you're doing all this for me."

"Later, Kate, I'll explain everything later. The main thing is you're safe now."

16

After Jason told her about the announcement of her death, Kate slept deeply and well, free of the nightmares which had haunted her. She continued to heal. Each day they spent together was filled with quiet joy, and they savored it, intensely aware that it would soon be coming to an end. They talked, laughed, traded stories, shared the cooking and fire-making, and played poker at Gran's scrubbed table.

One morning, feeling stronger, Kate led Jason to her secret place in the forest, where she had made the medicine wheel. He was entranced by the tiny mosses, the smooth lake stones, the silence.

"Oh, Kate, thank you for bringing me here. It's an honor to be in your sacred place."

She smiled and, to her dismay, felt her face grow warm. They then prayed and chanted together, something Kate had never done before with another person. *It feels so right*, she thought. Jason seemed pensive and nervous. Soon, they turned back for the cabin.

That afternoon, Jason shared more of his story with her. "After I got my MD from Johns Hopkins, I went home to Saskatchewan. I was confused about what Creator wanted me to do. So after the party my family had for me, I talked to my Granddad, who at 93 was still sharp as a tack. He asked me what was troubling me. 'You read me well, Granddad, you always have,' I told him.

"'You did all that work for so long and now you don't know what to do with it,' he said to me. Then he quoted Einstein: 'I want to know God's thoughts. The rest are details.' He told me what I needed was a Nitawayamih. That's Cree for 'go and pray', or vision quest. I canoed up the Pipestone River and went into the bush. I needed to sort out what I was meant to do with all I had learned from my grandfather, and also my new medical knowledge. I didn't want a fancy office in LA, but I didn't know what I did want. Something was calling to me, but what?

"So, I went to a flat rock that overhangs the river, stripped down, made a fire, took my cleansing dive into the river and then sat for three days. I didn't have anything but a few sips of water each day. I heard 'nitohtamowin natamakawin' – 'Listen and serve' over and over. I knew then that I needed to practice listening for guidance as well as listening to people that needed help, to serve in whatever way Creator guided me. I..." He stopped, looking embarrassed.

"Tell me," Kate said. "I'll believe you," with a warm smile.

"Well, I offered my life to Him to do with as He pleases. I learned to listen for Creator's voice in meditation. That's how I first 'heard' you."

"You heard me? How?" Kate asked.

"When we were both praying, I guess our prayers crossed the thought bridge. I heard you pray for strength. You were cold and alone and scared, but so brave and determined. You must have been undercover then."

"Yes, I did pray for strength and for Creator to guide me through the danger. And I felt as if someone was behind me holding my shoulders, whispering, 'It will all come right.' Was that you?"

His wide smile told her that it was. "And then," he continued, "there was the time we, uh, traveled."

"At the black bluff," she whispered.

Jason spoke quietly. "You were with me, Kate. You know that."

Over the next few days, Jason told Kate how his guidance moved him from place to place, wherever he was most needed. "And then I go home and practice medicine for a while, build up my resources. People need tending everywhere."

"So where is home now?"

"Well, that's a whole other story. When my grandfather died, I moved to Hawaii."

"Hawaii! I've always wanted to go there, but I never had the time. How did you end up in Hawaii?"

"Same way," he laughed. "I heard it in meditation, and just went. We have a home in Kauai, and have built a clinic there. Other healers have joined us, all with different skills. It's a holistic clinic and retreat center actually. It's called Ho'o pono pono, which means 'to make whole or to make right' in the Hawaiian language. The people of Polynesia practice it. If you have ever heard of it, it was probably as a blessing used with the dying, kind of a final gift. It is said back and forth by the person and someone close to them: It goes:

I love you.

Forgive me.

I forgive you.

Thank you.

Goodbye.

"People come to the clinic from all over the world. We use natural herbs and plants such as: noni and coconut, Lomi Lomi massage, healing waters treatments, different kinds of meditation, and personal healing retreats. We have surprising results. For some folks, our program is their last resort. Kate, you can shut your mouth now. You look gob-smacked, as the Kiwis say."

Kate's eyes got wider as she clicked her jaw shut, realizing she had been gaping at him in astonishment. "But how did you come *here*?"

"I do three months of service in Canada each summer with a mobile clinic, usually in the prairies. I still want to help my people. And I visit with my mother and sisters. This time I came to the Yukon for you. I knew you needed me."

"Holee!" said Kate, sounding just like Gran.

17

The next morning over breakfast, Jason said, "Kate, I want to ask you something. The other day, you mentioned that your Gran had a different experience in residential school than your mother Charlene. Do you mind telling me about that?"

Kate's mind went back to a time when she had wondered the same thing. "Why are you so different from mama?" the twelve year old asked her Gran one summer day at the cabin. "You went to residential school, didn't you?"

"Well, honey, yes I did, but I had a different experience."

"But didn't they cut your hair and make you stop speaking Tahltan?"

Gran said, "Let me explain this way. Yes, they cut our hair. It was easier to keep clean. And no, they weren't as rigid in our school. We learned English, but they didn't get mad if we spoke our own language."

Kate looked really puzzled. "I don't get it."

"Katy, people are people, even nuns and priests. You can't just put them all in one kettle of fish. The ones in my school cared, especially the headmaster, Father Simon, and young Sister Mary Joseph, who helped me to go on to the program at McGill. She loved me like a daughter."

Kate's eyes filled. "But then how could it have been so terrible for my mom?"

Gran shook her head and sighed. "Katy, your mom has a very sensitive soul, and unfortunately, she was taken to a school that was more, uh, backward than most."

"Backward, how?" she asked

"You're old enough to understand this, Kate, so I'm going to tell you what I know, and what I learned at McGill. The worst thing the government and the churches did to our people was trying to assimilate us. Do you know what that means?"

"I think so," Kate said, "How they tried to make the kids ashamed of being Indians?"

"Yes. It means the loss of our long hair, our names, our language, our family life, our culture. They taught us that it's better to be or act white. They believed, and most of them quite sincerely, that we were lost souls, that we had to become Christians and give up what they called 'our heathen ways'."

Kate sat back and said to Jason, "It was true identity theft -- stealing our sense of self, forcing us to repudiate our own race. They were trying to obliterate a whole way of life, and they did it in the name of God! I know most of them honestly believed they were saving us, but that doesn't justify some of the ways they abused the young ones."

Jason nodded, his eyes going darker. "The great sin of racism. For so many of our people, it bred an evil inside them that is still spreading, generation after generation. I've always felt as you do that the residential schools committed cultural genocide. The worst violation wasn't the physical brutality that some children went through, including your mother, I imagine; it was the spiritual theft, the loss of pride in oneself, in our people. It created a deep sense of shame -- the 'dirty savages' who needed to be hosed down. They tried, and too often succeeded, in breaking our spirits. So many of our people became 'apples' – red on the outside, white inside."

Kate felt a tight band squeezing her chest. "I can't talk about it anymore, Jason. It's too awful. It does make me appreciate what Gran and the rest of my family did for me. And I was really blessed to be part of the First Nations program at UVic which honors our people and is helping us retrieve our sense of who we are. Then there's Gran's experience, and she wasn't the only one. Her school saw potential in her and other kids, and really gave them a wonderful education and a leg up to go further if they chose to. Remember I told you about Gran going into that program at McGill, then coming home and starting the Women's Healing Center in Telegraph Creek? Now, that's a success story."

"You know, Katy, there's a prophecy among the Cree that the blue-eyed people must be part of the healing of our people. So the religious at your Gran's residential school did that. The University of Victoria and Harvard are doing it, as well. And a lot of money and resources are being poured into the Aboriginal Healing Foundation, which is offering recovery programs all across Canada."

Jason noticed Kate straining to keep her eyes open. "Oh, Kate, this is tiring you out. Thanks for telling me. Your Gran was a remarkable woman, who used everything she was given to give back." Kate nodded and agreed to have a rest.

The next day, as brisk winds whistled down from the glaciers, rippling the lake, and icy autumn rains began, Kate grew quiet. She pondered deeply and prayed within her medicine wheel in the morning and evening. Her heart felt heavy, not only because of the decision she had reached, but with unexpected grief at leaving Jason. She was amazed at how far she was now from her usual independent, almost monastic existence, feeling more and more connected to this beautiful man. She was overwhelmed at times by the yearnings she felt in her body and the images of them together which haunted her imagination.

In her dreams, she saw herself standing beside him with a circle of flowers in her hair. She talked sternly to herself, since Jason kept his distance and obviously didn't have those feelings for her. He had said, "we" when describing the clinic. Was he married? She simply couldn't ask him that. She pondered deeply about what she needed to do next and asked Creator to guide her. Once she came to a decision, she knew what she had to do, but she didn't feel it wise to tell Jason. He would want to go with her, to protect her, and she simply couldn't put him at further risk. *God knows he has given too much already,* she thought.

As Kate began to ready the cabin in preparation for departure, Jason knew they had to talk. What would she do next? Where would she go? He knew he was too involved with her already, so kept his silence until she chose to tell him. Before he went to sleep that night, he packed up his gear for the parting he now dreaded.

There was an emptiness already growing in his heart. *How can I leave her?* He realized that for the first time, he was so powerfully drawn to a woman that he could not imagine life without her. He kept picturing her beside him, a fragrant circle of flowers on her head, her long, glossy hair flowing down her back. He prayed for the strength and courage to leave her if that was Creator's will. At dawn the next morning, when the mist was just beginning to rise from the lake, and distant peaks began to glow gold and rose, he put on a heavy jacket and walked into the forest, to the clearing where Kate's medicine wheel was. As he chanted and prayed, facing the four directions, it struck him, *wouldn't she be safer in Hawaii?* His eyes lit and he asked Creator to confirm the thought. *Is this my own will or yours? A vain imagining or the truth?* In response, he heard, *her place is beside you.*

His heart pounding, Jason said a quick prayer of thanks and raced back along the deer path to the cabin, calling Kate's name. "Kate, Kate, I have something to tell you! I mean, to ask you!" As he burst through the cabin door, his voice rang into utter silence. He looked around and saw that her pack was gone and the cabin was already neatly secured. He ran to the shore and found that Gran's boat was missing. "Noooo!" he yelled at the Heavens. He ran back inside to grab his phone to call Milton, knowing it was already too late. Then he saw the note.

Throughout the night, Kate had had little sleep. She went over and over in her mind the plan to return to Toronto and finish what she started. She fought the desire to go to Jason and tell him everything, including her feelings for him. Now that she suspected he was married, she knew that once again, the love she longed for all her life was eluding her.

It is what it is, she kept telling herself, tears seeping down her cheeks into her pillow. The moment Jason crept from the cabin at dawn, she dressed quickly, packed and hastily neatened the cabin. She wrote a note and slipped it under a driftwood "sculpture" they had found and made their table centerpiece: "Jason, it's time to go. I'm not good at goodbyes, but I do want you to know I will always remember your kindness. You saved my life, Doc. Aloha and journey well. Gratefully, Kate"

Jason put his head in his hands. *Why, Creator, did you not warn me?* He rang Milton and asked him to pick him up. As they crossed the

114

lake to the town of Atlin, he held no illusions of following Kate. He realized this was probably all for the best and that his earlier "guidance" was probably just wishful thinking. *She doesn't feel that way about me,* he admitted sadly.

Jason spent the next two weeks traveling the Whitehorse area in his mobile clinic, throwing himself into his work to keep from feeling the deepening heartache of missing Kate. For a few cherished minutes, he believed that he had finally found his soul mate. He felt ripped by the separation, but was loathe to ask in prayer where she was. He didn't trust himself to keep from following her.

He stowed the vehicle in a friend's garage, and flew to Vancouver, then to Hawaii. When he landed on Kauai, there was Mama Moana, his manager and business partner, waiting for him with a huge grin. Her enormous frame was garbed in a bright coral muumuu; she had a hibiscus in the exact same shade tucked behind her right ear and a huge frangipani and gardenia tiara encircling her head. She held a lei ready to put around his neck. She took one look at him, her face fell, and she enveloped him in her huge arms. "Aloha, e kipa mai – come to me, dear one. Welcome home." He clung to her. As soon as Jason climbed into the passenger side of the Jeep Cherokee, she turned on the engine and the air con, and said, "I'll take you to the beach first, shall I? I don't think you're quite ready for the big Kahuna welcome." Jason just nodded, put his head down and began to weep.

115

As he knew she would, Moana just companioned him in silence as he poured out his story. He also knew she would have some choice words for him the next day after she had time to reflect on all he had shared. He spared nothing, including his intense feelings for Kate, and his worries about complicating her life.

"There's more," Moana said. "Spill it."

"Moana, you've always been able to read me like an open book." He took a deep breath. "I don't know if this is coming from my ego or my soul," he said, "but what will happen to the mana Creator has entrusted to me, if I join my light to hers? Would I be abandoning it? And Moana, I don't know where she is."

"Enough, now, dear boy, I'm going to pray on it. We'll talk tomorrow. Now you must join the 'ohana waiting to celebrate you home." After two hours of "emptying his cup", and a long, cool swim in the lagoon, Jason felt lighter, ready to face the friends and colleagues awaiting his arrival.

18

Kate burrowed under the pile of quilts in Uncle Willy's guest room, knowing that soon enough she had to get up and face what she felt called to do. Over flapjacks and bacon, with a supersized mug of coffee, she realized she needed to share her thoughts about the return to Toronto. "I have to finish what I started, Uncle," she said.

Willy frowned, but forced his expression into neutral, knowing his niece's fierce determination. "What's your thinkin' on that, Katy?" he asked, containing his own fear for her safety.

"Uncle, I knew I could count on you to give me the understanding and the space to think it through out loud. First of all, I met this man..." She told Willy all that had happened in Atlin and how, for the first time, she had met a man she could let in, one to whom she was powerfully drawn. "But he doesn't feel the same, Uncle. He kept his distance."

Willy grunted but chose to keep listening, not interrupting with his own need to comfort her out of what he considered an obvious misconception. "How'd you figure that?" he said.

"Well," Kate said, blushing, "we were alone in the cabin for weeks, and he never made a move. I'm pretty sure he knew how I felt."

"And he's a doctor, you said?"

"Yes."

"Do you think there might be another explanation for his not wanting to tamper with the doctor/patient dynamic?"

Kate looked startled, and Willy couldn't hold back any more. "Kate, look, any man in his right mind, if he had an inkling you were interested, would respond."

"Well, he did seem to dive into the lake a lot."

"My case rests."

"Oh, Uncle, if only that could be true. But I don't know where he is now."

"You're the investigative journalist, Katy girl, I'm sure you can figure it out."

"I can't do that right now, Uncle. I have to go back."

He sighed, wondering if this was the closest Kate would ever get to a chance for a happy life.

"So what's calling to you so strongly?" he asked.

Kate spoke of the work she had done undercover, the women and children she had met who worked for the mob. Their lives were destroyed by their addictions and the web of crime into which they'd been drawn. "I keep thinking about Lonnie", she said. "I just can't leave him there."

Leonard (Lonnie) Running Bear was a thirteen year old boy who left the Ojibway reserve in Ontario after his aunt told him to leave, saying she couldn't afford to feed him any longer. He had hitchhiked to Toronto with nothing but a small back-pack.

"He was a beautiful boy, Uncle. When he was sober, he talked about wanting to be a medicine man someday, and he had a smudge stick and wore a special shell necklace with a mother Mary medal. By the time I went under cover, Sabatano's men had taken him under their wing and made him think he was part of the family. They gave him as much crack and meth as he could take. Then they cut him off and told him he had to earn his way. All he could do to get his next fix was to work for one of their pimps. As he got more and more wrecked on meth, he started losing weight and looking bad. He couldn't produce the same profits, so they dropped him.

When I met him, he could only get the most horrid kinds of tricks, and was squatting with other homeless kids in an empty building that was boarded up. I met him when I was squatting there myself. His face was covered with sores by that time. I tried to get close to him, but he was just nodding off most of the time, between tricks. It took everything I had to talk him into entering a rehab program, and he really started getting better. He's a wonderful boy, very caring with the other kids. When I think of him and the other children, I just can't give up on them. I can't let all the information I uncovered go to waste. If there's anything at all I can do to help stop this, I have to do it."

119

Kate outlined her idea to return to CBC in Toronto to expose Sabatano, as originally planned during a show ostensibly to give people accused of crimes a chance to tell their side of the story. She felt Sabatano, with his huge ego, would find the idea irresistible. They would tell him a new hire would be interviewing him, and of course the new hire would be Kate.

"How sure are you that the mob believes you to be dead?" Willy asked.

"They have no reason to believe otherwise. I've been completely off the grid since my funeral in Atlin."

"So, where will you stay? How will you pull this off, Katy? That is, without getting blown away?"

"Well, a few days ago on a cell phone which I got rid of right away, I called Stan, the producer, and explained everything. Yesterday I called again, and he said the Don has agreed to an interview. The cops will be undercover in the live studio audience. If they read him his rights after the show, it won't be seen as entrapment. There is always the concern that his people are embedded in the department or even at the station, so the whole thing has been handled on a high security, need-to-know basis."

Willy just shook his head. "You know I'll be praying for you, Katy. Please be careful. You mean a lot to me and your aunties. And probably more than you know to this fella of yours." He handed her a pair of soft suede gloves, lined with rabbit fur. "Katy, these will help to keep you warm. I know how you hate the cold."

19

Kate sat alone in a private office at CBC, chanting a last prayer under her breath. She had gone over and over her notes, which she had reconstructed from memory, barricaded in a small safe house apartment in Toronto. She never went out. Meals were brought in to her. A shopper from the network brought her the clothes she needed, including a knitted tuque, cashmere scarf, heavy pea coat and gloves.

Refusing studio make-up for the televised interview, Kate wore a ribbed dove grey turtle neck with a silver chain and Haida eagle pendant, a navy blazer and a slate grey pencil skirt with her signature Manolo heels, for which CBC was glad to shell out. Her hair was held in her customary French braided chignon. A senior producer knocked and poked his head in. "Five minutes, Kate."

"Thanks, Arthur. I'm ready."

When Kate walked onto the small studio stage and sat in the interviewer's chair, there were startled gasps from the camera and boom operators as they recognized her. A murmur went through the live studio audience as well. Kate put her finger to her lips, looked around and smiled, and the noise immediately subsided.

Sabatano walked onto the sound stage escorted by a gorgeous blond producer who was distracting him with continual chatter until he was seated and miked. As he leaned back in the guest chair, he glanced over toward Kate, and his smile froze. He turned pale, and looked utterly stunned. "What the…?"

Immediately, the senior cameraman was holding up his hand and quietly counting down. "Five, four, three, two, live!"

Kate smiled into the camera, her violet eyes shining, and said, "No, I didn't die. Yes, there were attempts on my life. I guess Creator had other plans."

The producer in the control room looked wildly through the script and knew Kate was winging it. She instantly shifted into professional mode and began the interview. "Mr. Sabatano, welcome to The Fifth Estate. Today we will be talking about an enterprise in which you have a senior leadership role, one that is in control of the drug markets in Toronto and throughout the world. Most importantly, its prime activity is human trafficking.

"I'm talking about the 'Ndrangheta, now considered the top criminal organization in Toronto. It's a global syndicate based in Calabria, the toe of the Italian boot -- your home town, Mr. Sabatano. Care to comment?"

Sabatano leaned forward as if to escape but sat back down and crossed his arms over his chest. "You've got that wrong, Ms. Mackenzie. I deal only in fine wines."

Kate continued, "As you know, Mr. Sabatano, I spent six weeks as your personal assistant. Do you recall confiding in me about your cleverest move, to recruit children as young as nine years old, addict them to methamphetamines, crack or even heroine, then to use that habit to drive them into prostitution?"

"I have no idea what you're talking about. This is slander!"

Kate went on, looking directly into the camera. "When I started this undercover project, I posed as an addict myself. I discovered a world deeply hidden within the streets and abandoned buildings of Toronto, populated by children abandoned by family, or having run away from abuse only to end up becoming the most wretched addicts and worse.

It would be unwise and dangerous to show photos of the children I came to know in the cold squats of this city, but I have photos of other children taken several years ago in other North American cities, who were led along the same soul-destroying path. Here are their before and after shots – before they became addicted, then after. One of our CBC colleagues, also undercover, took these candid shots."

"What does any of this have to do with me?" asked Sabatano.

Kate simply stared at him with her violet eyes. When he said nothing further, Kate was off and running: "Johnny (not his real name) is a thirteen year old Athabascan boy who became part of a prostitution ring started by your cell." Sabatano merely stared at her coldly, refusing to speak. "Johnny's story is tragically typical. No place to go but the streets, hungry, and cold. Unwilling to go back to the foster care system or having escaped from juvenile detention, he is taken in by the 'Mafioso family', fed, given a job to do and praised for it. He is gradually given drugs, which he begins to crave. Then, when the drugs are suddenly removed, he experiences gut-wrenching, painful withdrawal and begs for them. He is willing to do anything. And this is how your 'family' lures a child into the back seats and back alleys to be used and abused by pedophiles."

"As I keep saying, what does that have to do with me? I have no idea what you're talking about. I'm just a wine merchant from the old country, and Canada has given me an opportunity for which I'm grateful."

Kate said, "Well, folks, I guess this is going to be more of a monologue. According to my research, Ndrangheta is the largest criminal operation in Italy and across the world, having cornered the market on cocaine distribution in Europe and here in Canada too. Unlike the Sicilian Mafia, which is the leading mob in Montreal, the 'Ndrangheta forms small cells called *locali*. They tend to work in the background, don't they, Mr. Sabatano?" The Don just shook his head and looked down.

Kate paused, then went on. "The Italian authorities call it the 'liquid mafia' because it filters into any hole and fills it. It was in one of these cells that I got to know our guest over a time frame of fourteen months, when I was undercover as an addict, then a dealer and for the last few months of that period, I was an assistant in Mr. Sabatano's private offices."

As Kate spoke, on the screen behind her and Sabatano, the photos of the children and teens wasted on meth and cocaine continued to appear, their faces pitted with sores, their bodies thin, the light utterly gone from their rheumy eyes.

"I want you to know that efforts are underway to rescue and rehabilitate these children. And you can help." A link appeared on the screen for a crowd-source funding site for retrieval and healing programs for young victims of human trafficking.

Kate ended the interview by saying, "This is the last public appearance of 'the Teflon Don', ladies and gentlemen. He will now be escorted elsewhere. Sad to say, you won't be seeing me again, either. I want to express my gratitude to CBC for their courage and integrity in supporting this highly secret and risky project."

The cameras continued to roll as Sabatano rose quickly from his chair and the authorities closed in with handcuffs. Then the show went to commercial. When the show returned, another journalist sat in the chair to close the show, but Kate had vanished.

Sabatano was immediately flown north in a waiting helicopter and placed in a safe-house far from the city in a holiday cabin in the Muskoka lakes district. His lawyer was flown in as well. For days, he roared at his keepers to put more logs on the fire.

20

"Kate, we only agreed to this because you assured us you had a plan for remaining safe after the broadcast," said Stan Levinson, the executive producer. "I know you won't tell me where you're going, but please take care of yourself. What can we do to help?"

Kate said, "Stan, I'm so sorry that this has to be my swan song. I want you to know I truly appreciate your trust in me to pull this off and willingness to follow my lead on how this went down." She sighed. "I don't know where I'll go eventually, but it won't be anywhere I've been before."

"Well, all the best to you, Kate. Now what do you need?"

"Thank you, Stan. There is one thing and it's a big ask…"

Within an hour after the broadcast, disguised as a janitor in green coveralls and a tuque, Kate shuffled out the back door of the studio and headed for a waiting SUV parked five blocks away. She carried her clothes in an old back pack provided by one of the janitorial staff. A private plane owned by a network executive awaited her on the tarmac at a small regional airport attached to Pearson International. Instructions were to drop her off on the west coast of

Canada. She had shed all electronics, including a cell phone and carried only a bag of old bills in twenties and fifties. During the flight to Vancouver International, Kate changed into jeans and a sweater, and put on a curly blond wig, lightening her dark brows with concealer. She took a cab to a private dock at the South terminal of Vancouver Airport and soon boarded a small seaplane, which had a suitcase of winter clothes and sundries waiting for her. The pilot asked her no questions, and she leaned back and slept all the way up the coast to the Queen Charlotte Islands.

Gran's cousin Agnes Johns was waiting for Kate in a mud spattered pick-up parked near the dock. She climbed out of the truck and came to help Kate with her bags. Kate waved off the pilot, and he smiled and turned the tiny plane toward open water. The first thing Kate did was to whip off the blond wig and free her long hair. "That's better," chuckled Agnes. They drove for half an hour through Masset until they arrived at Miller Creek where Agnes's remote cabin sat on a knoll above the water, surrounded by pines and firs.

"Let's park your gear in the back room and then have a cuppa."

Kate shivered and opened the duffle bag to find something warmer. To her delight, there was a hand-knitted Cowichan wool sweater, with brown, black and white designs of caribou, bear and wolf in natural, un-dyed wool. The indigenous knitters never removed the natural oils of the fleece, so their one-of-a-kind sweaters were waterproof as well as incredibly insulating. *Thoughtful of whoever did my packing. This is the only thing that has ever kept me really warm,* she thought.

"Well, Katy, you think you'll be warm enough?" Agnes laughed. "What's so mysterious about this visit? I was told to expect you but not to put it out on the tom-tom telegraph. Even the neighbors don't know you've come."

"Well, Auntie, it's a very long story, and much of it I can't tell you, to keep you safe."

Agnes looked even more intrigued. "Now, this is gettin' interestin'", she said. They refilled their mugs after Kate washed the breakfast dishes, and sat for several hours as she briefly explained her assignment with CBC and then talked non-stop about the strange Cree doctor who had saved her life.

Agnes listened, but when Kate seemed finished, she couldn't help herself from saying, "Well, girlie, what're ya doin' here? Why aren't you on a plane to Hawaii?"

"Auntie, I told you! He doesn't feel that way about me. And I think he may be married. What is it with you and Uncle Willy?!"

"Older? Wiser?" said Agnes, grinning.

The next morning, Kate watched Agnes preparing flapjacks and sausages on her huge Aga cast iron stove, which kept the room toasty warm. She looked so much like Gran standing there in her jeans, her waist long hair woven into a tidy knot at the nape of her neck, and sporting an apron down to her ankles. Tears clouded Kate's vision, and as Agnes turned around, she couldn't help noticing. Kate cleared her throat and said cheerily, "Breakfast smells wonderful, Auntie."

"Mm-hmm," Agnes mumbled. They ate in companionable silence and sipped strong coffee from large speckled blue enamel camping mugs, duplicates of the ones she and Gran had used at the cabin. "Katy, I never heard from you much after Elvira passed. What was that like for you?"

Katy nearly choked on her last gulp of coffee. "I never talk about that, Auntie," she said.

"Well, maybe it's time you did, honey." Again, Kate's eyes filled with tears, but this time they escaped, slipping down her cheeks. Sighing, she blotted them with a worn cloth serviette. "You know, Auntie Agnes, I've talked more about myself in the past weeks than in as many years. Not sure why, but maybe it's best I get it off my chest."

The first time Elvira fell, they were picking choke cherries near the cabin one afternoon. "She just crumpled all of a sudden. And she was unconscious for about five minutes. I kept shaking her and talking to her until she came out of it. I helped her back to the cabin, and she was very cross with me for leaving the buckets full of berries behind. 'Either the bears'll get 'em or we can make muffins and jam', she said. She insisted I go back to retrieve them. By the time I got back, the color had come back to her face. When I urged her to see the doctor in Whitehorse, she just pooh-poohed it, saying 'It was just one of my wee spells. I'm all right, Katy.'

"I was so worried Aunt Agnes. She was just never the same after that, and no matter what I said, she wouldn't see the doctor. You know how stubborn she was. I was only seventeen, and even though I was scheduled to start my freshman year at UVic that Fall, I didn't know what I would do if I lost her. You know how close we were. And she was the only one I ever..." Kate's voice trailed off into a sob, and she put her head down on her arms and let go.

Agnes didn't touch her, not wanting to disrupt her tears. *Finally*, she thought, *she's emptying that big cup of grief she carries*. Elvira had taught her that much. "Don't ever comfort someone out of their healing tears," she would say.

Kate sat up and continued, "I was really nervous about leaving her, and I tried to talk her into letting me stay in Telegraph Creek with her instead of starting UVic, since I was still young for a university freshman, but she wouldn't hear of it. For the first time, there was anger and tension between us, until one night she came up behind me, as I was sitting at my desk reading. She put her hands on my shoulders and said, 'Kate, let's talk.' And you know what that means – she talked and I listened."

Agnes's wrinkled face pruned up into a huge grin. She laughed, remembering her cousin's strong-willed determination.

Kate recalled vividly what Gran had said to her. "Katy girl, over the last dozen years, you and I have built something precious together. We have many summers of memories at the cabin, all our stories, and you have new stories to write in your life. I know there's something happening with my heart…" Kate interrupted her, but she shushed her. "Shh, Katy, I know you love me and don't want anything to happen to me. But that isn't the way of it. It's not Creator's plan. I'd rather die in my own bed here in the little town I love than in some big white hospital where I won't have any control over what they do to me. I know you don't really want that for me, either. So I need you to be brave. Be your unselfish, generous, caring self, and let me do this my way."

"And then, Auntie," Kate said. "I ran. I hid like a child for two days. I slept and ate with cousins. She knew where I was, but she let me be. I took long walks along the creek, and I prayed. I asked Creator to guide me and to let me do what was best for my Gran. By the time I came back to her on the third day, I had found the acceptance to honor her decision."

A few weeks later, I was in another world -- a small house on campus in Victoria that I shared with two other First Nations girls. Gran and I talked several times a week, and she seemed fine. She made it all the way through my freshman year, in time for the Year

One awards ceremony for the new program I had entered at First Peoples House. She sat there all dressed up in her green suede outfit, and looked so proud, but she was thin and pale, and over the summer when I was able to come home, I saw that she wouldn't last long. She wanted me to be at peace with it, and I did my best.

"We never went back to the Atlin cabin. She was just too weak to travel. As you know, that July she passed in her sleep. It was the gentle way she wanted to go. Just before she died, we were shelling peas on her porch listening to the Stikene bubbling past. Grandfather eagle was soaring around that day and we could hear his sweet warble. I pretended to be okay, but I was miserable. Then Gran said, 'Katy, this is a deep teachable moment for you, honey. It's time for you to start taking Vitamin T.' I knew Gran didn't hold with vitamins except what we got from natural foods and Indian medicine, so I said, 'What's that, Gran? I never heard of it.' 'Vitamin T is trust, Katy, trust in Creator. In the good book, the Prophet Isaiah says, 'Those who trust in the Lord shall renew their strength. They will mount up on wings as eagles. They shall walk and not faint. They shall run and not grow weary.'"

"I didn't answer her, just kept shelling peas. A few days later, she died, and I couldn't find a trace of 'Vitamin T'. After the funeral, it was like a tsunami wave picked me up and rolled me over and over. The grief just shattered me. And there was a huge hole inside of me, like that movie with Goldie Hawn and Meryl Streep as ghosts who shoot huge holes in each other."

Agnes nodded. "I know I should have contacted you, Auntie, but I couldn't talk to anybody, not even Creator. I couldn't pray for weeks. I told God that I didn't blame him, but I just couldn't talk to him like I did before Gran died.

One day I was walking and I looked up, and there was Grandfather Eagle right above me, singing that same sweet warble, as if he was consoling me. I started to cry, and asked Creator to forgive me. Then, I heard him say, 'I know you love me. You couldn't stay away long, daughter,' almost like he was pinching my cheek. And then the most amazing thing happened. I felt Gran right beside me, her soft cheek next to mine. And I heard her say, very softly, 'Don't get caught up, Sweetie. You're only a whisper away from eternity.' I knew she meant that I was being overcome by my grief, and that it was time to come out of it."

Kate stayed with Agnes for several weeks. Each morning, wrapped in her Indian sweater, she walked along Miller Creek. Her thoughts turned again and again to Jason – his smile, his plunges into the lake, their talks together, the times they had touched and laughed. As hard as she tried to banish him from her mind, he was at the center of her thoughts. Her heart literally ached for him from the time she awoke to the moment she was able to fall asleep. For the first time, love had slipped past her guard and was firmly embedded in her soul.

21

Moana shifted her huge bulk onto her side on the hammock and straightened her bright lime green muu muu, as Jason sat in a high-backed rattan chair across from her. The palms above them waved gently in the ocean breezes. "Well, my boy, how is it with you now? How are you, really?" She had watched him throw himself into clinic work for several weeks, the shadows beneath his eyes deepening, his usual glow of health fading. Jason sighed. "I just can't do it, Moana, I can't let her go. I can't sleep or eat or get her out of my mind for more than two minutes. And I keep going back to what I thought Creator told me: 'Her place is beside you'."

"So, what gives you the sense that you're meant to let her go? What keeps you from having her beside you?"

"I've never felt like this before. I don't know if my ego is trying to take over my soul. You know how we always ask our clients, 'Would you rather be driven by your ego or led by your soul?' I can't even separate them anymore. Maybe I've just been lonely too long."

Moana looked into his tired eyes. "So, what have you done before when you weren't sure? When you needed guidance?"

He sat up straighter and said, "Ask."

Moana rolled her eyes and shook her head, as if to say "That took you long enough to figure out," then warmed him with a loving smile

After clinic rounds that day, Jason told his colleagues he would be away for a few days and transferred his appointments to another physician. By two o'clock, he was climbing a little known trail up Mount Kapalaoa to his sacred spot. He knew his weakened state and had forced himself to eat a full meal for the first time in many days including haupia, Moana's coconut pudding which she called "Hawaiian penicillin". As he climbed, he swigged often from his water bottle. He didn't want to begin his fast dehydrated.

He set up camp under a rock overhang festooned with ferns, a dry dirt floor beneath it, as shelter from the afternoon downpours. The next day, he sat watching the sun rise in the rosy morning mist and began his prayer chant. "O Creator, make me a hollow reed, empty of self, purify me of selfish motives and help me to come to you with a clean spirit. I ask that the gentle winds of your will may stir me up and bend me into conformity with your plan for my life, directing my movement and my stillness, and my every decision. Set my feet firmly on your path. Give my eyes the vision to see, my ears the purity to hear only your voice. Make your will my will."

Jason opened himself and breathed in the silence. Three days later, as he made his way back down the mountain trail, he was smiling and moving swiftly, ready to act. And he was ravenous.

After a brief knock, Jason burst into Moana's private office. Finding her alone, he grabbed her in a huge hug. "Whoa there, fella! What's happened to you?"

"Moana, it was real! It's true! We *are* meant to be together."

She resisted saying, "I could have told you that," and just smiled at him wryly.

"Yes, I know you could have told me that," he laughed, reading her expression. "I just had to be sure."

"So, now what? What's the plan?"

"Well, I know Kate would have wanted to finish her project, and is probably back in Toronto. I won't stop until I find her, Moana. If it's truly Creator's will, I will find her, wherever she is."

"Then, God be with you, my boy. God be with you."

Three days later, Jason sat in the office of Stan Levinson, CBC executive director. Stan shook his head sadly. "I'm so sorry, Dr. Red Deer, we honestly have no idea where Kate intended to go after the broadcast."

Jason was torn by his pride in Kate for having completed her exposeé and the fear of losing her trail. *Why when I need guidance the most, do I panic that it won't come? Oh, ye of little faith,* he thought. He remembered something his grandfather had told him once: "Doubt your doubt before you doubt your faith."

"I can only tell you that a private plane dropped her off in Vancouver."

"Well, that's where I'll go, then," Jason said. He flew back across the country. When he arrived at the South Terminal of Vancouver Airport, he scoured the small dockside buildings for any information he could find. There wasn't a trace of her. He knew he needed to stop, pray and listen, but his anxiety was so intense that, for the first time, he didn't know if he could summon the peace he needed to empty his mind and be receptive.

He walked out to the marsh beyond the last hangar and hunkered on his heels. He breathed deeply, inhaling the ripe scent of boggy water and marsh grass. "Creator, hear my prayer," he intoned. "I'm lost. I need your hand to guide me. Give me the strength to follow your will, and the wisdom to know your voice. This I know. All things are connected like the blood that unites one family. Help me, Grandfather, to connect with Kate, if that is your will for us both. Protect her, guide her, and if it is your will, guide me to her. If it is not, give me the strength to detach and accept. All my relations."

Jason remained in silence until he began to feel numb. No visions came to him, no clarity. He had experienced this before, recognizing that the timing was always in God's hands. With a sigh, he remembered his own words to participants in a spiritual retreat. "God answers supplication prayers, petition prayers, in four ways: No, Slow, Grow, or Go! No is when what you are asking isn't right for you. Slow reminds us that only God's timing is perfect and we need patience. Grow is when it's all about soul learning, and Go! is when he flings open the doors right away." *I could really use a "Go!"* he thought, sighing.

He took a short cab ride to the Fairmont Airport Hotel and booked a room for the night. He needed a hot bath in a deep tub, a good breakfast, and time to quiet his soul. He longed for a vision in which he could see and feel Kate's presence. He was puzzled and, at some level hurt, that his usual gift of discernment and clairvoyance had abandoned him. The only thing he could sense was a need to return to Toronto. *She is somewhere on this earth*, he reminded himself. It was cold comfort.

The next morning, as he leaned back in his seat on Air Canada, once again crossing the country, it came strongly to him, to google hotels in the seedy part of town, where Kate had gone undercover. It was only a fragment, a hum in his mind, calling to him, but it gave him a glimmer of hope. He used his smart phone in the few minutes before takeoff to locate a low priced room to rent by the week.

He quickly scanned the worst reviews on trip advisor, and settled on the Dundas Square Hotel on Church Street in downtown Toronto. *Not exactly the Fairmont or the Royal York*, he thought with a weak laugh.

Once he settled into the meager room, he decided to get a can of Lysol foam spray. *At least I can have a clean bathroom.* He thought longingly of his sprawling home atop a green promontory overlooking the sea, with its wide veranda, gleaming wood floors and spacious rooms, and sighed. *There must be a reason I'm here. I sense Kate isn't here now. Perhaps there is something, some service I can do for her here.*

22

One morning when Kate came out for breakfast, Aunt Agnes was humming, doing a fry-up. She turned around, took one look at the shadows under her niece's eyes and shook her head. "Katy girl, we need to talk." Kate sighed and resigned herself to a lecture on self-care. She knew she looked dreadful, her sleep sporadic and fraught with dreams of flying through space with Jason, leaving her frustrated, confused and lonelier than she had ever felt in her life.

"Let's eat, and then we'll talk." As Agnes tucked into a hearty meal, Kate picked at the cheese omelet and home fries, and nibbled at the bannock on her plate.

"Honey, you gotta eat. I gave you half servings like you asked. People will think I didn't feed you proper," said Agnes.

To Kate, the food looked overwhelming, but then everything felt that way, as she tried to sort out her next step. She knew Agnes's beloved Haida Gwai was not her place, but only a stop-over on the way. But to where?

Agnes removed the dishes, shaking her head sadly at all the food left on Kate's plate. "Want another cuppa tea?" she asked.

Kate shook her head. "I still have some, Auntie." Again she sighed.

Agnes sat again, and took Kate's cold hands in hers. "Katy, I'm going to talk to you plain the way your Gran always did. You're getting weaker here, not stronger. I don't know what to do for you. Tell me, please. What's going on?"

"Just having trouble sleeping, Auntie."

Agnes recognized Kate's familiar evasion. "So, what's keeping you awake?"

Geez, thought Kate, *she sounds just like Gran.* "Okay. I keep dreaming about Jason."

"I knew it!" said Agnes. "Child, what is keeping you from him? Your pride?"

Kate was a bit startled, "What do you mean?"

"You obviously love this man, and to my way of thinking, he probably feels the same way about you. All them jumps in the lake and such!" She grinned and got a small smile from Kate. "But since he didn't come right out with it, you're afraid to risk, to trust. And I do understand that, honey, after all you've been through. But it's pride, Kate, and that doesn't suit you."

Kate frowned, and was quiet.

Agnes thought, *I've said enough, better shut me trap.*

"But Auntie, I don't know what to do. Am I supposed to go chasing after him?"

"Well, he would probably chase after you if he knew where you were!" she said.

Kate looked pensive. "I'll think about it, Auntie, promise." That evening, after making herself eat a portion of Agnes's salmon croquettes, Kate went on line and brought up a website for the Ho'o pono pono Clinic in Kauai, Hawaii. Her heart leapt as a photo of Jason appeared on screen.

She spent an hour reading through their services and decided that if nothing else, she would benefit from enrolling in one of their healing retreats. She thought, *I could tell him I've come for a treatment, and that I want to do an article about his clinic.* She spent another hour filling in the on-line application for a retreat starting the following week and agreed to a screening Skype call. Her heart pounded, but suddenly she felt enormous relief. She walked back to the front room where Agnes sat, a homemade Afghan on her lap, reading one of her Harlequin romance novels beside the large stone fireplace, where a birch fire danced and crackled.

"Well, you look a sight better, Katy. There's a bit of color in those cheeks."

Kate flushed more deeply and said, "Auntie, I want to thank you for your honesty. I've decided to go to Hawaii and enter Jason's clinic."

144

"Lord knows you could use it," Agnes said, "but I think the real medicine you need is the man himself."

"Never mind, Auntie!" Kate laughed. "But thank you, really, for your kindness in taking me in and loving me enough to tell me off."

"No problem, Honey. Now can I get you a cup of hot cocoa to help you sleep?"

"I'll get it, Aunt Agnes. You stay put. You look so comfy." That night, Kate had her first deep, dreamless sleep in days.

The next morning, she checked for emails under her new, assumed name, Maggie Johnson, and found she had been accepted to be interviewed for the clinic program by someone named Moana, offering a Skype time at two o'clock that afternoon. She sat by her computer, wringing her hands, trying to breathe. In the application, she had written an essay about why she wanted to attend the retreat, siting her need to decide a new direction in her life. The familiar dings startled her, but she clicked on "answer with video". An attractive, broad-faced Hawaiian woman with shining eyes and a huge crimson flower behind one ear came on the screen. Moana's voice was rich and warm. "Maggie, your application was very interesting to read."

What does that mean? Kate wondered nervously, for some bizarre reason remembering at that moment the Chinese curse, "May you live in interesting times."

"Thank you," Kate said lamely.

Moana went on. "I say that because you are a Tahltan and Tlingit woman with an unusual and, frankly, astounding educational background for one so young."

Kate replied, "I've been very blessed."

"Yes," Moana said. "Well, what we really need to understand is your personal reason for attending a retreat here. It's not a spa and beach kind of thing. It's a deeply intense process. So, what are you hoping for?"

Kate gulped and said, "Truthfully, I'd like to experience one of your programs personally. As I wrote in my application, I'm at a crossroads in my life, and I need time to reflect on a new direction. In all honesty, I may want to write a feature on your facility, with your approval of course. I'm a journalist."

"Well, actually, that would be fine, and the ten day Healing and Transformation Retreat would be ideal for your purpose. During the experience, the only writing you will be doing is personal journaling. So an article will have to wait. You need to leave everything and everyone behind to get the full benefit of this retreat. Maggie, tell me more about your personal reasons. What drew you to our program?" Moana asked, not letting her off the hook. "You wouldn't be allowed to simply observe. You would have to be fully present. What do *you* need, Maggie?"

If you only knew, Kate thought. She gulped, and fought back tears. She cleared her throat and went on. "I have a lot of stored up grief. I need healing."

"That's what we needed to know," said Moana, smiling gently. "Send me your arrival details, and staff will pick you up. Welcome to Ho'o pono pono, Maggie Johnson."

CBC had arranged a credit card for her in that name, and she had prepaid the retreat fees, which included meals, accommodation, and hiking equipment. She agreed to sign a medical waiver about her fitness to hike and do gentle to challenging climbs. She felt slightly guilty for not mentioning Jason, but it was far too complicated to talk about. When the thought pressed on her that she might actually see him within a week, she couldn't help smiling.

A few days later, she was on a flight from Vancouver to Hawaii, her long hair tucked up into a soft cotton hat. She wore dark sunglasses, a sundress and sandals, and a warm shawl for the plane. She agreed to leave her treasured Cowichan sweater in Agnes's keeping.

Kate's heart was pounding by the time the small connector plane from Honolulu circled Kauai Island Airport. She peered out the window, wondering if Jason would be there to meet her. The only person she had actually spoken with was Moana, during the screening interview, and subsequent emails were signed "from the Retreat Team". She was torn between dread and hope at seeing Jason again, believing that if by some strange quirk, he had guessed

147

who she was under her assumed name, he would be there to meet her. A part of her knew this was absurd, but still…

As she crossed the tarmac and entered the small terminal, Kate scanned faces while trying not to look as if she were doing so. She almost ignored the sign with "Aloha, Maggie Johnson" on it held up by a deeply tanned man who was almost as wide as he was tall, wearing a bright pink and purple flowered shirt. As she approached him smiling, he put a fragrant lei around her neck and gave her the traditional kiss on the cheek.

"Aloha, Maggie. Welcome to Paradise. I'm Bubba. I'll take you to the Center." Kate smiled and followed him to a shiny SUV. She breathed in the fragrance of the gardenias and frangipani in her lei. As Bubba turned on the ignition, Kate could hear the strains of a ukulele and the mellow voice of Kiale'i Reichel.

"Oh, I love his music," Kate said.

"He's my home boy, don'tcha know," said Bubba. "He's a cozziebro. We were raised on Maui by the same tutu vaine."

"Pardon?" Kate said.

"Oh, that means grandmother." Bubba didn't talk after that, but only hummed along with the music for the rest of the ride. Grateful for his silence, Kate took in the beauty of the island. After about fifteen minutes, they began to climb up a private road through waving palms and thick foliage. As they neared the top, Kate looked down on aqua blue water deepening to navy and purple, waves gently lapping the shore, and thought, "This *is* paradise." They pulled up before a large, elegant wood building with a wide veranda facing the sea, surrounded by the most colorful garden Kate had ever seen. Brilliant bougainvillea, looking like crushed paper, in shades of burnt orange, pink and red grew beside yellow and red birds of paradise and bushes laden with hibiscus in shades of cream, magenta and deep pink. Bubba said, "Lani is expecting you in reception. Your bags will be waiting for you in your bungalow."

Inside, Kate paused beside the desk where an attractive woman wearing a form fitting dress in the same flowered fabric as Bubba's shirt greeted her with a warm smile. "Aloha, Maggie. I'm Aolani. Welcome, welcome. You'll be staying in Serenity Hale (pronounced haleh). You have time to rest before the evening meal in the main dining room."

Kate left reception with an orientation kit, a key and a map showing her the short walk along a white gravel path through gardens and palms to her accommodation. A small wooden bungalow with a peaked, thatched roof sat on a raised platform above a koi pond, studded with pink water lilies. Five large, flat stones led gently up to the deck.

She unlocked the door and gazed around the immaculate space of gleaming teak floors and a high ceiling of woven flax supported by wide beams. The sitting area contained two high-backed rattan chairs and a couch with abundant overstuffed pillows covered in colorful Hawaiian fabrics in shades of lime and rose. Her bags were already placed beside a built-in closet. The queen-sized bed was covered with a white cotton spread, ornamented with fresh frangipani and hibiscus blossoms. Draped across it was a sarong in mauve and yellow.

All the screened, louvered windows were open, and Kate felt embraced by the perfect warmth of the gentle breezes carrying sweet, tantalizing scents. There was a tiny kitchen counter with an electric kettle, flowered porcelain cups, a plate of sliced mango, papaya, passion fruit and roasted coconut, and a small fridge with a pitcher of cold water and sliced limes. Kate peeked into the bathroom, and found it pristine as well, with a raised glass sink atop a black granite counter, with several amenities arranged in a large fluted seashell. A blue glass door led to a large outdoor shower with a huge nozzle surrounded by a high, wood slat privacy fence, draped with deep pink bougainvillea, coral hibiscus, and an overhanding branch of yellow and white frangipani blossoms. A potted lemon tree stood beside the shower. *Oh, I could get used to this*, she thought.

She undid the bun held tight to her head and let her thick, silky hair fall to the middle of her back. She folded down the light spread and lay down, feeling utterly loose and relaxed for the first time since she could remember. Soon she was sound asleep. What seemed like only minutes later, she was awakened by a steady tap at the door.

150

She hastily smoothed her hair and pulled the sarong around her. When she opened the door, a staff member spoke to her in Hawaiian. She looked puzzled, as did the young woman when Kate answered her in English. "Sorry, I don't speak Hawaiian."

"Oh, sorry, I thought you were kanaka wahine – Hawaiian lady. It's time for lunch." As Kate spent her first day at the retreat center, those words "kanaka wahine" echoed repeatedly in her mind.

After a delicious lunch of fresh-caught mahi mahi, papaya salad, and nu, the sweet milk of a coconut, Kate saw on the schedule that she had a meeting with her retreat mentor. Her heart started racing again as she wondered if it might be Jason.

She made her way down a gravel path beside a stream dotted with tiny floating purple flowers. She arrived at the Aloha Hale, the English translation carved beneath the Hawaiian: "Love House". *Well, this would be kind of perfect*, she thought as she walked through the high posts of the open entryway toward a counter behind which sat another striking young woman wearing a flower tiara encircling her hair and a sarong in the familiar pink and purple staff uniform. "Aloha, Maggie. Your mentor will be with you in a moment. Please have a seat."

Kate sat in one of the large rattan chairs padded with soft pillows and leaned back. Hoping to still her pulse, she focused on the sound of water falling into a small pool of koi surrounded by ferns and orchids. She breathed in the heady scent of the gardenias in a small

151

polished wooden bowl on the table beside her. Through the high-ceilinged, open hall she had a glimpse of the turquoise bay and distant horizon. She sat for several minutes, her heart pounding. Would she finally see Jason again? *Finally?* she thought. *I've been here less than a day.* Then a door opened and a large woman with a familiar face emerged, wearing a floor length muumuu in bright pink. She came toward Kate with a warm smile, and kissed her on the cheek. "Aloha, aloha, Maggie. I'm Auntie Moana. We spoke by Skype last week. Come in."

Kate covered her disappointment with a smile and followed her into a spacious office with a huge window shaded by palms and a magnificent 180 degree view of the lagoon. "Holee," Kate said, before she could catch herself. "This is the most beautiful place I've ever seen."

"Yes, the Lord has been good to us. We are very blessed," Moana said. "So, again I will ask you, what brought you here, Maggie? What is your deepest hope for this retreat?"

Kate swallowed and said, "Well, as I told you, I'm at a crossroads in my life. I'm between jobs, and I honestly have no idea what or where I will be from now on. So this sounded like a perfect way to sort things out."

"Yes. Well, as you'll soon learn, I'm not one to beat around the bush. You made a rather unusual request in your application. You asked that we not question you about your background. To be honest, that gave us pause. We had to think hard about admitting you to this program. Remember, the one boundary we set is that you tell the truth and only the truth to us and above all to yourself. For our part, we are committed to trustworthiness. Everything here is absolutely confidential. What is it that worries you?"

For the first time since she arrived, Kate knew that she was heading for a precipice. She took a deep breath and said, "Actually, my life would be in danger if certain people discovered where I am. But more than that, I've been packing around a lot of pain for a very long time. I need to deal with it." A tear slipped down her cheek.

"Now we're getting somewhere," said Moana.

23

Jason emerged from a dream of laughing with Kate at the cabin, rubbed his eyes and felt the stubble on his chin. One of his university friends used to say, "You're the only Indian I know with a white man's beard. Must be a throwback, half-breed," he would tease. Jason was startled to hear the wisdom voice he had been longing for: *Leave it alone. Let it grow.* His first reaction was relief at hearing the powerful inner voice of his grandfather, now one of his Spirit guides. *There you are*, Jason thought.

We have never left you, Grandfather said.

Jason closed his eyes and concentrated. *Guide me now, Grandfather*, he prayed. *What am I to do?* In the silence within the din of traffic beyond the grimy window he heard: *Find the boy, find the boy, find the boy...* As the message faded, he knew that was all he would receive for now.

His mind went back to the morning at the cabin, when Kate had told him the story of Lonnie, the boy she tried to help when she was undercover. She had made some strides with him, convincing him that he was not just an addict or a prostitute, that she could see his goodness and his idealism. "You have never lost your purity," she told him, watching Lonnie dissolve in tears. He sobbed in her arms for a long time. It was then she had convinced him that there was hope for the future, and that she would help him, but before she could get him into the rehab program he had finally agreed to, the explosion forced her to disappear. "It's like a thorn in my heart," she told Jason one night in the cabin. "I can never forget him. I have to find him, but first I have to speak out, as I always intended. The network went out on a huge limb for me. I'm so scared that Lonnie is lost in that city."

Find the boy. Jason felt invigorated by the crystal clarity of his guidance. Until it came, he felt painfully bereft and suspended in an unfamiliar space. Also, at a deep level, he was worried that his fierce, unbidden love for Kate was costing him the mission he had fought so hard to sustain -- his heart's deepest promise to use the powers Creator had given him to be of service. He never thought he could be with a woman and keep his vow.

"Worse than a priest!" Moana used to say. She never understood Jason's belief that he had to guard his chastity to keep faith with God. His magnetic feelings for Kate had blind-sided him, and he felt split like a tree struck by lightning. He felt off balance, uprooted, and was haunted by a Bible verse from James 1:8 "Their loyalty is divided between God and the world. The double-minded man is unstable in all his ways."

He allowed himself to recall the morning he stood within Kate's Medicine Wheel and received what felt like a distinct reprieve: *Her place is beside you.* He knew he had prayed with all the sincerity of his soul for God's will, not his own. Once again, the hope he felt then began to glow like a tiny flame. *God willing*, he thought, and turned his mind to how he would find Lonnie in this urban labyrinth. Once again relying on his inner guidance, he set out to look. He was following the flow, led by subtle shifts in the currents of thought, like steady, gentle gusts of wind in a sail.

He went to a coffee shop on the corner and sat at the counter. He stared into his mug of coffee, listening acutely to the murmurs of conversation, alert to words that might guide him further. He heard "underground" and "pool hall". He put some change on the counter and pulled up the collar of the thick, well-worn military jacket he had found at a Salvation Army store. He wandered intuitively until he came to a pool hall several streets away and walked in. The room was lit only by dim wall sconces and smelled of stale beer and cigarette smoke. He wandered over to the pool table and watched as several young men in their late teens laughed, smoked and polished their cue sticks.

"Hey Pops, want a game?"

Pops? I must look worse than I thought. "Sure. What are you playing?"

"Pool," they all said together, laughing uproariously at their joke.

156

"Oh, I thought you were playin' poker," he retorted. He took off his jacket and couldn't help noticing the boys' raised eyebrows at his muscled arms. He was wearing a sleeveless singlet under the quilted jacket.

"You open, Pops," said a tall, lanky, pock-faced boy called Stretch.

"What's the bet?" he asked.

"One of the boys blushed and said, "Jim doesn't let us…".

"Shush!" said one of the others.

"Don't you want to make it more interesting?" Jason said, pulling out a wad of bills.

Their eyes bugged out a bit, but Stretch said, "Sure, just wait a minute." He disappeared into a narrow hallway and Jason heard him knock on a door, which opened quickly. He returned after only a minute, his hand in his pocket. "Sure thing, Pops. Let's go."

Jason lost the first two rounds of Eight Ball, his shots sloppy and haphazard. Then they upped the ante and he won.

"How about a game of Bank?" he asked.

The boys frowned and narrowed their eyes. "Why not?" said Stretch, furiously polishing his cue stick with chalk. "First, let's get you a drink. Redskins like their beer, right?"

"Sure," said Jason. "I'm parched".

One of the boys whispered to another, "I need my fix. Where's that Indian kid?" Jason focused on the conversation while pretending to be restlessly awaiting his drink. He heard "Lonnie" and "tonight", and knew he was in the right place.

Stretch came back with a beer and a shot glass of whiskey. "Thought you might need some extra fuel," he laughed.

"After," said Jason. "That'll be my reward for creaming you guys. I'm feeling lucky."

Stretch winked at his cronies. Jason won the game easily and it looked like they were trying to lose. He had a suspicion of what they were planning. Stretch reached into his pocket and paid out the winnings.

Jason said, "I'm going to the toilet. I'll bring my drinks with me. He locked the door and poured both drinks down the sink, after taking a whiff of the shot, which was laced with something slightly more bitter than whiskey. He washed his hands and teetered out with the empties.

"Down the hatch, eh?" one of the boys said, leering at him. Jason acted as if he was having double vision and wobbled as if his legs were weak. As he made his next shot, he suddenly keeled over onto the table.

"Grab him," said Stretch "and bring him out back. Take his smelly jacket with you. I'll get Jim." Two of them carried him by his arms and legs out the door at the end of the hallway into an alley. He groaned and peered through half-closed eyes, sussing out an escape route. They lay him on the concrete amid the rank smell of garbage and started to go through his jeans pocket.

He knew he had to make a move fast, like a water moccasin. *Give me strength, Creator*, he prayed. Suddenly he leapt up and bashed their heads together. In the few moments he had left, he barricaded the door with an iron bar through the handle and held a sharp knife to the throat of the boy who was still conscious. "Unless you want to be scalped, white boy, you'd better tell me where Lonnie Running Bear is. If you don't, the tribe is coming for you."

"I, I, don't know."

Jason tightened his hold on the boy's neck and poked the point of the stiletto into his flesh. "You're killing me!" he shrieked.

Jason started counting, "1, 2, 3…" tightening his hold on the boy's neck.

He croaked, "All right! All right! Lemme go! I'll talk." Choking and coughing, he said. "He's at Teen Feed every night…at the Anglican Church in the square."

"You're lucky you talked. You'd better be telling the truth, or I'll be back. And don't you dare tell the others what you've told me."

159

As the pounding began on the other side of the door, the boy shook his head, blood dripping down his neck. Jason knocked him out again with a bang from the hilt of the knife. *For his own good,* he thought. He dropped him, grabbed his jacket and ran.

24

Once Kate started talking, she couldn't stop, nor could she stem the tears that flowed and dripped down her chin. She kept pulling tissues from the box on the low table beside her. Moana was very still, looking at Kate with a faint, compassionate smile as if nothing Kate could say would shock or disturb her. Kate began describing her time with Jason. "I was ill, and this amazing man took care of me." She didn't feel ready to reveal that it was Jason, wanting to protect his privacy, and left out elements such as her gunshot wound and Jason being a doctor.

Moana's eyes widened slightly and she thought, *Oh my God! This is Kate!* She quickly regained her receptive silence as Kate poured out her grief at finally having found a man she could love and trust, one who rejected her small attempts to show him how she felt. Kate paused, shuddering and hiccupping, and took a drink of water.

For the first time since Kate began talking, Moana spoke. "My girl, you have great courage. I appreciate your trust and openness. Now I know we were right to invite you here."

Kate felt a softening relief, as if someone had staunched a gaping wound in her chest. Moana's words were strangely restorative. *She's talking like Gran*, Kate thought, and smiled for the first time.

"May I ask you a question?" said Moana. Kate nodded, taking a deep quivering breath. "What gave you the impression this man was rejecting you?"

"Sometimes," Kate said haltingly, "I would touch him, and he literally jumped, as if he couldn't bear it." Tears once again coursed down her cheeks, this time silently.

Moana nodded, then said, "May I hold you?"

Kate looked startled and a bit frightened. "I don't usually..." Then, she sat up, straightened her shoulders and nodded. Moana moved to the couch beside Kate and opened her arms. Kate turned her body and curled her legs up onto the couch so that she faced Moana, and relaxed across her soft, ample chest.

Moana rocked her like a baby. "You're fine, Kate. You're safe now. Brave girl. My brave girl," she said stroking her hair. Kate just breathed in Moana's lemony scent and sighed.

After several minutes, she sat up and said, "Wait. How did you know my name?"

"Girlie," Moana said, sounding like Gran for sure this time, "We need to talk. Jason has told me about you, and your story is partly his. Be patient. First, it's time for some S & S therapy."

"What?" Kate said, feeling utterly spent and wishing she could just go back to her bungalow and sleep. "I'm not sure I'm up to any more today..."

"Come on. Time for sun and sea. You don't need to change." Moana walked Kate outside and pointed to the sheer drop off at the edge of the property. A young woman quickly appeared wearing the uniform of the day, a lime green flowered blouse and slit skirt, and carrying a large basket woven of green pandanas leaves over her arm.

Moana said, "Nané will guide you to a small beach, a tranquility zone. It's completely private. You can wear your sarong or nothing. No one will see you. Take the rest of this afternoon. If you wish, write in your retreat journal. You'll find it in your beach basket. Swim, sleep, walk, whatever your body wants to do. Then come for dinner at six. I'll see you then."

Kate gave her a hug and said, "I don't know how to thank you, Auntie."

"You just did," laughed Moana. "You'd better put on some sunnies first," and moved away with her elegant sway. Nané plucked sun glasses and a foldable hat out of the basket. Kate put them on and

Nané led her silently to the drop off, where she handed her the basket. She smiled and said, "Enjoy your afternoon."

Kate descended a flight of wide, wooden steps that wound down toward a tiny white sand cove. Her breath still hitched every now and then, but she felt incredibly calm and lighter than she could remember. She paused as she went down the steps to gaze out at the turquoise water deepening to azure and navy the farther and deeper it became. Lazy, white-crested waves lapped the sand. She thought, *He talked about me,* and smiled.

When she reached the cove, she found a legless beach chair and a rope hammock with plump pillows hanging in the shade of the cliff between two palm trees, creating a pale green bower overhead. There was a fresh water shower nearby with a wooden slat floor, and a small bench beside it with two fluffy, folded beach towels, mango and mint body wash, shampoo and conditioner, and a clean sarong. *They've thought of everything.* She put down the basket and moved the small chair into the sun. Her skin was greedy for the heat, as if breathing it in through her pores. *This is the medicine I need,* she thought, unwinding her hair from a high pony tail, and letting it fall heavily down her back.

She opened the woven basket and found sun block, coconut oil, a boxed lunch, a thermos of cold lime water, a cloth napkin, a small journal and pen. She suddenly realized she was hungry, opened the white cardboard box and started devouring the sandwich of fresh tuna on homemade coconut bread, with thinly sliced avocado, tomato and herbs, a small container of wild rice, followed by crisp macadamia and chocolate cookies, slices of papaya and a chunk of red, juicy watermelon. She drank deep from the thermos as well, then unwrapped her sarong and slipped out of her panties. She placed them on the bench beside the shower and turned around.

With a shout of delight she raced across the hot sand and plunged into the surf. The water was mercifully warm. *Oh, this* is *Heaven!* She looked up into the cloudless blue sky and prayed aloud, "Thank you, Creator, for this gift, this beauty. Help me to heal here, to put the past behind me, even my love for Jason, if that is your will." She could have sworn she heard rumbling laughter, like thunder in her mind. Leaping up to be lifted by the swells, she thought, *I can't believe it. I'm playing!* Something had shifted in her soul.

25

Jason followed the pungent scent of baking ham into the church basement and walked into the kitchen. "How can I help?" he asked.

A round-bellied, balding man with pink cheeks wearing a white collar and an apron threw one to him. "Hi, I'm Reverend Jim. Put this on. We need servers tonight. Thanks for coming."

Jason stood behind the counter, gazing around while waiting for the food to be ready. He noticed slogans on neon-colored paper posted around the walls. "Be determined: Never give up!" "Use your excellence! Give 100%". "Peace is giving up the love of power for the power of love." "Blessed are the peacemakers." "Humanity: there is no they, only us." "Unity: the honor of one is the honor of all." He looked at the line-up of kids, trying not to stare. There was a boy in a close-fitting sleeveless black leather vest and narrow pants, his arms showing elaborate tattoos. He wore steel-toed boots, and artfully draped chains hanging from unlikely parts of his body. He wore a Mohawk at least 5 inches high, dyed bright green. *Wonder how long it takes him to get ready in the morning*, Jason thought.

"How much should I give them?" he asked.

The minister said, "As much as they want. We've got plenty tonight."

Jason started dishing up thick slabs of ham, big dollops of scalloped potatoes. Another volunteer served green beans and apple sauce. Cutlery, napkins, condiments and glasses of juice were on each long table. At the back of the kitchen, apple pies were being sliced up for dessert beside a huge bowl of whipped cream.

When the line dwindled, Reverend Jim said, "Take a plate and go on out. The kids will show you what to do."

Jason was a bit puzzled as to what he meant, until he sat down across from a young family. A girl who looked about fourteen with milk pale skin was feeding a dirty faced toddler who sat on her lap. Beside her sat an older boy of mixed race, thin and wiry, with a pock-marked face and long dreads, wearing a hoody. A macramé necklace dangled from his neck with several strange objects woven into it. Jason introduced himself, and they mumbled their names to him – Sara, Virgil, and baby Emily -- and continued focusing on their food. He pointed to Virgil's necklace and said, "Interesting. What does it mean?"

That's all it took for the young man to look up, smile winningly, and begin holding forth about his Rastafarian beliefs. His partner looked on adoringly, nodding her head, as the baby stuffed potatoes into her mouth with her fist. All Jason had to do was to sit and listen. Then he said, "Seems like you're a man of wisdom."

He nodded. "Well, I *am* the leader of our Rasta community. Emperor Selassie is my spiritual ancestor." He launched into another long speech about Haile Selassie -- "the Emperor of Emperors, the Lion of Judea".

Jason dared to ask, "How are you living?"

"We get by. We have a good squat. Lots of protection," answered Virgil.

Jason sensed it was premature to ask about Lonnie. "Well, thank you for your illuminating words, Virgil. You've taught me something," he said. Virgil smiled broadly for the first time, and Jason could see him mouthing the word, "illuminating".

Jason moved on to the piano, where a thin, listless Indian boy who looked about twelve was playing lilting chords. "Mind if I listen?" The boy shrugged without making eye contact. "That's beautiful," Jason said, "Did you compose it?"

"Nah, I'm just fooling around."

"So, you made up those chords?"

"Yeah, I guess."

"How did you start playing?"

"Just comin' here for grub."

"Really. Well, you have a gift, do you know that?"

The boy looked up and said, "I'm finding my roots."

"Your roots…"

He lowered his voice, conspiratorially: "Yeah, my people are First Nations."

Jason nodded respectfully. "I'm of the Cree Nation," he said.

"Really?" The boy looked interested and said, "Well, I had to run away to find my people. I'm still looking."

Jason wondered how this young boy was existing but called himself back to his mission. "Maybe I can help you," he said.

The boy frowned and said, "How?"

"Well, do you know how to use a computer?"

"Nah, at the home they didn't have stuff like that."

"Well, I could do some searches for you and come back and tell you."

"You don't want me to come with you?" he said suspiciously.

"No need. I sense you are a man of honor, and if you say you'll be here, you will."

The boy blushed. "You do?"

"Yep. Now, just tell me what you already know. And by the way, what's your name?"

"Kevin Josephs."

Thirty minutes later, after taking notes on Kevin's memories of his family, Jason went over to where Reverend Jim was visiting with some teen girls, and said, "If it's okay, I'll be back tomorrow. Can you use the help?"

"Always," he said. "And I can see the kids take to you."

The next evening, Jason came in carrying a large envelope. He had done some research using his android tablet, following the small leads Kevin had given him, and used a printer at an internet shop to compile it. Kevin waved from the piano bench when he saw Jason.

"I need to serve up some grub," Jason said, "but we'll talk after dinner."

"You got somethin' for me?"

"I think so."

Kevin's eyes brightened.

They sat together, and Jason explained the research he had discovered. Kevin was of the Michipicoten First Nation. The biggest clue he had given Jason was something he mentioned in passing -- the teasing he received in Juvenile Detention when other boys made fun of the town where he remembered living years before -- Wawa, Ontario. He had casually mentioned the way other boys had chanted, "Wah, wah, big baby!"

Jason said, "The town of Wawa is north of here, near Lake Superior between Sault Sainte Marie and Thunder Bay. Does that ring any bells?"

Kevin frowned in concentration, and said, "Yeah. I think so."

"Do you remember the names of any of your relations up there?"

"I...I had an Aunt Mable, Mable Sport. I remember because she called me her 'little sport'. I remember!"

"Good on you, Kevin. We have something to go on now. I'll do another internet search and see what I can come up with."

Suddenly, Kevin's face clouded, and he asked, "So, whatta you want? What I gotta do for you?"

Jason closed his eyes and said, "Nothing that would disrespect you, Kevin."

"You respect me?"

"Yes. You're loyal to your people, and you're modest. You have talent and you don't take it for granted."

Kevin looked startled and then his eyes misted. "Nobody never said words like that to me before."

"Well, I can see lots of good in you, but that's enough for now," Jason smiled. "There is something you can do for me. I am searching for someone, and I hope you can help me."

"Okay, if I can, I will."

Jason told him he was looking for Lonnie Running Bear, who had been hooked on Meth.

"What do you want with him?" Kevin asked. Jason realized these kids had never had a reason to trust anyone.

"Actually, a friend of mine asked me to find him. She used to hang out with Lonnie."

"You mean Janie?"

"Maybe. Describe her to me."

"Well, she has these weird, amazing eyes."

"What color are they?" Jason asked, holding his breath.

"You tell me," said Kevin with a sly smile.

"Well, they're sort of purple and sometimes dark blue, with little gold bits," Jason said.

"Yes, that's Janie. So, is she the one you mean?"

"Yes," Jason said, noticing his heart beginning to pound.

"None of us knew what happened to her. She just up and disappeared one day. Is she dead?"

"No, Kevin, she's alive. But I don't know where she is right now. What I do know is that she is really worried about Lonnie. So, I made a promise to her in my heart to find him and help him. Can you help me keep my promise?"

"Well if you're a friend of Janie's, then I'll tell you what I know."

"I'd really appreciate it, and tomorrow I'll bring you more info on your people."

That night, following Kevin's directions, and wearing black, Jason slipped into an unheated warehouse across town. He moved around silently until he heard the soft snores and coughs of several people sleeping in a small storage room. He hunkered down until dawn. Then he started softly singing a song Kate had taught him -- one she had made up and used to soothe Lonnie and others to sleep or when they were crashing after a bad high. She had changed the words of Ten Little Indians to include virtues. "One little, two little kind little Indians, three little, four little peaceful Indians, five little, six little brave little Indians…"

A tousle-haired, reed thin boy, with sores recently healed on his face sat up and stared at him. "Who are you?" He pulled out a pistol and aimed it at Jason's heart.

"I have a message from Janie."

Slowly, Lonnie put down the gun, and said, "I'm listenin."

26

Kate awoke on the second morning of her retreat and stretched luxuriantly. She had slept deeply, and felt an unfamiliar serenity. *All that crying yesterday. Maybe Moana's right. Maybe emptying my cup is a good thing.* After a warm shower, she toweled off, letting herself breathe in the sweet scent of the frangipani blossoms hanging over the privacy fence. She plucked one, and tucked it behind her ear, then put on a fresh sarong. Then, she went down the steps of the bungalow and placed her feet gently on the grass.

She made a small medicine wheel with shells from a basket on the deck and chanted, facing the four directions. She added a short prayer: *Guide me, protect me, Creator. Show me your will, and keep Jason safe, wherever he is.* She wondered why those words had come. Wasn't Jason here? Then, she sat on the veranda, gazing up into a cloudless blue sky, lingered over a mug of green tea, and ate some dried coconut, ripe mango and passion fruit. As instructed, she opened her journal. On the inside flap was a message: "Tell the truth. Do it now." She recalled that this phrase came out of the EST movement of the seventies. She had researched it for an article she wrote on "Realizing our full potential."

She turned a page and began to write. *I am seeking truth, Creator, the truth of my life and my new direction. You alone know my path and you are the light I follow. Give me the strength to face my past, and the wisdom to discern my future. Thank you for all the blessings you have given me and for saving my life. Thank you for bringing Jason into my life as my healer and...whatever he is meant to be to me. Give me the eyes to see your purpose for me, and the ears to hear your voice. Let me not be a wind chaser. Free me from illusions. I seek only to know the truth, your path of truth for me.*

She laid down the pen and closed her eyes, letting her mind open, knowing that prayer was only the first part of a conversation with God, stilling her mind to meditate on His answer. *Go to the water, my daughter. Learn the ways of the sea.*

She swiftly wrote the words in her journal, then put on a one piece bathing suit, some shorts, a t-shirt and a pair of waterproof sandals. She carried a pack with a water bottle, light windbreaker and her journal and pen, and went off to the main lodge. Moana had told her this was a free day, to start by journaling and then follow her instincts. She went up to the fit young man staffing the activity desk and said, "I've never sailed, and I only have experience with a canoe, but I'd like to go out on the water today. What would you recommend?"

"I know just the thing," he said, smiling warmly. "I'll have Peter show you." He said a few words into his cell phone, and said, "He'll be here in a moment." Peter was a well-muscled young man, with blue eyes and white blond hair. He had a slight German accent. He led her to a boat house on the beach and said, "Cal recommended a sea kayak for you. I'll take you out and show you the basics, and then you can go by yourself. The only rules are you have to wear a life preserver and stay within twenty feet of the shore your first time out."

"Fair enough," she said. "By the way, where are you from?"

"I'm from Austria", he said. "Ho'o pono pono hires staff from all over the world to give us experience in working with kids, adult programs and hospitality. We all have skills they need, too."

"Hmm, sounds like a great opportunity."

"It is. Now, these kayaks can tip over, so let me show you how to resurface. You might want to change into a bathing suit." She quickly removed her shorts and T Shirt and stuffed them into her pack, which Peter stashed in a water tight container. After several trials where she rolled upside down in the gentle waves and righted herself again, smiling broadly each time, she felt ready. Peter showed her where to place her hands on the two-bladed paddle and how to pull it through the water smoothly. "Become the water," he said. "Ach, I never told anyone that before."

Kate laughed. "It's meaningful to me, thank you," she said, and made a mental note to record that in her journal. She relaxed and began to paddle with easy flowing movements, remembering not to grip the paddle too tightly.

Peter paddled behind her for about fifteen minutes, then pulled up beside her. "You're a quick study, Maggie. You're ready to solo now." Kate thanked him and took off, pulling the blades of her paddle, deep and slow, then speeding up until she felt she was the water, she was the wind. She glided through the swells effortlessly. A clear thought came, *don't grasp for the truth. Trust; hold it lightly. No need to strain. Be calm. Be ready. Ride the waves. Follow the flow.*

She remembered canoeing with Gran over the turquoise water of Atlin Lake when they fished for lake trout. Everything she had learned about stopping, slowing, and maneuvering applied to kayaking. She felt an acute, unaccustomed awareness. She searched for a word to describe it. *Freedom. Freedom makes change possible. It means leaving the past behind like the wake of a boat, and moving forward with a new rhythm.*

She wondered longingly if Jason would be part of her future. "Lord, I'm pining for him, and that's the truth. What do you think of that?" she asked aloud, and realized she had arrived back at the cove where she had played and rested the day before. She pulled into shore, and chuckled to herself as she struggled to get out of the kayak without tipping it. To her surprise, there was a picnic hamper waiting for her. She read the note, "For you, Maggie. Enjoy!"

She had worked up a good appetite and happily tucked into the bowl of cold noodle salad with peanut satay, caramelized onions, tiny green leaves of baby arugula, bits of mango, and lumps of tender chicken, followed by a moist chocolate cake and fresh fruit salad. *Mmm, they sure know how to feed people around here.*

She read a second note which was under the dessert dish. "The truth shall set you free." She smiled at the synchronicity, and fell asleep in the hammock beneath the palms. She dreamed of Jason -- his face, his smile, his laugh, and awoke with a deep knowing. As she made her way back to the boat house, the thought came clearly, *this is my truth. I love him. I want to be with him. That's what following the flow is for me!* She raced back to the bungalow, and wrote all the thoughts she could recall in her journal, ending with her confession of love. She decided to ask Moana about Jason when she saw her that evening at dinner.

27

Lonnie had a deep, chesty cough, which erupted in visible clouds in the icy air, and when Jason sang Janie's song to him, the lump in his throat made it worse. He hacked so loudly, the others awoke. When he caught his breath, he quickly told them that Jason was a friend. He took Jason to another small storage room, with a door and closed it behind him.

"Is Janie okay? I haven't heard anything from her. She just disappeared. I was so scared she was dead."

"She's not dead, Lonnie, but I'll be honest with you. At the moment, I don't know where she is."

Lonnie's face fell. "Then you don't really know if she's okay! Well, what's her message?"

"She wanted to know if you were sticking to your recovery program. She wanted to know if you were safe."

"Yeah, I'm doin' good. Except for this chest cold."

Jason looked pensive, "Why are you in this cold squat? Can't you go to a shelter? At least you'd be warm."

"Oh, man, you have no idea what happens to kids like me in those places. I tried, but had to practically knife an old guy to keep from…you know."

"Well, what's your plan, son? Maybe I can help."

"Look, man, I'm just going day to day. Being off the stuff is hard enough. Why are you asking me all these questions? Where's Janie?"

"I told you the truth. I'm pretty sure she's fine, but I don't know where she is at the moment. I have an idea. Let me ask you something. Are you a brave Indian?"

Lonnie said, "Yeah, man! If you knew some of the shit I been through, you wouldn't ask me that."

"Okay, I believe you. I have a proposition. Can you get away from Toronto for a while? I have a place where you can be warm for the winter, and I'll do my very best to find Janie and bring her there."

"What about my program?"

"You can actually continue it where I have in mind."

"What's this all about?" Lonnie asked, doubt clouding his face.

"Have you ever been to Hawaii?"

28

Kate put on a yellow sundress and white sandals, placed a gardenia in her upswept hair and went to dinner at the main lodge. When she walked in, Moana made a slight head nod, inviting her to sit beside her. There were several others at the table already. Kate realized that these must be the participants in the ten day retreat. Once the tenth person was seated at the large round table, Moana tinged her water glass with a spoon and called them to attention. "We'll begin with introductions and a brief prayer. Please introduce yourself by your name, a hope you have for this retreat, and one of your core strengths. What gift do you bring to this circle?"

Kate was thankful Moana started herself, saying, "My hope is that each of you will have the courage to delve deep. The gift I bring is truthfulness" and then waved her hand to the man sitting on her other side. "Mathew…Matt, and my hope is that I will discover a reason to live. The gift I bring is wonder." As people continued to share, Kate thought, *this isn't just some guided island tour.* She took a deep breath and said, "I'm Maggie. I'm at a crossroads. My hope is to find my true path. The gift I bring is loyalty." Her thoughts went to her mother, and she struggled to hold back tears.

"Thank you all for your openness," said Moana. "This is a good start. I'll see you all at the Hibiscus Room in the lodge tomorrow morning at 5 AM. We invite you to be trustworthy. Each activity begins precisely on time, so we will actually start at 5, and we'd love to have you with us. Now after this brief prayer, enjoy your dinner."

Dinner was served and Kate said, "My, my, the chef sure knows how to stir up an appetite!" She heartily forked into tender grilled yellow fin tuna with a lemon pepper sauce, macadamia and date risotto, fresh asparagus and star fruit salad. Moana said, "Yes, we cherry picked our chefs from the Bellagio and the Aria in Vegas. They were happy to come to Hawaii and to, let's say, enjoy a better benefit package."

"You really are world class on this little island, aren't you?"

"Absolutely," Moana said. "Our fees are high, but what people receive is well worth it. You should see the raves on Trip Advisor."

"Oh, believe me, I have," said Kate. "Moana, there's something private I'd like to talk to you about. Could I see you briefly after dinner?"

"Sure thing," Moana said. "I can give you ten minutes."

Kate perched on the couch in Moana's office. "Sit back and relax, Kate. Talk to me."

"I need to tell someone or I'll burst. I spent today diving into the truth. I thought and prayed about Jason. He's the one I was talking about." She paused, watching for surprise from Moana, but she merely smiled as if she already knew. Kate continued, "I realize I love him. I want him in my life. I've never been in love before, but I know this is real. And Creator seems to be confirming it."

"Well, Kate, this is quite a momentous decision, and your retreat has only just begun."

"I know! This is the first time I've stopped working or running since Jason and I were at my Gran's cabin, the first time I've really looked inside." Moana grinned and continued to sit quietly.

"So, Moana, where is he? Is he here? Can I see him? Where…"

"Calm yourself child. No, he's not here, but he will be back. And don't ask me when, because I don't know. So, did you come to this retreat hoping to see him?"

"I didn't realize it fully, but yes, I'm sure that was in the back of my mind. When he wasn't at the airport, I noticed how disappointed I felt, even though I used an alias when I registered. We got so close at the cabin, I guess I thought he would know it was me."

"Well, since he isn't here, what do you want to do?"

"Oh, I want to keep going with the retreat. It's been amazing already."

"That's what I hoped you would say." Moana stood and pulled Kate up into a hug. "Okay, 'Maggie', we meet just after dawn tomorrow, so I hope you'll get some good sleep. Have a cup of Chamomile tea before you go to bed."

"That's what Gran used to give me." As she walked back in the moonlight filtering through the palms, Kate mused, *Moana never said a word about Jason. She was so non-committal. I wonder what he said to her about me. But then, she would keep it confidential. Lord, guide me, keep me safe in Your will. Don't let me get my hopes up if I'm not right for Jason.*

The excitement and adrenaline Kate had experienced before dinner drained gently away as she sipped the herbal tea. Soon after climbing into bed, she took a whiff of the mesh bag of lavender the turn-down staff had placed on her pillow, nestled into smooth, clean sheets and fell deeply asleep. She set her alarm for four AM and was just waking as it went off.

After a shower, she scanned the retreat schedule, which listed what to wear each day. This one called for a sun hat, good climbing shoes, walking stick, which she found outside on the deck, her canteen, light rain gear, the retreat journal and pen. She packed her gear and had a cup of Kona coffee, some fresh fruit and a feather light cheese scone left in the bread box by the night staff.

When she reached the meeting room in the lodge, several people were already there sipping coffee, and everyone arrived before five.

Moana, looking refreshed and wearing a scarlet and white flowered muumuu came in and greeted them all. "Each of you is here because you felt a calling to come. Life is a sacred opportunity, and pausing in this place of beauty, our island of Kauai, is a way to bring fresh perspective to your own life journey."

Several people nodded and smiled. "Kauai is geologically the oldest of the main Hawaiian islands with an area of over 560 square miles. It's the fourth largest island in the Hawaiian archipelago, and we think of it as "the garden island". The name comes from the legend of Hawaiiloa, the Polynesian navigator who discovered these islands. He named the island after Kauai, his cherished son. So here is where you will discover what your heart most deeply cherishes. Kauai also means 'food or harvest season.' May your commitment to enter this retreat yield a rich harvest. Now, I leave you in the capable hands of your guide, Marianna. You will find that she has many healing tools in her basket. She's a native wahine and a psychologist. We are blessed to have her on our team."

A tall, fit Polynesian woman in her forties stepped forward, wearing shorts, a T-shirt, and hiking boots, her dark hair in a high ponytail. Standing very erect, her hands clasped behind her back, she said, "Aloha, everyone. I will serve as your guide on this retreat. It is highly likely that you chose this particular experience, not in spite of but because of the rigor it requires at every level – physically, emotionally, and spiritually. You will do well to dive in, dive deep, and trust that when you surface, you will be made new.

"So let's dive right in. One of our practices is to focus on one virtue each day. Virtue means strength, essence, or power. Virtues are the gifts of the soul, the content of our character, the legacy of our ancestors. The virtue of the day is Mindfulness."

She began to read from a card: "Mindfulness is living reflectively, with conscious awareness of our actions, words and thoughts. Awake to the world around us, we fully experience our senses." The reading ended with a quotation from the Tao Te Ching: "Can you cleanse your inner vision until you see nothing but the light? Can you step back from your own mind and thus understand all things?" She then read the affirmation, "'I am thankful for the gift of mindfulness. It keeps me present.'

"We will be on a trek this morning, which will be spent in silence. I'll let you know when it's time to speak, and unless you need help during the hike, there is no need to talk. Each of you is on a personal, individual journey. Today you will open your inner vision by focusing on your outer senses. Quiet your mind. Be deeply present. Feel all your senses – touch, sight, sound, smell. Notice your own breathing. Feel your body. I will say a prayer in our native Hawaiian to start our hike and then say it in English.

"Spirit of sky, land, sea, and mountain, guide us with your wisdom, protect us with your power, show us the path we are meant to travel in this world. Awaken us to truth. Give us the courage to explore within and to embrace life as it unfolds according to your many blessings. Amen.

"Silence begins now. Before we depart, we will do a Qi Gong stretching exercise called Eight Pieces of Brocade." She led them through the gentle standing exercises, which Kate found flowing and calming. It seemed to stretch every muscle in her body effortlessly.

"Good. Now, please stay hydrated through the day. You all have canteens, so please drink some water now. You can refill them later, and there are places to relieve yourself along the way. Now, we'll move on. Begin by feeling your feet on the ground with each step. Quiet your mind. If thoughts come, don't judge or become distracted. Simply watch the thought come and watch it go, like a leaf on a stream. Let it come, and let it go. Bring yourself gently back to your breath and to your feet on the path. Ride the breathing body."

Kate wondered why Marianna didn't call for questions, but then thought, *Hmm. We're being asked to trust.* She chided herself, *now, stop thinking. Just be here now.* She smiled to herself, remembering the classic book of that title by Baba Ram Dass, which she had found on Gran's shelf and read as a twelve year old.

The ten men and women silently climbed into the bed of a large truck and sat on the wooden slat seats. The truck slowly rumbled off through a forest track and stopped fifteen minutes later beside an enormous Banyan tree with roots nearly a foot tall spread out around it. Beside it was a rock pool into which poured a waterfall from high above.

Marianna indicated that they were to follow her up the trail. Thick ferns and bracken as well as ironwood trees and palms hugged the trail. There were bushes of red, pink and peach hibiscus, and red and yellow Birds of Paradise among the ferns. Rushing water could be heard as the trail became steeper and more winding. After about an hour of climbing, Kate noticed more light ahead and heard a soft gasp from the people in front of her. As she emerged from the forest canopy, there was a spectacular panoramic view of mountains with water falls plunging into the sea, and waves cresting far below on the Na Pali coast. Marianna sat cross-legged in a flat grassy field, waiting for them to join her.

"Before we have our morning kai, please write in your journal some words, questions, impressions, whatever you experienced on the hike. Then when you're ready, find a partner and share. Listen with receptive silence, and make no comment other than to acknowledge a virtue in your partner after he or she has finished. It's natural for tears to come when we hit the bedrock of truth. Let the tears flow. Don't touch one another unless asked to do so, as it can disrupt the process. Remember the Art of Boundaries – Assertiveness to speak your truth, Respect to be present without advising, teasing or interrupting and Trust to keep everything confidential."

After journaling about her experience, Kate turned to her left and smiled at a slender, blonde woman in her early thirties.

"I'm Michelle," she said in a thick French Canadian accent. "Would you like to start?"

"I'm Maggie. Yes, I'll share." Other than her time at the cabin with Jason, Kate was used to solitude and secrecy, and rarely spoke of her feelings, even with Gran. Her initial outpouring to Moana two days before was like entering a deep, dark sea cave, fearing the unknown dangers, then suddenly emerging into the sun. Yet, she had spent her whole life keeping her own counsel. She found herself trembling, suddenly anxious. "Uh, maybe you should go first," she said, blushing.

"All right. Ce ne fait rien. It makes no difference," said Michelle. "Well, at first I had trouble not thinking. I find it very difficile to have an empty head."

Kate nodded, already feeling more comfortable. Michelle went on to describe the fragrance and colors of the flowering trees, which had absorbed her attention, and then suddenly said, "I have lost someone very close, and I am here to heal." She spoke of her mother, who was also her closest friend, and how she had died from brain cancer. "I lost her before I lost her," she said, "She was not herself. She didn't even know me." Her eyes and Kate's filled with tears. Michelle put out her hand, and Kate took it.

"Michelle, you're really brave to be vulnerable, to let yourself feel your grief, and coming here is a kind thing to do for yourself," Kate said. "And I see your love and devotion for your mother."

Michelle thanked her and gently withdrew her hand. "Your turn," she said.

Kate took a breath and then said, "Okay. I have been in danger all my life, even from my own mother. I've kept to myself, gotten comfortable being alone, and I'm used to numbing myself and working hard, because that's how I feel safe. On the trail, and really ever since I arrived, I *feel* too much. The smells, the tastes, the lushness of the beauty, and the things going on inside me -- I'm just not used to it, and I just feel…overwhelmed."

She held her hand out to Michelle, who took it in both of hers and looking deep into Kate's eyes, said, "What courage for you to come here. I admire your openness to these new things." Then the two of them hugged and smiled.

They sat quietly in the circle waiting for others to finish sharing. Then, Marianna said, "After our kai prayer, keep your silence while you have your food. Eat slowly, and taste every bite. Savor the flavors. When I ring a bell, you may chat, if you wish, for about fifteen minutes. Then I'll guide you to what comes next."

They were silently invited by an attendant to refill their water canteens from a chilled container, and helped themselves to the food laid out on a trestle table covered with a flowered cloth, with mesh umbrellas over the food – hard boiled eggs, a huge bowl of tropical fruit, flaky croissants, rich cheeses, plates of fresh mahi mahi, taro, and small clusters of the chef's signature dark chocolate with macadamia nuts. After about fifteen minutes, Marianna rang a small bell, and invited them back into a circle. "Please share a bit of your experience if you choose to. What was meaningful for you?"

Kate noticed her heart pounding as each person around the circle spoke of some insight or observation which was meaningful for him or her on the hike. As Michelle shared, Kate felt nauseated. When it was her turn, she opted to say, "I pass". She felt ashamed, but was simply too terrified to open up in the circle. Silence had been her protector for as long as she could remember. Flashbacks of sudden slaps, walking on broken glass, freezing and shaking, kept surfacing. She had to take deep breaths not to run away from the circle. A silent scream seemed to be building inside her.

When everyone else had shared, Marianna said, "Now, do you have any questions?" *Finally*, Kate thought, but realized she had none. She breathed easier, realizing she wouldn't be put on the spot. She felt a strange contentment in taking things as they came. A man named Geoff raised his hand and in a British accent asked, "Why the chocolate?" Everyone laughed.

Marianna said, "Actually, chocolate is perfect for the strenuous hiking we're doing. It's rich in fiber, iron, magnesium, copper, manganese and a few other minerals. Cocoa, particularly in the form of dark chocolate, is full of antioxidants, more than most foods. The bioactive compounds in cocoa can improve blood flow to the skin and protect it against sun damage, lower blood pressure, and reduce the risk of heart disease. There is even evidence that it improves brain function. And since we're all about Mindfulness today, it fits! And of course, as we Hawaiians like to say, 'It's yum!'" Everyone laughed.

A woman named Edith raised her hand. "Do you answer all questions in such depth?"

"Nope," replied Marianna, "only the ones on chocolate."

29

The hikers returned to the Center by early afternoon, invigorated yet tired. They were given a break for a swim, snacks, and a siesta until the next session at 4:30. Kate floated in the lagoon, and then headed up to her bungalow for a shower and a nap. She fell sound asleep and had a dream.

She and Jason were at the cabin. This time they were touching. She wound her fingers into his long thick hair and ran them down his muscled arms. She awoke to find herself deeply aroused and jumped out of bed, embarrassed despite being alone. *Marianna wasn't kidding about being open to all our senses*, she thought.

The group met back at their customary room and Marianna opened the circle by saying, "This is a healing circle. It's time to open further, trusting that each of us is safe in this circle. So we're going to practice deep presence to one another. Put your hand on your heart and picture a strong, protective, tightly woven shield of compassion and detachment. With compassion alone, we often amplify the emotions of another with our own. With detachment and compassion, we can walk intimately with another without taking on the other's feelings." She allowed that to sink in, and then asked a question. "First let's share thoughts. How has mindfulness connected your body and spirit today?"

Two of the men immediately raised their hands. Marianna called on one, who blushed as he said, "I had no idea a virtue could make me horny."

The laughter of the group was long and loud. "So, did others have this sensory experience?" Most of them nodded. She said, "We really are one – body, mind, and spirit. They are all connected. Sexual awakening is a natural part of that. So, now I invite you to call on your detachment, and gently bring yourself to this present moment. Okay, now put your shield over your heart and be completely present, with receptive silence. The quality of your attention is directly proportionate to the degree of your concentration. In this experience please be mindful to follow my lead.

"Now, I'd like to hear from Maggie. Maggie, it's time for you to share." She gazed at Kate, kindly expectant, as if saying, "Trust me." Kate was stunned. She opened her mouth, and found there were no words. "Show us Maggie, with words, or a movement, or a sound."

Kate shut her eyes and slid out of her chair. She found herself on the floor in a tight fetal position, hands over her head, then gradually uncurled her body and lay spread-eagled. She put her hands over her face as guttural sobs shook her.

Suddenly she felt hands gently supporting her, her head in Marianna's lap. The group was echoing the sounds Kate made until there was a crescendo of moans and cries. Then a plump, fulsome woman gathered Kate against her and began to hum and rock.

"Mama," Kate cried as the others softly moved back. Gradually, her shuddering breaths quieted, and various voices, led by Marianna, started speaking to her: "You're safe, little one." "Mama loves you." "I'm so sorry." "Everything's going to be okay." "You're such a beautiful child." "You're very dear to me."

Kate gradually sat up, and the others dropped back into their positions in a small semi-circle around her on the floor. Kate grabbed tissues from a box placed beside her and blew her nose. She looked up to see each person smiling at her.

Marianna asked her, "How are you, Maggie?"

"Actually," Kate said, "my name is Kate. I feel amazing – light, free. I felt your love. Thank you all so much." Marianna asked her if she was ready for virtues acknowledgments. She nodded.

Marianna began. "Kate, you trusted us with your inmost feelings. That took profound courage." Each of the others named a virtue they saw in her – her strength to survive, her loyalty to her mother,

her endurance, her beauty. It was as if she had opened a deep fissure of pain and drained it, and now it was being refilled with love.

Kate felt elated. She had no idea how much time had elapsed until Marianna said, "It's time to stop. Supper is in one hour. Thank you all for your amazing, loving attention. You have the evening to yourselves. The activity sheet is on the board in the lobby. Or you may choose solitude -- whatever helps you to re-balance. Given the feelings that arose today, I am reminding you of the boundary about mixing socially. Remember the purpose for which you came. You're all strong. You can take it!"

Kate walked back to her bungalow, feeling startlingly alive. She took a cool shower and noticed that her awareness was acutely vivid. Every drop of water in the shower stream glimmered. She saw, as if magnified, the stamen of tiny yellow flowers projecting from the center of a coral hibiscus draped over the privacy fence, and then was awestruck by witnessing the flower gradually closing for the night. It was like slow motion photography, crystal clear in the midst of a time warp. She was immersed in a strange emotion. With a laugh, she realized it was joy.

After smoothing lightly scented coconut oil on her body, she changed into a white and crimson sarong laid out on her bed, and draped a light shawl over her shoulders, leaving her long hair loose down her back. She plucked a white flower and placed it behind her right ear, meaning she was "single and available". *My darling Jason, you have no idea how available I am.*

30

Lonnie thought Jason had to have some kind of angle, *like some fuckin' sex slaver, or human trafficker.* He didn't know him from Adam. But how did Jason know Janie's song? He resisted Jason's suggestion to move to a cheap rooming house where he could be warmer.

"Hey, man, what about my homies? I can't just up and leave them. I bring in meals from the van that comes around from Sally Ann and they…uh, they need me."

Jason was moved by Lonnie's loyalty to his buddies, some of whom were still toking, smoking meth or shooting heroine, and the incredible discipline Lonnie showed to resist falling back into it himself. "Lonnie, I see your loyalty, and I respect you for it. If two of these guys were willing to get clean and you could bring them with us, who would it be?"

Lonnie rubbed his chin and thought. "I guess I'd bring Carlos and Annie. They both really want to kick it in the balls – sorry. And they've been in and out of rehab trying. But man, this is gonna cost megabucks. I ain't got it. And I'm not gonna get it!"

"Listen," Jason said. "I run a program that has grants for kids like you three. If we feel reasonably certain that you really intend to get clean and stay clean, there is money to transport you."

"There's no way, man. How the hell am I supposed to trust you, comin' in here, talkin' smooth? How can you prove you're not taking us to some sex commune or somethin'? If Janie comes and tells me you're okay, I'll believe it."

Jason thought for a minute and said, "What if I show you some photos of our program?"

"Better not be some generic 'Up with people' crap!" Lonnie was so tense, Jason could practically smell his fear. *The things some of these kids have gone through,* he thought.

Jason said, "Look. I respect your caution, your wisdom. You have good reason not to trust me. And I can see you feel responsible for your homies. What if I bring you my tablet later and show you?"

"I'll see. I got group and individual today, so it'll have to be after six."

"What are you doing for dinner?" Jason asked him.

"Oh, we've got reservations at the Royal York," he said, snickering.

"Well, what if I bring in dinner?"

"Cool, man, whatever. See you when I see you."

When Jason returned at six, there was a group of seven kids in the alley of the old building where they were staying, squatting or standing around a fire in a garbage can, warming their hands. Most were coughing. *Good thing I brought extra,* he thought. He put down three large pizzas on a crate, as well as plastic containers of lasagna and salad. "I don't think I brought enough plastic forks" he said.

"No worries, mate," said a very large boy beside Lonnie in a strange accent. "We don't need 'em."

Jason broke out the large bottles of juice he had brought as well. He had his tablet in a travel bag over his shoulder, but decided to wait until they had eaten and perhaps dispersed to show Lonnie photos of the youth retreat he had led the winter before. He knew he could only manage three young ones on this trip.

They dug into all the food as if they were starving, *which they probably are*, Jason thought. After they had eaten, Lonnie handed him the last piece of Meat Lover's pizza.

"Hey man, you gotta eat too."

There wasn't a noodle, or a lettuce leaf left, and every drop was drained from supersized bottles of juice, which they had passed around, (Jason wincing at the spread of their flu germs).

Lonnie said, "Man, that was cool of you. Thanks."

"You're welcome," Jason said.

"Now, you guys get going. I have a meeting," Lonnie said. They all vanished but the big guy, whom Jason assumed was there for protection. Lonnie said, "You too, Big Roo. He's cool." Reluctantly, the boy trundled off.

Jason brought out his Android tablet and turned it on, thumbing through icons until he got to a photo file labeled "Youth retreat 2014". He handed Lonnie a small bottle of hand sanitizer and indicated for him to use it before touching the tablet. "Ooh, aren't we careful," said Lonnie, grinning. "I understand, man, electronics have to be looked after. This would bring in a good price," he said, feinting as if he was taking off. Jason stood quietly. "Just ribbin' you, man," he said.

"Trust goes both ways," Jason said.

"Yeah, yeah, I know."

As Lonnie thumbed through the photos his eyes got wider. "Holee. This is where you want to take us?" There were photos of kids sitting in a circle in a sunlit meadow with Jason surrounded by waving palms, leaping from a rock into the sea, repelling down a cliff, playing basketball, Jason on the sidelines with a whistle, and in his office where he was using a stethoscope on a skinny young man. "So who are you? What are you anyway?"

"I'm a Cree from Saskatchewan. I'm also a doctor. I started this healing and retreat center in Hawaii. It's for adults as well as kids, and there's a program we call Hokopua, to give kids who have had trouble in the past move on with their lives. It includes scholarships for education, and...um, other benefits."

"Man, if you're for real, this is like what Janie said all the time. 'Never give up hope.' This is like a bloody miracle! So what do I gotta do?"

"Three things. First, you have to get well. As I told you, you can bring two friends. I can only take you if you are all over the flu. Second, I do expect you to move into the boarding house I've found for you and start antibiotics right now. As I said, I'm not taking you to Kauai until you're well. Third, you all have to be clean and sober for at least two weeks."

"You twisted my arm, mister, or I should say, doctor. But I'm still not sure. Maybe tomorrow. I wish..."

Jason waited. Then he said, "What do you wish?"

"That I could talk to Janie first."

"As I told you, Lonnie, I don't know where she is at the moment. May I suggest something?"

"I guess."

"Do you pray?"

Lonnie frowned and said defensively, "Yeah! I'm a good Indian, ya know."

Jason smiled and said, "How about you ask Creator what is the right thing to do?"

"I'll do that," said Jason, glowering. "But don't count on it. This ain't just about me."

That evening, which he knew was afternoon in Hawaii, Jason rang Moana on her private cell. "What a surprise!" she said. "I thought you fell in a hole."

He told her about how he had started looking for Kate in Toronto and decided to stay to find Lonnie, and what Lonnie had said about talking to Kate, aka Janie, before entering their program. He sighed, "So, I have no idea where she is, but I'm still hoping Lonnie and two of his friends will come. Once the kids are settled there, I need to leave again, so I'll need you to look after them. Moana, I have to find her! I know I'm asking a lot of you, but…"

Moana started giggling, then roaring with laughter. Jason could picture her belly shaking. "What!?" he asked sounding flustered.

"I have a surprise for you, my boy. She's here."

"What?! Why? When…?"

Still laughing, Moana said, "Now you sound like Kate. Look, she came here to enter our healing retreat, and I would imagine, hoping to see you."

"Oh, my God!" he said. He closed his eyes and just breathed for a few moments. "Well, that…that, uh, solves so much. Can you ask her to talk to me later tonight?"

Moana sat with Kate at dinner and when they finished, she asked her to come to her office. Kate noticed others going off with her in the evening apparently for private sessions, so thought nothing of it. She sat down on a comfortable chair across from Moana.

"Well, Kate, I won't beat around the bush. There's something I need to tell you."

"Oh, God, what is it?" Kate sat up suddenly vigilant, her pulse speeding up. "Has he found me?"

"You mean Jason?"

"No…never mind. What do you want to tell me?"

Moana cleared her throat. "Well, I just heard from Jason today."

"Really?" Kate reddened. "Where is he?"

"Hush a minute, and I'll tell you. He's been looking for you. He's in Toronto. When he lost your trail, he decided to do something for you. He went looking for Lonnie."

"Really? Is Lonnie okay? How...?"

"Lonnie is fine. Jason is trying to convince him to come here and enter our youth program."

"You have a youth program?"

"Girl, if you'd let me finish a sentence without more of your questions, I'll tell you the whole story."

Kate sat back and tried to calm her breathing. "Okay." She made a gesture of zipping her lips.

Moana told her about Lonnie entering rehab and Jason's attempts to convince him and two of his friends to come to Kauai. "But Lonnie is afraid. If he can talk to you, he'll probably come."

"Of course I'll talk to him!" Kate said. "Uh, when would they be coming?"

"In about two weeks if they follow Jason's boundaries. You'll be finishing your retreat in another week, but you're welcome to stay and wait for them. No extra charge," she smiled. "If you're okay with it, Jason will be calling in about a half hour. You can wait here or take a walk."

"I'll walk, thanks. I'll be back soon." Kate nearly ran out of the room, leaving Moana shaking her head and chuckling. *Something is definitely going on with those two.*

Kate raced to her bungalow, grabbed a bottle of water and drank it all. Then she took a whiff of lavender to calm her down. *Oh Lord, I'm all twitterpated*, she thought, using Gran's expression. It was almost too much to take in, first knowing she was going to speak to Jason again, and that Lonnie was safe. She patted her face quickly with a cold wet cloth and headed back to Moana's office. After just a few minutes of the two of them staring at the phone, it rang. Kate jumped and told herself to breathe.

Moana answered, "Kate is here with me. Do you want to speak to her?"

"Yes, please Moana." Jason said. She handed the phone to Kate.

Kate held the phone to her ear and said, "Hello? Jason?"

"Janie, how good to hear your voice. Are you all right?"

"Yes," she whispered. "I am now."

He cleared his throat as if he wanted to say something else. Kate understood why he had called her by her alias. "There's someone here who wants to speak to you."

"Okay, I'm ready."

"Janie?" a small voice asked incredulously.

"Yes Lonnie, it's me." She could hear him sniffling and it set her off as well. "Are you all right?"

"Yeah, Janie, I am. I did what you said, and it's working for me. I'm cleaning up my act."

"Oh, Lonnie, I knew you had the strength to do it!" she said, brightening.

"Say, I need to ask you something," Lonnie said. Then she heard him turn away from the phone and say, "Hey, a little privacy here, okay? Okay, he's gone off a ways. Say, Janie, what do you know about this Indian? Is he for real?"

"Oh, yes," Kate said, "He sure is. And you know the place he wants to bring you? That's where I am."

"Well, why the fuck's sake didn't he say so?!" he yelled.

"Lonnie, language! And he didn't know."

"Well, that's just weird," he said. Then, it struck him. "Oh my God! If we do come, will you still be there?"

"Yes, Love, I'll wait for you to come."

"You can come back now!" Lonnie called out, wiping his arm across his eyes. After a few moments, Jason came back on the phone.

"Ka, er Janie, will you still be there when we come in about two weeks?"

"Of course, Jason. I wouldn't dream of being anywhere else."

"Well, all right then. See you soon," and he hung up. He turned back to Lonnie who was still wiping his eyes.

"I don't usually do this, ya know."

"Hey, real men aren't afraid to cry. It just means you have strong feelings. That's a good thing in my book."

"I bet you never cry."

"When I do, I feel better afterwards."

"Oh," Lonnie said, "Well, anyway, Janie cleared you."

"And what about Creator?"

"I did ask, and I didn't exactly hear anything, but I felt something funny in my gut."

"Like what?"

"It was weird. It was, um, a weird sort of good feeling."

"Would you call it trust?"

"No, but you would," and he smiled.

By nine that night, Lonnie, Carlos and Annie had scrubbed themselves in long, hot showers, put on freshly laundered new pajamas from Walmart, and were snug in their warm, clean bunk beds.

"Is this Heaven?" Annie said.

A stout Native woman wearing an apron knocked on their door, and when they sang out, "Come in," she brought in a tray of lemon tea, bananas, and fresh baked ginger snaps.

"This snack will help you sleep," she said, and then handed out their antibiotics to be taken first.

"Hey thanks a lot, Mrs.," Lonnie said.

"Please call me Auntie Belle," she said.

They downed the pills and swigged from water bottles on the bedside table. "Now I know we're in Heaven," Annie laughed as she tasted the first bedtime snack in all of her eleven years.

31

The day after speaking with Jason and Lonnie, Kate awoke at dawn to the roosters' crowing. She stretched and smiled. *Jason is coming.* She sensed he wanted to say more to her on the phone, something personal, but not in front of Lonnie. *And I'll get to see my Lonnie.* Life was definitely changing. For the first time, Kate dared to hope that Jason might have feelings for her, beyond his role as a healer. The thought both terrified and thrilled her. *I'd better get moving*, she thought.

After a quick shower, she smoothed natural repellent over her body, made of coconut oil mixed with essential oils of lavender, peppermint, citronella and a drop of tea tree oil. It had a pleasant aroma, but the mossies didn't like it. She put on her hiking clothes and checked the equipment list for the morning hike, then brewed some Kona coffee and opened the bread box to find fresh baked coconut muffins studded with chunks of pineapple, banana and macadamia nuts. Slices of toasted coconut were on a plate in the small fridge. *This Hawaiian food is so delicious! I could get used to this.* Kate felt joy bubbling up within her – a sense of a whole new vitality. *I think it must be the work we did yesterday, and then hearing Jason's voice.* She checked her pack, grabbed her hiking stick, and went to join the others.

"Today is Justice Day. Let's pray," said Marianna. "Oh, Jah, Allah, father mother God, we come before you today to ask your guidance as we find the courage to explore our betrayals, those that have caused us pain, and those we have committed that have caused pain to others. Give us the humility to open to the teachable moments. We thank you for the opportunity to heal and this place of beauty you have created. Amen." She paused to allow some silence and then said, "Today, we will be hiking, rappelling and swimming, and will do some exercises to reclaim and restore justice. Let me read a bit from the Virtues Reflection Card of Justice. Hold these thoughts in mind as we climb the path in silence.

"'Justice is being fair in all that we do. We continually look for the truth, not bowing to others' judgments or perceptions. We make agreements that benefit everyone equally. When we wrong another, we take responsibility to make amends. If someone is hurting us, it is just to stop them. It is never just for strong people to hurt weaker people. With justice, we protect everyone's rights, including our own. Sometimes when we stand for justice, we stand alone.' And here is the quote on the card from the Holocaust Museum in Washington D.C. 'Be not a victim. Be not a perpetrator. Above all, be not a bystander.'

"We will be on a new path today. Does everyone feel ready to climb to new heights?" And she smiled. "As you climb, you can simply invite the spirit of Justice or the angel of Justice to be with you. Notice your bodily responses and your thoughts as you reflect on justice.

"We will take time today to think about when you have felt victimized in your life, when you have been a perpetrator, and when you have been a bystander. As you can imagine, this day of Justice requires deep truthfulness. Trust that you are strong enough to take this inner journey, or you wouldn't be here. This morning, as we climb, think about a time you felt betrayed or victimized. Let the feelings in. We'll be doing some work together on these experiences."

Kate's eyes widened as she thought of the word "victim". Her mind went back to the times when she had contemplated suicide as a teen, overcome by a deep longing for her mother, despite knowing that Charlene had been her greatest danger.

32

Charlene had a violent hangover the day her husband Hiram finally
tracked her down to the lakeside shack where she and little Kate
were holed up. He picked up the tiny, bruised, shivering four year
old in his arms and in a cold, hard voice, said, "Woman, you had
better get clean and stay clean, or you will *never* see Katy again, and
I mean that. Don't even *think* about trying to find her until you do.
I'm getting a restraining order on you this time. If you dare to come
anywhere near Katy, I will throw your ass in jail." Then, he turned
and left with Kate in his arms.

Two days later, the local cop came by and started a fire in the stove.
He said, "Charlene, you're really in trouble this time. Hiram could
have filed charges. He did put a restraining order on you going
anywhere near your daughter. You'd better shape up. You're
killing yourself here. Do you want me to call somebody?"

She lifted her head from her arms as she sat at the battered kitchen
table and just shook her head, so he left. Twenty minutes later, he
called Social Services from his office. He asked for his cousin
Mark, one of the supervisors. "Coz, there's a woman in a shack up

here on the lake and she's in a bad way. She needs help today. Can you send someone to get her to hospital? Tell them to come to my office first, and I'll take them there."

Hiram drove Katy down to Chemainus in southern British Columbia to her Aunt Esther's house, wrapped in a blanket, with the heat turned up high. He stayed with her for a week.

Early one morning, he came into the little room where she was snuggled under a warm comforter. He gathered her into his arms and said, "Sweetheart, Lady Kate, I have to go." Katy tried hard not to cry. She looked alarmed, but said nothing.

"Honey, are you worried" She nodded. "About mommy?" She hid her face against his shirt. Hiram held her tighter, and said, "You know Daddy loves you, and so does Aunt Esther and Gran, and all of us. Your mommy is sick. She should never have hurt you or let you get cold and hungry, but she's very sick. She didn't know what she was doing. She's not coming back to get you, I promise."

Katy looked up with a questioning look, but still, she said nothing. Hiram went on, "I'm going to leave you with Auntie Esther for now, but when I come back, I'll stay longer. Would you like that?" She nodded again and wound her little arms around his neck. "I'll see you soon, my darling, okay?"

Hiram drove north, sighing about how his and Katy's lives had been filled with so much pain. He desperately wished he could create a home for her, but his work as McCain's overseer for distribution across Canada forced him to travel. His father insisted that he retain the role "rather than turn back into an aimless hooligan", or he would be cut off from his inheritance. He wouldn't budge. "Bloody stubborn Scot," Hiram grumbled to himself. For the sake of Katy's future, he held on.

Hiram was the son of Douglas and Aileen Mackenzie. He was born and raised in the Orkney Isles of Scotland. The Mackenzies had a successful livestock business, then expanded into fisheries, and finally offshore oil and gas. Hiram and his five siblings were all expected to assume roles in the family business.

Of all the Mackenzie children, Hiram was the most restless, the one who would run off into the hills and woods for hours not letting anyone know where he was. He resisted any sort of control or authority, treasured his solitude and independence, and had little regard for pleasing his parents. He adored his mother, Aileen, but she knew better than to put restrictions on her wild child. Being a quiet, retiring woman, she secretly admired his adventurous ways.

Hiram would often find a good tree with sturdy limbs in which to lean and read the books he loved: *Robinson Crusoe, Moby Dick*, the works of Aristotle, and C.S. Lewis, especially *The Lion, the Witch, and the Wardrobe.* He hated the rules and boredom of school, and it was all they could do to get him to pass the exams. He graduated from sixth form by the skin of his teeth. At the same time, he was known in the family as "the charmer". Aileen used to say, "When he turns it on, he can charm the birds out of the trees".

Despite or perhaps because of his detachment, he was popular amongst his peers and considered a heart throb by the girls. His broad shoulders, thick black hair and unusual violet eyes were irresistible. Aileen worried about him constantly. Privately, she thought of him as her smartest child, yet wondered if he would ever settle into a career or any viable path. He got through high school by the skin of his teeth, then stubbornly refused to attend Orkney College, except to take a few classes in philosophy and landscape architecture, because they interested him. He had a few close friends, who took the initiative in picking him up for rugby games and parties.

His magnetism meant nothing to him until he was about sixteen, at which point he sacrificed solitude for the mysterious and sensuous pleasures he found with local lassies. He would take out one of the farm trucks until all hours and often slept the day away.

For Hiram's father Douglas, a serious and ambitious businessman, Hiram's self-indulgence was intolerable. One day he came to Aileen, uncharacteristically cheerful, and said, "I have an idea for the boy." Of course she knew which one he meant. In Hiram's growing social fluency, his unself-conscious attractiveness, Douglas recognized a potential asset to the sales side of the burgeoning business. He knew he had to use every iota of tact and wile to get

Hiram to agree. And so he came up with a plan. One evening at dinner, which despite all his lollygagging, Hiram never missed, Douglas sat back and said, "Son, I want to talk to you after dinner, in the den."

"But, Da, I was going to…" One look at his father's stony face, one eye-brow raised in challenge, and Hiram relented. "Yes sir, I'll change those plans."

"Very wise," said Douglas.

Douglas knew that it was useless to compare Hiram's unrepentant free-wheeling life to the career paths of his older siblings, all of whom either aspired to work for the company while earning relevant degrees at university, or already held positions. He had already tried that approach, countless times. Guilt had absolutely no impact on Hiram. His father knew there had to be something to catch his interest. "Son, it's time you made some decisions about your future."

Hiram sighed, but remained sitting upright in a chair in his father's den.

"I've given a lot of thought to this, and here's what I've noticed. You love your freedom. You're smart. You like to learn. You're good with people. You're quite, em, magnetic, Lord only knows why. Perhaps it's because you don't seem to need anyone. But what I do know is that you could use that ability to serve this family." He paused, trying to read Hiram's cool expression.

"I'm listening."

"Here's what I'm thinking. You give two years to the company, see how you like the work, find your place, and I'll shout you a trip overseas, wherever you want."

Hiram looked intrigued in spite of himself. "And if I don't?"

"I will no longer support lack of effort or an aimless existence. Your financial trust will be frozen until such time as you have selected some career path and shown that you are serious about it, about something besides your own personal pleasure. I won't ask you to leave the house, but you'll be completely on your own for money. Look, I don't want to fight. What do you say?"

"So, what do you have in mind? What would I do?"

"I'm thinking you would be a good fit in the international sales division. You might even enjoy it."

To Douglas's amazement, Hiram grinned and said, "You've really given this a lot of thought, Da. I'll give it a shot."

Douglas released the breath he wasn't aware he was holding, and stuck out his hand, which Hiram took.

By twenty-one, Hiram was second in line to the role of Sales Director of Mackenzie Enterprises. He discovered that he loved the work. He had a genuine interest in people, enjoyed learning about other cultures, and became a skilled and crafty negotiator. It happened that he was assigned as the contact person for the McCains when they flew to Orkney to talk about a joint venture.

Hiram researched the Canadian frozen foods conglomerate before they arrived and learned that in the 1950's Harrison and Wallace McCain had co-founded McCain Foods in their small hometown of Florenceville, New Brunswick, one of the maritime provinces of Canada. The brothers had followed in the footsteps of their father, who owned a seed potato exporting business there. They opened a plant, hired thirty employees, and sold $152,000 worth of french-fries in their first year.

By the time they were scheduled for the meeting with Mackenzie enterprises, they were producing more frozen french-fries than any other company in the world. The McCains turned what was initially a potato plant into a multi-billion dollar frozen foods empire. The company was now expanding into other countries through more than a dozen joint ventures.

The parallel though less grandiose success of Mackenzie Enterprises attracted the interest of the McCains. Hiram impressed his father during the meetings with the McCain team, and apparently, his quick witted negotiations and Scottish charm impressed the McCains as well. Without consulting his father, Hiram agreed in a private meeting to oversee the joint venture by joining the McCains at their New Brunswick headquarters for at least a year.

Later that evening, Douglas paced the floor, shouting to Aileen, "He's leaving me in the lurch! I can't believe it, after all I've done for him."

"Doug, you know how he is. He wants to be free. He does things his own way. It will still be good for the company. And he said it's only for a year. Let him go."

"What choice do I have?" he said, already obsessing about how to maneuver Hiram back home.

Hiram spent the first year driving across the endless Canadian prairies, meeting with outlet executives, taking side trips on weekends to tour the bistros and jazz clubs of Montreal, fishing the bountiful rivers of Saskatchewan and hiking the majestic Rockies in Banff, Alberta. He exulted in the happy solitude of traveling across the expanses of Canada, contrasted with the rich, multi-cultural offerings of its cities.

Toward the end of his one-year contract, he discovered British Columbia on the West Coast, with its rainforests, mountains, and islands, which echoed the natural beauties he had left behind in the isles of Scotland. One bright morning, he stood on the deck of a huge BC Super Ferry headed for Vancouver Island, the wind ruffling his hair. Sun-lit peaks sparkled in the distance, and sun dollars twinkled on the sea. When the ship entered Active Pass, between rocky, forested islands, he knew he would never go back to Scotland. Shortly afterwards, he attended the pot latch where he met Charlene and was instantly smitten. They married a few months later, to the consternation of his father, who refused to attend the wedding.

Hiram decided to apply to become a permanent resident of Canada, and he signed a long-term contract, which McCains enthusiastically offered him. He had amazing rapport with people, and the distributors across Canada had never been happier.

Kate was born a year after Hiram and Charlene were married. Now in a fury at losing his son to "that barbaric country", Hiram's father put a legal freeze on his substantial inheritance, with a condition that if he ever wanted to see a dime of it, he had to remain in the employ of McCains to prevent him from "going back to a feckless life".

McCains used this condition as leverage to keep Hiram on the road, which was a hardship for his young family. Even though Hiram missed his wee girl and his beautiful wife, he was secretly thrilled that he would not be losing his freedom, until Charlotte's drinking became progressively worse. He knew his absences were putting Katy at risk, and he threatened to take her away from Charlene.

"And do what with her? Keep her in the back seat with a blanket and a bag of chips?", Charlene snarled. When she absconded with Kate to an unknown Northern location, Hiram knew he had to take action.

~~~

Hiram always wanted Kate to have her First Nations side honored, something that Charlene had rarely experienced except in her first few years, before the residential school had taken her. He decided to make one more attempt to convince Charlene to sober up, with a wisp of a hope that she could remain part of Katy's life.

After leaving Katy with her Aunt Esther in Chemainus, Hiram drove back north to the shack at Teslin Lake, where he found Charlene

224

comatose, emaciated and nearly frozen to death. There was a pot of soup on the front step, which she hadn't touched. He picked her up and carried her to his truck, took her to the hospital, and asked the doctor to transfer her to a treatment center in Vancouver as soon as she could travel.

He said, "I'll make the arrangements," and left. He rang the police and said, "I thought we agreed you'd take care of her."

"We tried, Mr. Mackenzie. But she checked herself out of the hospital and just went back to her usual ways. We can't force her to change. Believe me, she's not alone. There are others…"

Hiram stopped him, "I know. Thanks for trying. I'm arranging for her to go to Vancouver now."

Hiram continued to visit Katy at Aunt Esther's every few months, and even though she had plenty of delicious food, especially porridge and peanut butter toast, had clean clothes to wear, and Aunt Esther never forgot "Lamby", the hot water bottle wrapped in a soft lamb's wool cover to keep her bed warm, she still felt lonely. And she never sat on Aunt Esther's lap. She just…couldn't. But her Daddy had always been safe. He was the only one she would allow to hold her.

During one August visit from Hiram when Kate was about to start kindergarten, Esther called him aside and said, "Listen, Hiram, I'm sorry to tell you this, but I need to move. My mum is sick and she needs me. As much as I love little Katy, I just can't take her with me, and I don't think it's good for her to keep moving around anyway. You've gotta make a better plan."

Hiram scratched his head and said, "Well, Esther, you've been very good to her, and I thank you for it. What do you think I should do? You know I can't take her with me on the road. That's no life for a child."

Esther put one hand on her hip and the other on her cheek. "Well, you know who has always wanted her, is Charlene's mum, Elvira, up in Telegraph Creek."

"I know that, Esther, but I'm worried Charlene will get her hands on her again if Katy is with her mother. God knows where she might disappear to."

Esther shook her head and said, "Elly would never, ever allow it. She knows better than anybody what that troubled girl has been through, but she would never expose Katy to her. I just know it. Why don't you call and talk to her?"

That night, Hiram talked with Elvira. She told him, "First of all I would never let Charlene near this child, and second of all, she's picked herself up and has good work out in Alberta. Would you believe she's driving a big truck and she's joined AA too? She's really ashamed of what went on, and she knows Katy is scared to death of her, for good reason. I want you to trust me, Hiram. We have a real good school up here, believe it or not. It's small, and it's perfect for our Katy."

Hiram agreed to give it a try. Once again, he and Katy were on the road. Katy still didn't talk much, but after about two hundred miles and many country music songs, she did say in a small voice, "Will mommy be there?"

"No, Lady Kate, she won't. She's living far, far away."

Katy didn't know why that made her feel like crying. She was real scared of Mommy, but she still missed her. She loved her Gran more than just about anybody, and had enjoyed visits to Telegraph Creek in the past. Knowing she would be staying with Gran calmed her heart.

My sad little girl, Hiram sighed.

33

Charlene spent six months in the Women Into Healing treatment center outside of Vancouver, finally coming to terms with her alcoholism, which had started in her early teens. She came to understand that the hateful racism she experienced in high school reinforced the sense of shame and worthlessness planted in her at the residential school.

When she was first mandated to attend group therapy, Charlene sat there with knees drawn up, grasping her legs with both arms, head buried and long hair covering her face. She kept her silence despite gentle words from the counselor welcoming her into the circle. She felt rotten inside -- angry, alone, and helpless. The first ten days, she had a bad case of the shakes, but gradually they abated.

Each afternoon, she would trudge to the group room and "assume the position". But she did listen. As other women shared their stories, she felt the first stirrings of empathy. Then one Wednesday morning, she sat up, pulled her hair behind her ears, and looked into the eyes of another woman across the circle. The woman nodded and Charlene reciprocated. When the counselor opened the circle, asking "Who would like to start?" she opened her mouth and said, "My name is Charlene, and I'm an alcoholic." As she disgorged the depths of guilt she felt toward her mother, Elvira and her husband, Hiram -- "the saints" -- and especially her little daughter Kate, she began to understand why she often felt she just didn't want to be here, and why she drank to oblivion. It was as if she were retrieving bits of her soul that had been shattered and drifted away. She started eating nutritious meals and gaining weight. She worked out in the in-house gym -- walking, then running on the treadmill, lifting weights, strengthening her physical core, as her will to live grew stronger.

A medicine woman named Vera Gray Eyes came in several times a week to offer smudging -- a sacred practice among many coastal nations, in which a stick of sage branches tied together was lit, producing aromatic smoke with which individuals could "cleanse" themselves, using their hands to sweep the pungent smoke over their bodies.

Vera also gave private sessions she called "Indian counseling". Her office walls were full of posters:

"Get over it!"

"It's your choice."

"The red road or the dead road."

"It's your pity party and you can die if you want to."

229

There was a cartoon entitled "Single Session Therapy" in which a therapist slapped his client across the face, saying "Snap out of it!" There was also a poster of Monet's Water Lilies inscribed with words of the Sufi poet, Jalal'u'din Rumi. It caught Charlene's eye, and she stared at it during each session. "If God said, 'Rumi, pay homage to everything that has helped you enter my arms', there would not be one experience of my life, not one thought, not one feeling, not any act I would not bow to."

Charlene sat in silence until Vera would say, "So, how's my favorite boozer?" Charlene would laugh and tell her about what was happening in the group sessions. Vera listened quietly, occasionally asking a question such as, "Where do you feel that in your body?" or "You keep crossing your arms, Charlene. What are you protecting yourself from?" And she demanded answers. Vera ended their sessions with a smudge, fanning the burning sage with an eagle feather. As Charlene cupped the sweet smoke over her face, her head, her ears, and the rest of her body, she breathed in the scent of sage as if it were her last hope. Then Vera wrapped her in a long hug, murmuring "You can do this, Charlene."

One day, the group counselor, Jane, introduced a guest visitor. Jane started the session as always with the motto of Women Into Healing: "We will love you until you can love yourself." Then, she looked at the guest and said, "This is Annie Standing Bear. I mentioned to you yesterday that she would be coming. She has some tools we're going to start using in group, and she's here to share them with us."

Charlene wasn't alone in rolling her eyes. Annie was a plump, brown-skinned woman with long, thick braids, and her body was wrapped in what seemed to be several layers of skirts and a shawl. She wore Birkenstock sandals with wool socks, and carried a huge woven basket with handles, which she lay at her feet. In front of her was a low table.

First, she took out a scrolled poster and attached it to the wall behind her with putty. It was entitled "Virtues: the Gifts Within" and listed fifty-two virtues, from Assertiveness to Justice to Wisdom. Out of her basket she pulled a neatly folded cloth of dyed batik in soft reds and browns with designs of elk, moose and bear, and spread it over the table. Then, she placed various items from her basket on the table: a small woven basket with some cards inside, an abalone shell in rainbow colors, a sage bundle tied with red string, a box of matches, a box of stones, and a long cloth-wrapped bundle, which Charlene suspected was an eagle feather.

When she was finished setting everything out, Annie said, "Good morning, good women. First, I want to thank the Kwantlen people, the original owners of this land we are on for the privilege of being here. Now, let's begin with a healing prayer. Please stand with me."

231

She closed her eyes and started a keening chant in Cree. As the pitch of her voice rose, high and yearning, it gave Charlene chills to the roots of her hair. Then, Annie opened her eyes and said, "All my relations."

She took a breath and looked around making eye contact with each of the seven women in the circle. "I'm here because I'm one of you. Six years ago, my life was in pieces, and this place was a lifesaver for me. I was wrecked on alcohol and heroine. There isn't one thing any of you have done that I haven't done, and I'm here to tell you, it will get better. You may never get over your grief about the past, but you can get through it. I honor you for the courage to do this inner work. It's the best way. It's the right way. It's the red road of recovery.

"Now, I want to tell you something. Just as the winds that encircle the earth connect the breath of all people, we are all connected spiritually too. That means, that this soul work you are doing, to come back to yourselves, to learn to love yourselves, is helping other women too. You're not just doing it for yourself. You're doing it for all of us -- for your daughters, your mothers, and your sisters across the world. Nothing could be more important. I love the line in the movie, 'The Help' where the African-American maid says to the little white girl, 'You is kind, you is smart, you is important.' Remember that.

"So this morning we're going to call on the power of the human spirit we all share. This power is a treasure you carry within you, one that can only come alive by being used, by being practiced."

Despite herself, Charlene felt curious to know what this woman was talking about. Annie picked up the small basket on the table. In it were some colorful cards a bit larger than playing cards. She said, "These cards are called Virtues Reflection Cards. Each one contains a description of a virtue. Do you know what a virtue is?"

The youngest woman in the circle, fifteen year old Janine, raised her hand and spoke up. "We had something about it in school. I think virtues are, um, what's good about us."

Annie lit up in a wide, brilliant smile. "That's one of the best definitions I've ever heard. Thank you for having the confidence to speak." The girl nodded and smiled shyly. "The virtues are the link between us and Creator. They are the qualities of the Divine and the content of the human soul. You know how Dolly Parton sings that song, 'You can be a beacon if you let it shine.' That's what virtues are. Hope, Kindness, Honesty, Loyalty, Gentleness, Creativity. They are all the good things inside of us. The reason you're here at Women Into Healing is to reclaim the good within you. Look, I know that many of you have reached a very low place. That's a place of humility -- owning our mistakes, taking responsibility. It's probably the hardest thing you've ever had to do. It's the best place – the only place -- to start climbing up to where you belong. Okay, enough talking. Let me show you how to do this Virtues Pick. First, each of us will wear the Shawl of a Thousand Prayers."

She took out another bundle and reverently unwrapped the thin, soft rawhide covering. It was a shawl in hues of red and black with fringes beaded in yellow white and black. She unfolded it and put it around her shoulders. "Now I'm going to go first, so you'll know what to do when it's your turn. You keep a receptive silence while listening to me, and I'll feel it. When I finish, please acknowledge me for a virtue you notice in me and how you see me acting on it. You can use this poster on the wall, or think of some other virtue."

Annie briefly shared her story, how she had lost her children over the years to foster care because of her addictions. She talked about her recovery, how it was an ongoing struggle. Then she reached into the basket and randomly pulled out a card. Her face lit up. "My virtue is Hope."

She read the card aloud. "Hope is looking to the future with trust and faith. Without hope, we lose our will to live fully. Hope gives us the courage to keep moving forward..." When she finished reading it, she said, "The way this virtue speaks to me is, hope was the only way I survived. I nearly lost my will to live, but hope pulled me through. Well, that's me."

The women looked around, and Charlene raised her hand. "Annie, I see your virtue of determination. You never gave up. You kept going in your healing journey." Annie nodded and smiled. Several others, studying the virtues poster, followed suit. Then, each in turn shared something of her story and did a Virtues Pick.

One woman drew Detachment. "What the fuck is that?" she said. "I never heard of it."

One of the other women said, "Donna, read it and see if it makes sense to you." Annie nodded.

As Donna read it, she murmured "Hmm." Then she said, "Yeah, this is me. It says, 'We let go and accept what we cannot change…we step away from harmful cravings.' I've bloody well done that since I've come here!" Everyone laughed.

When it was time for the others to acknowledge her, several hands went up. Bonnie, a large woman with a halo of flaming red hair and generous curves, who described herself as "Reubenesque", said, "To tell you the truth, Donna…"

"Uh, oh, here it comes," Donna laughed.

"To tell you the truth, I see your detachment. A couple times when some of us got into a fight, you kept your distance. You detached. And yes, you've been drug-free for weeks. I honor you for that detachment, that letting go."

Donna grinned, and said, "Thanks."

After each woman had a turn, Annie said, "I want to thank you all for calling on your confidence to share today, and you gave excellent virtues acknowledgments! What was helpful or meaningful for you about this morning?"

The women's smiles shone with a new light. Myrtle said, "Wearing the prayer shawl while doing our virtues pick felt so special. All those prayers you told us were said while it was being woven."

Donna said, "This was awesome! It's like you introduced us to ourselves in a whole new way. I guess we're virtues virgins!" All the women laughed.

Charlene said, "I knew I was gonna need a new lifestyle when I get out of here. This is it. You said the virtues belong to us, right? We're gonna need all of them when we're on our own again."

Annie nodded and said, "Thank you for being so open today. I see your hope for a new way of life. I'm leaving a set of Virtues Cards here for you all to share. And now, please pass around these virtues stones and take one as a remembrance of today." The women nodded in appreciation and passed the small cloth bag. Charlene reached in and pulled out a small smooth river stone in which was carved the word, "Purity". She thought to herself, *that's what I'm trying to do -- clean up my life.*

" I'll be back in a few weeks," Annie said.

Charlene was suffused with a positive emotion very new to her. She had no words for it, but felt a deep shift inside. She knew that nothing would ever be the same again.

34

As Kate climbed, reflecting on when she was a victim of injustice, she had mixed emotions. After the joy she'd been feeling, she was surprised at the flow of tears, which she continually wiped away with her long t-shirt sleeves. She kept thinking back to the terrible cold. She even shivered a few times despite the growing heat of the tropical morning and perspiring from the strenuous climb. She remembered the ache she used to feel for her mother and a sense of deep shame, even though Gran always told her it wasn't her fault that her mother was sick and had to go away.

As she got older, she wondered where her mother was and why she never came, ever, to see her. She swiped at more tears and finally sat on a bench at the side of the trail, buried her face in her hands and sobbed. A man behind her on the trail suddenly sat down and put his arm around her shoulders. She shrugged him off. "Don't!" she said. The last thing she needed was to be touched when she felt so vulnerable.

"Sorry, sorry," he said and left her to sit alone.

When she arrived at the top of the trail, her face was red and her eyes were swollen from crying. She took a long drink of water from her thermos and sat on the logs arranged in a circle, with her head down. Marianna said "Okay, dear ones, you've been climbing. What has the inner 'climb' been like for you? What was happening in your body? Remember to put on your shields now as you listen."

A man from the mid-west named Rick responded first. "My stomach was clenched the whole time."

Marianna waited, then asked, "What are you clenching in your stomach?"

In a shaky voice, he said, "I'm so angry...at my Dad. I used to have to clench my stomach muscles, because if I didn't, his punches 'to toughen me up' really hurt."

"How old were you when this was happening?"

"It started when I was five. 'You gotta be a man,' he would say. My mother used to try to stop him, but it just made him worse. He was always drunk."

"Come into the center, Rick," Marianna said. He went and stood beside her, a bleak look on his face. Marianna gestured to one of the attendants, and he brought a bat and a low table into the center of the circle. Marianna handed Rick some safety goggles which he put on. She said to the group, "Hold onto your shield of compassion and detachment. Let your own feelings come while you stay focused on

Rick." Then she handed him the bat and said, "Show us that anger clenched inside. Let it out now."

He began swinging the steel bat onto several large stones of shale on the table. They made a loud crunching sound as they disintegrated the more he swung. Then the small table broke and he kept swinging and began making a low growling sound. He was sweating profusely. Then suddenly he stopped and threw the bat down, his chest heaving.

Marianna brought him to a sitting position beside her. "Now close your eyes, and talk to your father. Picture him sitting in front of you. Tell him what you wanted to say but couldn't then." Marianna placed her hand in the center of Rick's back.

He shouted, "Why were you so mean? How could you hurt a little kid like that? What the fuck is wrong with you, you fucking bastard?!" He sobbed and went on, "I would never do that to my son. Why couldn't you just love me? Why should I have had to protect myself from you? You were supposed to protect me!" He was breathing heavily.

Marianna asked him to lean to his right side and explained to him that this was a dialogue with his father. He took several deep breaths. Then, Marianna said, "Now answer as your father."

Rick was silent for several moments, then said, "I'm so sorry, son. I didn't know what I was doing. I was out of my mind, drunk most of

240

the time. I was so ashamed. I couldn't work, couldn't support you and your mother as I wanted to. There's no excuse. I was just lost. I wanted you to be strong, not weak like me."

Marianna gently pulled Rick back to center. He opened his eyes, looking shocked by the words that had come. He turned to Marianna and said, "He just wanted me to be strong."

"Tell us all," Marianna said. There was a long silence, and then he looked out at the group, and repeated in a soft voice, "He just wanted me to be strong," a small smile on his face.

"Okay for us to acknowledge you now?" said Marianna, and each one around the circle named the virtues they saw in him. His sense of justice, his love for his own son, his endurance.

"I see your strength," said Kate. "You grew strong in love instead of hate."

When it was Kate's turn to do the exercise, it wasn't anger at her mother that emerged, but grief. She leaned over her knees and wept. Marianna asked her, "What do you need to do with your body? What do you need to say to your mother?"

Kate stood and raised her arms to the sky. "Why, Mama? Why couldn't you just love me? I was your gift from Creator! Why did you leave me?" Then she crumpled, and Marianna and a man she had beckoned over, held her up.

"Kate, what do you need to hear from Mama?" Marianna asked.

"I already have," Kate said in a small voice. "She stayed away to protect me."

Marianna didn't push Kate as she had done with several others. She said, "Kate, you seem to have bypassed the anger that often protects us from our grief. Such sorrow at the injustice of your mother abandoning you."

"Yes," Kate whispered.

The group then acknowledged Kate for her loyalty to her mother, her faithfulness at wanting her mother in her life in spite of all the pain and neglect she had endured, her lasting love. She looked surprised. Marianna whispered, "Let it in." And she did.

During the next exercise, the men and women went in separate directions -- the men to a large pond at the base of a waterfall, the women to a zip line. The men let go of the pain they had carried by throwing stones as large as they could hold into the deep pond, bellowing out "Anger, I release you!" (Or whatever they wanted to let go of). The women harnessed up and imagined leaving their emotional burdens behind as they "flew" through the green canopy. The men stripped and entered the pond to cleanse their pain and reclaim their sense of justice. Then the activities were reversed. While other women threw stones gathered at the water's edge, Kate needed quiet. She thought about the letter her mother had written so long ago, which Gran had given her when she was ten years old. She whispered to herself, "Let it in."

Marianna came and sat beside her, gently touched her shoulder and said, "What's happening with you, Kate?"

Kate said, "I've cried more in the last few days than I have in many years. I guess it's helped me to let go of something. I'm realizing that I want my mother in my life, no matter what she's done. I've lived without her long enough."

"You know something, Kate? You're a step ahead of us. Tomorrow our theme is Forgiveness."

That evening, after dinner, the group came back together in the lodge. Marianna had them journal about a time they had been a perpetrator or bystander of injustice, whether bullying another child, cheating a friend or partner, or witnessing violence without intervening. Some found that they had deeper emotions around their own acts of injustice than when they had been victims.

Marianna invited them to form triads with two new partners as they explored times they had been bystanders. Kate was in a triad with a slender, elegant blond woman named Mary Sue from South Carolina and a Jerry, a short, stocky, man with a handsome face from New York. Mary Sue drawled, "Shall I begin?" The other two nodded.

"When I was in Elementary School, segregation was new to our school, and to every school, for that matter. Listening to my

Daddy's rants every night at dinner about my having to fraternize with, um, negroes – that wasn't the word he used – I knew he expected me to be equally incensed about it, but something strange was stirrin' up inside me. I didn't like seeing that little group of black kids who had to bus across town to our school shunned, laughed at, even spat on. One afternoon, when I had finished after-school tennis, I was heading back to the gym, and I caught some boys dragging a ten year old girl into a janitor's storeroom. She was screaming and thrashing around. I stood there, frozen. I just stood there and let them take her. It's a horrible memory for me. I'd do anything to change what happened. They raped that little girl, damn near killed her. She never came back to our school after that."

When Jerry spoke, he cleared his throat, and said, "As you can see, I'm on the short side. I'm also Jewish, and I went to a mixed school in Brooklyn with Catholic and Protestant kids. I had my share of bullying, but then Robert, an older boy, took me into his clique – it wasn't exactly a gang – and for the first time, I felt safe. I found out later, he wanted me to write his essays for him, and I'm not proud of that either. I was so desperate for protection, for belonging, I sold out. I sold my soul. Anyway, he used to make these awful racist comments, loudly in the cafeteria, aiming them at whatever minority might be around, including my cousin Herman. He called him a Kike, and told a really nasty Jewish joke. I laughed as loud as the rest of the guys, but it made me sick."

Kate struggled to think of a time she had been a bystander, and then it came to her. When she had been at Harvard in the Leadership program, she was having lunch with a few other students, when one whispered behind his hand, "Don't look now, but here comes that savage, Mathew Eagle Feather. He's just a dumb Indian. Can't imagine what he had to do to get in here," and snickered. "I just sat there and didn't say a word. Because I'm a Mackenzie, most people had no idea…"

When the sharing circles finished, everyone was feeling down and guilty. Many hung their heads. Marianna looked around the group, and said, "Look at me, everyone," making eye contact with each person. "How was this session for you?"

"Tough, even worse than remembering being a victim," one man said. Everyone nodded in agreement.

"What has been a teachable moment for you, a lesson from today's work?"

The ample woman who had held Kate in her lap spoke up. "It's been a bit mind-blowing to realize that we have been all three – victim, perpetrator and bystander."

Marianna said, "Yes! Any other thoughts on that?" An animated discussion followed. Then, Marianna said, "You have really dived into the truth today. And you're experiencing the humility that comes from realizing you have been all three. The point is not to humiliate yourself but to heal, so now we're going to close the day with something that is genuinely healing. Each of us will identify an act of restorative justice."

Each of the group members spent time journaling a commitment to never again stand by, to always speak up for justice, and to make amends unless it caused further harm. They stood in the closing circle, eyes shining, stating aloud, "I commit to never again participate in or allow an ethnic put-down in my presence," said Jerry.

Kate said, "I empower myself to do what my heart calls me to do. I commit to speak up in the face of prejudice. And I fearlessly reach out for the love I need and deserve." Her cheeks were flushed, and a sense of energy tingled throughout her body. She looked around the circle. Others had the same look. *What is this,* she wondered. *Oh, it's Hope.*

That evening, Kate took out the time-worn, deeply creased letter from Charlene written more than a decade before.

Dear Kate,

Every word I write here is the truth including the word "dear". You are the most precious gift of my life, and believe it or not, you are and always will be very dear to me. I have sent this letter to Gran because she knows you best and I trust her to give it to you when she feels you are ready to read it.

First, Katy, I want to tell you how very, very sorry I am for having hurt you when I was sick and out of my mind. None of it was your fault. Some kids think the bad things that happen to them are their fault. I always believed that myself. I thought if I was good enough, and quiet enough at the residential school, bad things would stop happening, but I have come to understand none of it was my fault. Sometimes grown-ups do bad things to innocent children. And what I did to you was never because of anything you did wrong. I was very sick from alcohol, and I drank so much I lost my mind, I lost myself, and I lost you. I miss you so very much, but what makes it easier for me is knowing that you have found a better life with your Gran. My greatest hope is that you are a happy girl and that you know you are loved. I know that you are kind, you are smart and in ways you cannot imagine now, you are important.

You lost me at a very young age, then when you were still so young, you lost your Dad. So much grief for a little girl. I want to tell you now that I am better. Your Dad sent me to a healing place that really helped me. He was such a generous man, and I know he loved you more than anything.

I have been sober for six years now, and I intend to stay clean and sober for the rest of my life, with Creator's help and the help of other people struggling with the same addiction. I really want to stay on the healing path. I have moved to another province and I won't be coming to see you. I don't want to stir up those bad memories of when we were together. Please believe that the reason

*you won't see me is not because I don't love you. It is because I do
love you very much and want to give you the best chance for a better
life. Katy, here's what I hope for you.*

*I hope you never lose yourself in drugs or alcohol. I wish you
sobriety.*

*I hope you can heal the wounds you received when you were young.
I wish you wholeness.*

*I hope you believe you are good. You are full of good virtues like
kindness, compassion, courage and honesty.*

*I hope you find your calling, your special song, using the talents
Creator has given you.*

I hope you find love and stay loyal to it all your life.

I love you, Katy, and I always will.

Your mother Charlene

Kate refolded it for the hundredth time and tucked it back into her
jewelry case. This time felt different. As she read her mother's
words, she was suffused with compassion, and said aloud, "I forgive
you, Mama." Then, she slept.

35

When Kate awoke the next morning after a deep restful sleep, her first thought was, *where is my mother?* She had often wondered what happened to Charlene, what kind of life she had now, but she was too wounded to actually do a real search. She Googled Charlene's name occasionally, without success, aware that she was probably not into social networking, and also that she may have remarried and changed her last name.

She sighed and stretched, wondering what the day would hold. Her next thought was of Jason, a longing that came from deep inside. *I want him*, she thought, and jumped out of bed, not willing to frustrate herself by dwelling on this heavy-hearted and deeply stimulating feeling. When she imagined seeing him again, she nearly trembled with anticipation. She felt skittish, *like a cat on a hot tin roof,* she thought, aware that Jason would soon be flying to the island. Her stomach tightened with anxiety, and she felt an unfamiliar yearning edged with fear. *What if he doesn't want me? What if this is not his path? How will I live without him? Stop it!* she told herself.

By the time she set out for the lodge, the weather had clouded over. She wondered if they would be trekking in the rain, but the program didn't advise a pack, so probably not. Walking in the cool morning air, she was glad she had put on her soft angora sweater and brought a rain jacket. When she arrived, people were already forming a circle with Marianna.

After the opening prayer, Marianna said, "Yesterday we focused on justice. We explored how each of us has been the giver and receiver of injustice. The balancing virtue to justice is forgiveness. Without justice, there can be no lasting forgiveness. The Dalai Lama says that to truly forgive we need to protect ourselves from those who harm us." She read from one of his books: "Nothing in the principle of compassion—the wish to see others relieved of suffering—involves surrendering to the misdeeds of others. Nor does compassion demand that we meekly accept injustice. Far from promoting weakness or passivity, compassion requires great fortitude and strength of character."

Marianna went on. "Even the Baha'i Faith -- a religion that focuses on unity and peace -- is very clear about this." She picked up another book, and read: "The Kingdom of God is founded upon equity and justice, and also upon mercy, compassion, and kindness to every living soul. Strive ye then with all your heart to treat compassionately all humankind -- except for those who have some selfish, private motive, or some disease of the soul. Kindness cannot be shown the tyrant, the deceiver, or the thief, because, far from awakening them to the error of their ways, it makes them to continue in their perversity as before."

"Yesterday we focused on how to restore justice by making amends, by changing ourselves. One of the most important ways for us to restore justice to ourselves when we have been betrayed is to set clear boundaries. So, how do these Buddhist and Baha'i teachings apply?"

Marjorie, a tall, amply endowed African-American woman with tightly braided hair in zig zag designs, raised her hand. "This totally makes sense to me. Many of us were victimized by our own parents. Their addictions were...*are*...a 'disease of the soul'. And it doesn't serve them, or anyone who is a perpetrator, to be indulged. It doesn't serve them emotionally or spiritually. So we have to do whatever is necessary to protect ourselves – and them—from repeating the injustice."

Marianne said, "Marjorie, what a clear understanding of the need for boundaries. Anyone else?"

Dietrich spoke in a thick German accent: "Ze image you gave us last night, of having one foot in one virtue and the other in its balancing virtue, zat is our holy ground, yes?" Marianna nodded. "I like zat. I'm German. I need things to be orderly," and he laughed. "But really, it seems the truth."

"Yes. Thank you, Dietrich. So, as we look at how forgiveness fits with justice, let's do some work on boundaries. What are some examples of boundaries you either have created or need to create in your life?"

Marjorie said, "My boundary is with my ex-husband, who picked up where my parents left off. I was drawn powerfully to that bad boy. His mean and nasty ways were so inside my comfort zone, until I wised up. Now, I don't allow him any contact at all anymore, because he is simply unwilling to talk reasonably, and does all he can to grab me back. I ain't goin' there again. Doesn't mean I can't forgive him, but I won't forget. And I won't open that door again."

She paused and continued, "I had an epiphany last night. Forgiving others doesn't mean what they did was right or that it didn't hurt. It means we're no longer carrying that pain. It doesn't belong to us. We can let it go, like tossing the stones into the pool."

Others talked about boundaries with their teenager children, who were in chronic tantrum mode. "I told my daughter," Mary Sue said, "If she can speak to me with respect, I'll listen to anything she has to say. Otherwise, she has lost my attention. So, when she starts ranting, I walk out of the room. I take a time out myself." Others laughed and nodded. "She actually came around, and found out that if she speaks reasonably to me, I really do listen and take her feelings seriously."

Once again the group divided into triads and supported each other to create specific boundaries to restore justice in their relationships. After lunch and a rest, they reconvened to reflect on forgiveness.

Marianna began with a story. "A man who had committed all kinds of crimes, including violence, went to a spiritual master and asked him, 'Will God ever forgive me?' 'Of course,' the master said. 'He is the ever-forgiving.' 'How will I know when I am forgiven?' the man asked. 'You know you are forgiven when you don't do those things anymore.'"

She continued, "This afternoon, we are going to do some work on a deeper level." Kate's eyes and several others' widened as if thinking, *how could we go deeper?*

"Psychologist Bill Plotkin speaks of the "sacred wound" that comes from early betrayal. He says that when we get to the root of the pain, we can release the old story that has put us in the role of victim or perpetrator. You're doing real soul work in this retreat. It's actually freeing you to write a new story."

By now, the tension in the group was palpable. "Do you feel like running out of the room?" Marianna asked with a twinkle in her eye. They all nodded. "Well, guess what. We're going to have a party.

"Today, we're going to play 'Statues'. How many of you played that game as kids?" Most raised their hands, including Kate. "This time we're going to meld that game with a Parts Party, a kind of family sculpting developed years ago by a family therapy pioneer, psychologist Virginia Satir. She said, 'Life is not the way it's supposed to be, it's the way it is. The way you cope with that is what makes the difference.' Here's what we're going to do. We'll have two sessions this afternoon. This can be as meaningful for those watching as for those actively involved.

"You've all shown amazing determination in this retreat, some of you exploring aspects of your lives – of yourselves – you've never explored before. Satir believed that we own everything about ourselves -- our fears, our hopes, our words, our thoughts, our choices, our history, our way of experiencing the world.

"What allows the original wound to become sacred? Plotkin says, 'The wound becomes sacred when you are ready to release your old story and become the vehicle through which your soul story can be lived into the world.' He speaks of the goal of healing as 'dis-identifying' from the wounded self. We're going to do a virtues version of the Parts Party, because identifying our strength and growth virtues is the most direct path to transforming pain into healing. Satir said that only when we befriend all the parts of ourselves can we be truly free. So let's get this party started!" The group looked visibly relieved.

"I've been pretty locked into my old story all my life, so I'll volunteer to go first," said Jerry, the short, solid man Kate had worked with earlier. He had piercing dark eyes and a neatly trimmed

Van Dyke beard. He chose different people in the group to represent parts of himself. As Marianna instructed, he gave each part a brief description and wrote a "title" on large blank sheets of paper with loops of yarn to be hung around the neck of those in the psychodrama.

Jerry chose Kate as the unavailable fantasy that tormented him -- a beautiful woman who lived in his imagination and continually shamed and rejected him. He wrote out a label, and Kate hung it around her neck: "Impossible Dream". He chose a somewhat short man to play his isolating, lonely self and gave him the label of "Orphan". There were other parts: "Genius", the brilliant boy who skipped grades and always felt out of place socially in contrast to his soaring academic career. "Mensch" was another -- a normal guy who had buddies and was comfortable in his own skin. The parts were asked to walk around as they might at a party and move toward other parts they were naturally drawn to, then to dialogue. Kate found herself drawn to "Orphan."

Marianna said "Statues!" and the parts froze in place. Then Marianna moved toward Kate and the man playing "Orphan".

"Just talk to each other. Trust what comes. The rest of you relax and remember your shields of compassion and detachment." Marianna said.

Kate surprised herself by saying to Orphan, "You think you can't have me, but have you ever tried? What gave you the idea you have to be alone?"

Orphan answered in an angry voice, "You're the ice queen. How could I ever expect you to even notice me? You're way out of my league. And besides I have no idea what to say."

Kate struggled to hold back tears. She recognized herself in his words, and had been called "ice queen" before. Other students at university couldn't understand this cool, beautiful woman who was never seen with a man. Marianna moved close and whispered, "Let it come."

Kate's tears began to course down her cheeks. Orphan and Jerry himself began to weep as well. Kate realized she identified with both the Orphan and the part she was playing.

She said, "That's in your head, Orphan. I'm just as lonely as you are!" They moved toward one another and held each other in a long hug.

Marianna, watching Jerry's face, asked him, "Jerry, what just changed?"

"She's human! She's a person."

"So, what virtue just helped Orphan and Impossible Dream to connect?"

He said, "Empathy", and Marianna asked the two to turn their signs around, and wrote Empathy on them. "Now, Orphan, ask Impossible Dream how it feels to be her."

"How does it feel to be you?" he asked.

"I'm so lonely. I've always been alone, because everyone thinks I'm untouchable."

"Would you be interested in someone like me?" Orphan asked in a hushed voice.

"Of course! You're interesting. You're smart and funny. I don't care if someone is an Adonis or just a regular guy."

"Wow," said Jerry.

Marianna instructed each part to tell Jerry what virtue it needs from him in order to be a healthy part of his being. Orphan said, "Yes empathy, and also confidence."

"Mensch" (regular guy), Jerry's assertive, comfortable, funny self, said "Let me run the show a bit more. So I'm asking for trust and a bit of audacity."

Marianna asked each part to take a deep breath, remove their labels and step out of role. "Now, let me remind you of our boundary that guests are not meant to connect while here in any physical way other than affectionate hugs. Satir said we need lots every day!"

Jerry's eyes shone as each person in the group honored him for his openness, his courage, and his truthfulness.

He said to Marianna, "Thank you for your wise guidance and this amazing process, and I thank Virginia for her creative genius too!" Everyone applauded.

During a debrief where each person spoke in turn, including observers, those that played parts expressed what he or she was taking from the experience.

Kate said, "I own my loneliness and I claim the gift of love and friendship."

Jerry said, "I own my specialness and my fear, and I claim my mensch-hood! And my empathy," he said, smiling broadly.

The group did another Virtues Parts Party with Violet, a woman who had been raped when she was six. It was another powerful, moving experience for everyone there. After each person shared their own inner experience of the work done that day, Marianna said, "I applaud every one of you for your trust in this process. The observers were totally present as well. Could you feel it?" she asked those who played parts.

They nodded. Marianna concluded by saying, "We have done this soul retrieval work as a form of self-forgiveness, which is essential in order to forgive others. By accepting all aspects of the self, we honor our own experience, we claim it and own it. This inner work takes huge energy, so enjoy the buffet that's being served tonight."

Conversation was lively over dinner, and plates were piled with lobster, small tender steaks, huge mounds of salad, fresh corn on the cob, fluffy yeast rolls, and bowls of tropical fruit salad.

"I'd better watch my waistline after retreat," said Gwen, a slim, athletic woman from California as she popped a mini chocolate éclair into her mouth.

Kate laughed and said, "I think we're all burning major calories here!"

Marianna stood and announced that, after dinner and a rest, there would be a beach volley ball tournament. "You need to reconnect with your bodies now after all the soul work we did together today. Those who really don't want to play can swim or toss a Frisbee. Our last activity tonight is a special fire ceremony." People groaned.

"We don't have to walk on hot coals, do we?" Dietrich asked.

"No," Marianna laughed. "That's Tony Robbins' shtick."

Jerry roared with laughter, and said, "Hey, Marianna, you're catching on to Yiddish!"

As they ate, the energy in the room bubbled with laughter. Their joy was palpable.

Kate thought, *this place is amazing, and the pace is perfect. Someone has thought carefully about this program.* She immediately pictured Jason, in a sleeveless singlet, leaping for a ball. *Let's just see how untouchable the ice queen is when he gets back! If he's interested..."*

36

A brisk breeze was blowing as the group gathered on the beach at sunset that evening, veils of rose and coral flowing across the sky. One large cumulous cloud was limned in gold. Kate pulled on a thick cotton sweatshirt, fending off the loss of that luscious early evening heat she had felt during the volley ball game.

Marianna called the group to attention as they sat on logs around a fire pit. "Dear ones, tonight we will do some private work. I'm going to invite someone to serve as our fire-keeper, and someone to serve as the water bearer when we have completed this exercise. Anyone?"

Twenty-five year old Joseph, a First Nations man from Canada, and a woman named Alicia in her "fit and fabulous fifties", as she liked to say, volunteered.

"This is a Forgiveness fire. Let's start the fire and when it's going strong, I'll hand out pads of paper and pens. Think of your biggest regret in life and write it down, for your eyes only."

As the fire flickered and crackled, they sat silently, each one reflecting on the past. Kate realized that she had only one great regret in her life -- that she had never made the effort to find her mother, Charlene. As she wrote it down, she found that the act of admitting her own responsibility for the ongoing separation somehow calmed her, and felt oddly liberating.

When everyone seemed finished, Marianna said, "When you're ready to let go of it -- truly let go of it -- and forgive yourself once and for all, toss it into the fire. As it burns, think of it as rising to the Heavens. You will no longer carry it."

One at a time, they solemnly stood and threw their wadded paper into the flames, watching as their sins burned to ashes.

Marianna asked everyone to stand while she prayed, "Creator, forgive us for these sins, these times in our life when we were off the mark. In your tender mercy, bless our mistakes, help us to receive the lessons they teach, so that we will learn and grow from them. We now release them to your Divine forgiveness. All my relations." Kate smiled at the homage to the First Nations way of prayer.

"Now," said Marianna, "similar to what you did last night, write down one virtue that will atone for the regret. Write how you will practice that virtue from this time forward. Again this is for you alone, not to be shared with anyone else. You will keep this paper as a marker for your new commitment." The group wrote quietly.

Kate made a clear decision. She wrote, "I will find my mother, God willing, and I will offer her a loving relationship. It's time." For several minutes, they sat quietly, gazing into the flames.

Marianna started singing in a rich, contralto voice, "I'm gonna lay down my burden, down by the waterside…" The group joined in.

Then Jerry spoke up, "Say, where are the S'more's?" Others laughed.

Marianna said, "Are you kidding? Do you think we'd dream of making a fire in Hawaii without them?" Sure enough, in a covered basket were the marshmallows, chocolate and graham crackers. Kate just shook her head, smiling broadly.

As they munched, they chatted, then sang camp songs for another hour. "Row Row Row Your Boat" in rounds, "Dona Nobis Pacem", and Alicia surprised everyone by singing in her sweet soprano voice, "Ave Maria". As they wandered off to bed, Kate felt a new lightness. She pondered how long it had been since she had ever felt this way. *This is the first time,* she smiled. Her thoughts quickly went to Jason. *If Jason wants me, that will be my first time too.* The excitement that quickly arose felt like a small, happy bird, flitting inside her chest.

As the days of the retreat went on, Kate and all the participants were awed by the variety of ways to explore their inner world. Each day they learned a new way to meditate: walking meditation as taught by

Thich Nhat Han, which Kate already practiced, visualization by imagining a place in nature they had seen before and welcoming the presence of Spirit, then what Marianna called "a Spirit Walk" where something in nature spoke to them. They were all amazed when clear messages came through to them.

As Kate walked contemplatively that morning, her attention was drawn to an old stump out of which was growing a slender young green shoot and several ferns. She had her journal with her, the instruction being to be open to a calling from something in nature and to spend several minutes observing it, then to ask, "What is your message for me?"

She saw that the stump, with its rough faded bark, looked dead, yet out of it sprang new life. When she journaled the question, the response came swiftly. "You have deadened yourself to your longing for your mother, and for love itself. Now out of the old pain, new life, new love has already begun to grow." She walked back to the lodge finding other retreatants there, writing in their journals.

The second question was, "What do I need to do?" She began to write "I need to be brave enough to open fully to love with Jason, to take the risk, to be vulnerable. The treasure of love is worth anything, even more pain. I also need to keep my commitment to locate my mother, and do some 'peace and reconciliation' work with her." Kate took a deep breath, and looked around. Her gaze connected with Michelle, and they nodded that they would partner to companion one another about the Spirit Walk. They chose to sit outside on a patio overlooking the blue lagoon. Michelle said, "This time, would you like to go first, Mag…I mean, Kate?"

Kate said, "I'd love to." She described every detail she could remember about the stump and its offshoots, then shared what she had written. When she finished, Michelle looked deep into her eyes and said, "Kate, you are radiant. You have made a huge shift. I see your hope, your optimism, your forgiveness, and such loyalty to your mother." They hugged each other tight.

Then Michelle shared, "I was drawn to a gull. I followed it to the edge of the cliff, and realized the cliff was where I needed to be. I am on the edge of change. It is time to release my grief over losing ma mere, and to open my heart to love again. I sent my man away. I had nothing for him. But he has never given up. It's time for him to come home."

After a pause, Kate asked, "And what did the gull say to you?"

"My mother needs me to do dis too. She needs to fly free, and she cannot as long as I am so sad. I never realized I was holding her back with my tristesse."

"Oh, Michelle, such humility you have to open yourself to this truth. And faithfulness to your mother. " Michelle nodded, smiling. Again, they embraced.

By the last day of the retreat, each individual had partnered with everyone there. They had worked as a team during the Virtues Parts Party. They felt as if they had known each other for years. To their surprise, after Marianna had asked each one's permission privately, she said, "You have all given permission for others to have your contact information, except for one, who for professional and personal reasons is not free to do so. If that changes, that individual will contact you." Somehow, they knew it was Kate. She gratefully received their nods of acceptance. She had not gone into any of the details of her work or the danger she'd been subjected to, but perhaps because of her false name at the beginning, they seemed to understand without needing to know.

On the last day, there was a Hawaiian luau at noon, with traditional fare -- poi, kumara, fresh blue fin tuna, bowls of tropical fruit salad with mango, papaya, starfruit and watermelon, and for dessert, Kona coffee with Hawaiian wedding cake. Some of the staff played the ukulele and sang during the sumptuous meal.

After everyone but Kate was packed up, their bags brought to the vans ready to take them to the airport, Marianna led them one last time to their final gathering. They stood in a circle within a grove of palms, the afternoon sun dappling through the fronds. In the center of the circle was a small table covered by a flowered sarong cloth, with a crystal bowl of water. Marianna guided them in "the anointing ceremony", in which pairs stood face to face, and honored

266

one other by naming their virtues, ending with what they saw as the other's core virtue.

Jerry dipped his fingers in the water and said, "Bless you, Kate, for your loyalty to your family, your mother, yourself." Some made the sign of the cross on each other's foreheads. Jerry made a circle. "This is for your medicine wheel, dear Kate."

When it was her turn to honor Jerry, she made a sign for the six-pointed star of Judaism. Jerry laughed, and they hugged each other tight. Then the group reformed the circle and did a round of gratitude. Each briefly shared a gift they were taking and a commitment they were making.

When it was Kate's turn, she looked around into the loving eyes of each person, and said, "The gift I'm taking is joy, and the commitment I'm making is to let love in."

Then the group sang, "Spiritual Companions", a song by composer Radha Sahar of New Zealand. "Spiritual companions on our way back home."

As Kate sat with Moana that evening sharing a light supper of seafood chowder, biscuits and fruit salad, Moana asked her, "What do you think it will be like for you over the next few days, now that the others have gone?"

"You know, Moana, truthfully, though I feel closer to them than to any group of people I have ever known, I'm ready for some solitude.

I need to process the last ten amazing days." Moana nodded and smiled. "Also, I'd like access to a computer, if I may. And to make some long distance calls."

"Of course," said Moana. "Hiroshi will set you up tomorrow in a private office, if you like. You can use Jason's." Was it Moana's imagination, or at the mention of his name, did Kate's eyes suddenly deepen from violet to indigo?

37

Kate sat cross-legged on a towel in the sand at Tranquility Beach, the tiny sheltered cove where she had spent time on the first day of her retreat. She reread her journal, underlining key phrases and words, taking time to pause and reflect, soothed by the gentle hiss of lacy sea foam spreading on the sand. She breathed in the salt air. Then she unwrapped her sarong and dove into the water. It felt like silk over her naked body. *Still cleansing*, she thought.

After a cool shower from the nozzle beside the palm tree, she dressed and once again sat with her journal, this time in the low beach chair. She picked a virtues card randomly from her personal set in a flowered bag given out during the retreat. It was Honor.

The photograph showed Mount Fuji in Japan, with a small red gate at the base of a shrine. Within the definition it said, "Others can trust us to keep our word of honor. When we do things we are ashamed of, we restore our honor by making amends. We do our duty, whatever sacrifice it requires."

She wrote in her journal, "By staying away, my mother was being honorable! She was sacrificing to make amends." The quote on the card from Oprah Winfrey struck Kate with fresh understanding. "If you seek what is honorable, what is good, what is the truth of your life, all the other things you could not imagine come as a matter of course." She wrote, "The Truth of My Life" and underlined it. The insights she received over the past ten days took form as she wrote.

I want to love and be loved.

I am ready to be touched.

I am willing to be safe.

I am open to every blessing Creator has for me.

I am happy.

She pondered "willing to be safe" -- a curious way to say it. An insight occurred to her. She had put herself in danger – in the cold wasteland of the Toronto underground -- to replicate her experience with her mother. "It was the only way to revive my time with her."

Kate turned the page and wrote a new heading: "Find My Mother". She quickly wrote out a plan, step by step. Feeling energized and keen to begin, she gathered her things and went back to the bungalow. She quickly changed and went to find Hiroshi.

38

Charlene's years as a long distance semi driver across the prairies suited her, despite the loneliness that could suddenly cut into her like a knife. Because it was a kind of penance, it also felt right, as if the guilt and pain at losing Katy were being expiated one infinitesimal moment at a time. And it was lucrative. Within a year, she had saved enough to buy a used rig. Sustaining her sobriety was essential to the job, and she attended AA meetings whenever she could.

Charlene found thoughts of the past unbearable, except for consciously reminiscing about what she had learned in Rehab. She recalled the story she heard from Annie Standing Bear about two wolves. The story went that a Cherokee elder told his grandson, "My boy, inside all of us there is a battle going on between two wolves. One is evil. It is anger, jealousy, regret, greed, arrogance, self-pity, guilt, resentment, inferiority, lies, false pride, and superiority. It is the ego.

"The other is good. It is joy, peace, love, hope, serenity, humility, kindness, empathy, generosity, truth, compassion and faith. It is the soul."

The grandson thought about it for a minute and then asked, "Grandfather, which wolf will win?"

The old Cherokee replied, "The one you feed."

The AA slogans Charlene had memorized became her mantras: "Easy does it." "Keep the plug in the jug." "Let go and let God." "Live in the now." And her favorite, "Expect miracles."

To keep the sanity she had fought so hard to attain, she focused on the future. Long distance driving was a meditation for her, and from time to time, intriguing ideas would surface. A dream began to take shape. She pictured a fifties style diner, completely campy and retro, serving juicy burgers, crisp fries, old fashioned malteds, and ice cream sodas, as well as "Indian food" – like caribou burgers on fried bannock. Her diner dream began to morph into a plan.

Charlene took to heart her favorite song, "Hero" by Mariah Carey, especially the lyric, "when you feel like hope is gone, look inside you and be strong. And you'll finally see the truth that a hero lies in you." She often remembered one of Vera's posters that said, "Dare to dream. With God's help, anything is possible."

In the back pages of her journal, she drew up plans for the diner with black and white checkered tile floors, red vinyl seats, a Formica counter and polished wood tables, a juke box with Billboard hits from the Platters, Bobby Darin, Elvis, Bill Haley and the Comets, and Patti Paige. There would be photos of Hollywood legends like

Elvis, Marilyn Monroe and Frank Sinatra, as well as cowboys (and girls) like Tex Ritter, Roy Rogers and Dale Evans, and of course Indians from history too – Cochise, Crazy Horse, and Maria Tall Chief, the ballerina. She once saw the front of a vintage car hanging from the ceiling at the Hard Rock Café in Calgary, and pictured a metallic orange '57 Bel Air Chevy complete with fins and side stripes rotating on a large neon sign outside the diner. She would call it "Gran's Place". She realized that the capital she needed to build it was still a distant possibility. No bank was going to finance a female Indian alcoholic in her first business venture.

One morning, at a truck stop known for its gargantuan breakfasts, she was reading the paper over coffee and flapjacks. Other truckers, their plates piled with bacon, sausage, steak, eggs, toast and flapjacks, teased her about the fact that she never indulged in the "Trucker's brekkie". Suddenly, her eyes widened as she noticed an ad for big rig drivers at a Manitoba mine. The high risk job offered more than triple what she was earning doing long distance hauling. She made a split second decision to apply for it, and just for a while, to stop running.

Within a few weeks Charlene had sold her eighteen wheeler, adding another twenty thousand to her growing nest egg. She found a furnished three-room lakeside cabin for rent on the outskirts of Flin Flon, a tiny town in the lakes area of northern Manitoba.

She transferred her Bank of Montreal account to the local bank after easily qualifying to drive the gigantic mining trucks. The hiring boss said, "To tell you the truth, we find that women keep the rigs operational longer. They're more careful. Are you?"

Charlene said, "My record as a big rig driver is clean as a whistle. No accidents. Yes, I'm careful, and I am absolutely fine sitting on 2000 plus feet pounds of torque."

He grinned at her with respect and shook her hand. She knew she had to be hyper-alert to move the supersized truck around without doing damage, and said a silent prayer of gratitude for the strength Creator was giving her to maintain her sobriety.

Charlene had chosen Flin Flon after checking that it had an AA chapter, and she attended meetings three times a week. She kept away from any sort of social life, knowing in her gut that it would take just a single step on that slippery slope for the bottle to lure her back. The "as is" cabin needed minimal refurbishing. It cost her a few grand to repair the plumbing, buy a new mattress, sheets, towels and a down duvet. She also installed Wi-Fi.

She continued to save the bulk of her ample wages. Her hourly rate was more than she earned waitressing in high school, in a good month. After work, she headed straight home, took a shower, and prepared a quick supper of fruit, cheese, and crackers, sometimes a bowl of popcorn, or scrambled eggs. Then, she turned on her laptop to log onto a long distance learning site. She was slowly earning an associate's degree in business management. She went to bed early, after faithfully writing in her spiritual journal, a practice she started at Women into Healing, said a prayer for Katy, snuggled under the covers and quickly fell asleep, lulled by the crackling embers in the wood burning stove.

One evening, at an AA meeting during her second year in Flin Flon, she met a man. The tall, lanky, well-built Cree, with classic chiseled features, was a recovering alcoholic, and a counselor. He wore jeans, snakeskin boots, and a cowboy shirt. It was as if a door that had slammed shut and stayed locked for a very long time suddenly banged open. Charlene began to take care with her appearance, washed her long black hair with special shampoo that made it shine, and for the first time, looked -- really looked -- into someone's eyes.

The night he came up to her and said, "Hey, good lookin`, want to get together later?", she barely managed a nod. Her cocoon stage was at an end.

Charlene and Phil started going for coffee after Meeting, then saw each other on Saturday nights for several weeks. They talked about his work as a school counselor and hers as a driver. As she began to trust him, she shared her vision for "Gran's Place". He found the idea fascinating, and in the hours he was away from her, Phil began to think about how he could help make her dream a reality. To his surprise, he couldn't picture a future without her, but recognized a skittish quality in her response to him, and didn't want to scare her away with premature talk of commitment.

Charlene could hardly stop herself from touching him, and their hands stayed locked together even when they ate. They avoided further intimacy, having been burned by their own violent pasts, both still carrying a load of guilt. One night, Phil invited her back to his cabin. As they walked in, Charlene turned to him, finally lifting her face for a kiss. "I don't want to hurt you," Phil said.

"Me neither," she said.

"Then we won't," he said, covering her mouth with his own. They moved against each other, groaning with desire and new hope. Phil touched her tenderly, then more roughly. His mouth went to her breast and he knelt and bit down gently. "Oh, dear God," Charlene moaned.

Within moments, they were pulling at each other's clothes, leaving a trail through the living room. Phil pulled back the covers of his bed and they fell, Charlene's legs wrapped around him. They couldn't get close enough. Their first love-making was wild, and fast, bringing a torrential release. They lay together, legs entwined, smiling.

"Well, that was worth the wait," said Charlene stroking his chest.

"Next time it'll last longer," laughed Phil. Charlene didn`t leave until the next day after a night of love-making and a breakfast of Phil's "famous" sausage bannock.

"Do you have to go?" he asked.

"If I don`t go now, I never will."

"Okay by me," he said, holding her close and nuzzling her neck. She couldn`t believe hot desire could be kindled again so easily.

"Whoa, Trigger," she said. "I have to go get some things done, then I need to stand on mother earth and ground myself. You just flew me to the moon."

39

Charlene and Phil were soon married. They freely discussed Charlene's dream for "Gran's Place", and one day, Phil said, "Honey, it's time."

"Time for what?"

"Time to get serious."

"Hey, we got married, didn't we?"

"I mean about 'Gran's Place'."

"Really?" Charlene said, her pulse quickening.

"Yep. I've got quite a nest egg set aside, been saving for years, little by little. Didn't know what I wanted to do with it, but I knew deep down, something would come along. This is it."

"Oh, Phil, I've got one, too! Do you think we can pull it off?"

The next spring, they bought two acres near Provincial Trunk Highway 10, heavily traveled by big trucks, and the building started. Charlene had to cut her hours as a driver to oversee the subcontractors, making sure they followed her designs to the letter, and to order the posters, frames, vinyl seats and black and white marble tiles. She discovered that she loved it. Seeing the bits and pieces come together gave her great satisfaction, and as she regaled Phil each night with the daily dramas and victories of building, he would frown or chortle in empathy. He loved seeing his wife so animated.

It took until the following Fall for the diner to be up and running. The day the '57 Chevy was hung by a giant crane on the sign outside, all the construction workers as well as friends gathered around to whistle and applaud. Charlene was in her glory, and Phil was overjoyed for her. He put his arm around her and whispered, "Best investment I ever made."

Charlene hired Johnny Williams, a Cree chef from Saskatchewan known for flipping the best, juiciest burgers and his "bannock specials", with ground Caribou steak. Charlene told him never to stint on quality. The word soon spread through the trucker community by CB. "Wanna meet up at Gran's Place? They got a special on Moose stew." The diner was full at all hours.

Phil had pretty much stayed away during the building phase, as he didn't want to cramp Charlene's style or have the workers defer to him. But, when he heard about the teens making it their after-school hang out, he started coming around.

"You oughta hang out a shingle saying 'Psychiatric help, 5 cents'", Charlene told him laughingly one evening over burgers and fries. He had started informal one-on-one counseling with individual teens. He would sit alone in a booth, nursing a cup of coffee, and gradually one young person would slip in across from him, and they would talk.

Charlene found that she was particularly drawn to the thin, malnourished, shabbily dressed kids who quietly showed up at the back door late in the evening before closing, trusting she or Chef Johnny would put a brown bag together of leftovers for them. Her heart was moved by these kids, so sad and grateful.

After about five years of steady success with Gran's Place, Phil noticed that Charlene was getting restless. She would hunker over her nightly journal, looking more and more pensive.

One Saturday morning, after they made love, Phil said, "Honey, we need to talk."

"Uh oh, what does that mean?" Charlene said, running her hand over his back.

"Let's have breakfast, and I'll tell you," he said.

As they finished a second cup of strong coffee, Phil said, "I've noticed, Char, something's on your mind. Will you tell me?"

Charlene sighed and said, "I keep thinking about these poor kids, who need so much help. Feeding them just isn't enough anymore. I want to do something more…I don't know, just more. But, it feels selfish or unreasonable to want more or different, with "Gran's" doing so well and all."

"Honey, do you honestly think I wouldn't welcome any idea you have? "Gran's Place" turned out better than we could have imagined. And you know how much I care about the kids."

Charlene jumped up, hugged his neck and said, "Oh, Phil, you're the best! Let me show you something."

She left the room and came back with a magazine, the cover featuring a beaming teen in a cowboy hat astride a horse. "Phil, have you ever heard of equine therapy?"

40

Kate's thoughts of Jason were as constant as the sea breeze. After a while she just surrendered to the longing. What helped her to have a semblance of patience was concentrating on her search for Charlene. She rang Uncle Willy, Aunt Rose, and others in the family, letting them know she was safe. "Please don't ask me about where I am. I promise to fill you in when things settle for me."

What a strange thing for me to say, Kate thought to herself. *I wonder what settling means?* "I've made a decision that I want to find my mother. It's time she and I let go of the past. I want to meet her on new ground," she said. She asked their help in tracking Charlene down.

No one seemed to know anything, but Aunt Rose gave her a glimmer of hope. "I heard from Cousin Sadie out in Alberta that Charlene got married again. Maybe she knows her married name."

"Oh, please find out, Auntie, and call me back, collect."

"How come you're in Hawaii?" Rose asked.

"Please have patience, Auntie, I'll explain everything soon." *I will?*

The next day, Rose rang Kate on the newly purchased "untraceable" cell phone Moana had purchased for her. "Well, Katy girl, you're in luck. I found out that for a long time Charlene was driving a truck cross country, then stayed for several years in Flin Flon, Manitoba. She met a man there and married him. His name is Phillip Pelletier. She opened a business -- a diner -- and then apparently sold it a few years later. Sadie doesn't know where they moved to after Flin Flon, but it's something to go on."

"Aunt Rose, I can't thank you enough for your help."

"No problem, Honey. Just remember your old auntie when you decide to let us know what the Sam Hill is going on." Kate laughed.

After a swim at the cove, she went back to her bungalow to shower and to offer a prayer at the small medicine wheel she had made in front of her bungalow. "May the grandfathers and grandmothers help me to find my mother."

She unlocked Jason's office with the key she'd been given, and closed the door. She leaned against it and inhaled deeply, as if she could capture his scent. She caught a whiff of sage, and smiled.

His shelves were full of books on medicine, psychology, youth, and sacred knowledge, from Native spirituality to the Bible, several books of Vietnamese monk, Thich Nhat Han and the Dalai Lama, *Wellsprings* by Jesuit Anthony de Mello, the ancient Zenda Vesta of Zoroastrianism, the Tibetan Book of the Dead, and the poetry of

Pablo Neruda and Jalalu'Din Rumi. She reverently ran her finger over the spines.

There was a large mahogany desk, pristine and gleaming, a sitting area with a rattan couch and two large chairs, with plump cushions covered in a grey and white floral print. There was a small, well-tended Bird of Paradise in one corner, its deep red and bright yellow offsetting the less flamboyant colors of the furniture. A low glass table held a box of tissues and a bowl of polished stones. She reached in and pulled one out. On the bottom was carved, "Love". *Perfect,* she thought. *How am I going to get anything done in here? Focus, girl, focus!*

She took out the laptop Moana had loaned her, and decided to sit at Jason's desk. As she sank into the high backed brown leather chair, she sighed, acutely aware that Jason had sat in that very space, that she was placing her hands where his had been on the arms of the chair. *Man, I've got it bad.*

She spent the better part of the morning doing searches for Charlene Pelletier without success. Then she googled Phillip Pelletier and dozens of individuals came up. She explored a few of the names which had Facebook accounts, then went back and took a deep breath.

She scanned the remaining individuals until suddenly, she stopped. There was a tiny photo beside one name. She tapped it and an article came up from the Provo Daily Herald in Utah. It had a photo of a tall Indian with high cheek bones and a greying braid holding the bridle of a horse on which a teenaged boy was seated, smiling broadly. The caption read, "Equine Therapy Last Hope for Troubled Teens."

As she read the article, she felt her pulse racing. "Thank you, Creator" she whispered. As she read further, she saw a link for a profile of Young Eagle Strength Project also known as the YES Project. Her finger tips were beginning to tingle. She went to the YES Project website and surfed through the categories, noticing that the project was endorsed by the Boys & Girls Clubs of America, and funded by the Provo Community Foundation as well as United Way.

When she clicked on About Us, she held her breath. There were photos beside each of the staff members along with their bios. Listed among the counselors was Charlene Mackenzie Pelletier. The photo showed a curvaceous, dark-haired woman in her forties wearing a western shirt tucked into slim jeans, with a strong resemblance to Kate. She lit up in a huge smile.

Kate felt the stirrings of elation. She had to tell someone! She raced to Moana's office down the hall. The door was closed, so she went to the front desk and asked, "Lianne, is Moana busy right now?"

"She's writing this morning, so I wouldn't want to disturb her, but if you like I can let her know you want to see her."

"No, that's okay. I'll wait until I see her at lunch. Um, do you know what she's writing?"

Lianne looked around as if imparting a secret, and said, "She doesn't say much about it, but she's a very successful romance writer. She turns out quite a few novels each year. I can tell you, it helps to pay for this place!"

Kate walked away chuckling to herself. She went back to her bungalow to journal her experience of the morning and to offer thanks. The journal had become a genuine companion in which she could share anything and everything. *I hope no one gets a hold of the steamier bits,* she thought. Then, it occurred to her it might be useful to Moana in her next novel. She laughed out loud.

It felt surreal to know where Charlene was. *It didn't even take long once I decided,* she thought. She recalled what Gran used to say, "Creator never steers a parked car. Once you decide to open to His will, there's a shift in your spirit. Change can come real quick. God will guide when you decide."

As she sat in stillness on the deck, lulled by the soughing of the breeze in the palm fronds, and the chirping of birds, she suddenly sat up straight. It dawned on her that for the first time in her careful, compulsively planned life, she was suspended in the unknown. She had no idea where she would go, what she would do, what life she would build, now that her career path was disrupted by a success that forced her to disappear from the scene.

That was one thing she hadn't planned on. Would the Mafia don and his cronies keep searching for her? Could she ever feel safe, knowing Hunter was out there? Would she have to live under an assumed name? It occurred to her that the need to disappear into an unfamiliar life was *like mother like daughter*.

Of all the questions that began swirling in her mind like a sudden hurricane, her relationship with Jason was in its very eye. She really had no idea what his feelings were for her, yet how she longed to hear his voice, to talk it all out with him. She looked at her watch, to check the date. He was due to fly back in two weeks.

For whatever reason, she knew she didn't want to take any further action about contacting Charlene until she had a chance to talk to him about it. *Well, Gran*, she journaled, *I think I know what you'd say*. "Go with the flow, Katy. Trust in the Lord." Once again, the words of the prophet Isaiah came to her: "those who wait on the Lord shall renew their strength. They shall mount up on wings as eagles." She closed her eyes and envisioned herself on the back of grandfather eagle. All she could see for miles as they soared was the sea -- the deep, ever moving, powerful sea. *Creator, help me to be patient*, she wrote. *I wait on your will. Shape my life as you want it to be.*

41

Jason paced his room at the Hilton Doubletree in Toronto, where he had moved once Lonnie, Carlos and Annie were settled in the "safe house", walking distance from his hotel. The days until they would all board the plane for Hawaii crept by at a painfully slow pace, and felt to Jason more like two years than two weeks.

He passed the time transporting the kids to rehab and appointments at the clinic treating them for their colds. He was on tinder hooks waiting for the physician to pronounce them well. He went back to the squat where the other youth remained and talked with them about rehab. None of them felt willing or ready.

He returned to help out at Teen Feed. He took long walks around the city, shared an evening meal with the kids, and returned to his room. The relative lack of activity combined with his longing to see Kate unsettled him as nothing ever had before. He had no idea if she felt as he did, but didn't trust that he could restrain himself once he saw her again. Whether or not they were meant to be together, at least he was doing this one last thing for her, bringing Lonnie out of his troubled life to one that had the potential to launch him in a whole new, healthy way.

Finally, the children were cleared by the clinic, and Jason secured tickets for them all to fly to Kauai. One morning, he arrived at the house and gathered them up after breakfast. "Listen up, kids. It's time for a pow wow." They sat in the small living room, looking a bit nervous. Jason said, "Let's start with a prayer. Anyone want to offer one?"

To Jason's surprise, Lonnie cleared his throat and said, "Yeah. I'd like to." He took a breath and then began to chant in a high, reverberating voice. Then he said, "Creator, thank you for all the blessings you've given us, for healing, for a new chance. Thank you for sending Janie." He had to pause as his chin was trembling, then he continued. "Thank you, God, for Jason's caring and for giving us a new life. Give us the courage to take this journey and keep us strong. All my relations."

Listening to the purity of this child who had been to hell and back touched Jason's soul. There was a long silence as he collected himself. Then he said, "Lonnie, Carlos, and Annie, I honor you all for the courage and strength you've shown to come back from addiction, to hold onto your hope, to say yes to a new life in a strange place. I promise to help you, and trust you to use this opportunity as a gift from Creator." They all nodded. "Now it's time to go to Walmart and get ready for our trip!"

"Yay!" they shouted.

"We're going to Wally's World!" Lonnie said.

Jason handed each of them $100 and a small notebook and pen. "Okay, here's what you need to get: a couple of tee shirts and shorts, a bathing suit, a hoody for cooler evenings, good hiking shoes, a pair of flip flops, something dressier for church or ceremonies, and rain gear as well as a back pack. See what you can do with this, and if you need more I can handle that." They wrote it all down.

The kids had huge grins on their faces, as they pushed their carts around the store. They ticked off each item and about forty-five minutes later, arrived at the checkout where Jason waited.

Annie looked nervous and started blushing. Jason looked at her. "What is it Annie?"

"Is this okay?" she said, holding up a frilly pink summer dress.

"That will look beautiful on you," he said.

She started to cry and Lonnie put a hand on her back. "It's okay, Annie. She never had nothin', uh, anything, like this before," he said. "It's her first time."

After Jason paid for three duffle bags in different colors, one in a bright pink, he introduced the children to a friendly cashier named Helen, whom Jason had briefed. One by one, they placed their new purchases on the counter. She was very patient with them, waiting to ring up each item as they wrote its price on their lists before putting them on the counter. The only thing that exceeded their budgets was a $30 pair of hiking shoes.

Helen waved away Jason's attempt to pay the difference. "Consider it our contribution," she said. Jason looked at her nametag, which said, "Manager".

"Kids, what do you say?" he whispered. Lonnie spoke up first, "Helen, thank you for being so generous."

"And kind," Annie added.

"Yeah," said Carlos, "I didn't know there were so many nice folks in the whole world." He held out his hand, which Helen shook.

"You kids take care," she said, her eyes filling. She turned away and dabbed at her tears.

The next day, they carefully packed and repacked their bags. Annie's dress was the last thing in so she could take it out first and "hang it up right away" when they arrived. They peppered Jason with questions in the taxi en route to Pearson airport.

"What's it like there? Is it hot?"

"Will we still get to be in the same room?"

"Do we have to go to school?"

After about fifteen minutes, Jason said, "When we get to Ho'o Ponopono you'll get an orientation, and all your questions will be answered. You'll also meet the other kids."

"Other kids?!" they shouted. "You mean it won't just be us with old people like you?" Carlos asked, suddenly slapping a hand across his mouth. "I mean..."

Jason laughed. "No worries, kiddo. And no, you won't just be with old people like me. We have about twenty children and teens in residence at the Center. There's a good school nearby. There are dorms. One for boys, and one for girls." Annie's eyes widened.

Annie, you'll meet Laurel when you get there, one of the older girls who will be like a big sister. She'll show you around, and you'll sleep near her room."

"There are rooms?"

Jason nodded, trying not to laugh again. The children followed him through the airport like ducklings, shy yet proud in their crisp new jeans, tee shirts, hoodies and sneakers, which squeaked across the shining floor.

They loaded their duffels into individual carts until they reached the ticketing area. Jason said, "Now we'll consolidate. We'll just use one cart." The kids rolled their carts to where others were nested together, and came running back to Jason. He was quietly in awe of the innocence in their enthusiasm.

He leaned down and said, "Let's offer thanks now." They formed a huddle, and Jason said, "Creator thank you for your grace in bringing us together, for helping Lonnie, Annie, and Carlos to heal.

Bring us safely home. All my relations." Out of the corner of his eye, he noticed Lonnie silently mouthing "home".

"Now, let's stick together. This is a big airport. Do you want to carry your passports yourselves?" They nodded, as he brought the stiff new documents out of his backpack. They all looked a bit awestruck as they opened them to see their photos and names beneath.

"So, that's why we took those funny pictures with the man in the Pharmasave, and weren't allowed to smile," Carlos said.

"And here's some things to put in your backpacks too," Jason said, bringing out three comic books, packs of gum, bags of Sun Chips, apples, and Snickers bars.

"Cool!" said Lonnie. "Jason, you're really a…a good guy. And you're not *too* old."

As they entered the ticket line, faces shining, people saw the little band of Indians and began to smile. The children smiled back. Jason felt as if his heart might grow out of his chest. *I love this work*, he thought. *And you love these young ones,* he heard in the sacred inner voice that often came.

42

Sitting beside Moana at lunch, Kate restrained herself from throwing her arms around her and blurting out the news of finding Charlene on line. She wanted to give Moana a chance to eat first. After a few spoonfuls of pumpkin soup topped with a huge dollop of coconut cream, Moana suddenly put down her spoon turned to Kate and said, "What?"

"What, what?" Kate said.

"Kate, you're practically thrumming and you've hardly touched a bite of your salad. Now spill it, girl!"

She laughed, "You know me so well, Moana. Okay. This morning, I found my mother!"

"Really? Tell me."

"She's remarried, and she's living on a ranch in Utah and they work with kids and…"

"Slow down, child, and take a breath. I can see you're really excited about this."

Kate stopped to breathe. "I think we should eat now, and I'll come to your office when you have time and tell you the rest."

"Yes, that's a very good idea. I'm open right after lunch. Now try to eat something, little bird."

They walked together to Moana's office and Kate wondered how she would manage to digest the half cup of soup and the salad she had force fed herself to please Moana.

"Now," Moana said, as they sat across from one another in oversized cushioned rattan chairs. "Tell Auntie everything."

"Well, first of all, I was amazed at how Creator guided me to the right name." She recounted the long listings of Pelletier and how she had followed the tingling sensation.

"I learned from one of my Aunts that my mother had remarried, and I found her husband Phillip, from a lot of other Phillips, and then traced him. And they've started an equine therapy program, like a last chance for kids in trouble, in Utah and…"

"Just breathe a moment, Kate."

She gulped in some air, not aware she'd been holding her breath as the words came tumbling out. Moana was quiet and alert, waiting for Kate to speak again.

"She looks, she looks," her chin quivering, "she looks like me."

Moana sat patiently. "And?" she said.

"And really for the first time ever I want to see her, but I'm just not sure."

"What aren't you sure about?"

"I'm not sure she wants to see me," she said in a small voice.

"What's it like, not knowing if your mother wants to see you?"

Kate thought a moment and said, "If that's true, then it's really sad, but I discovered on retreat that that could be my own 'vain imagining'".

"Hector projector?" Moana said, smiling gently.

"Yes. My deeper knowing is that she was protecting me by staying away. For her, it was an act of love and sacrifice."

"What would allow you to trust that wisdom, Katy?"

"I guess I need courage," she said.

"And we know you've had plenty of that in your life," said Moana. "Leaning into trust takes a deep level of the courage you've known and practiced for so long."

Kate nodded.

"So, what is the excitement you've been feeling?"

"I guess it's the possibility of actually seeing her again, of connecting with her. Retreat has changed me, changed my heart, and I want her. I need her. I always have."

Moana remained silent, waiting.

"Truthfully, Moana, I want to talk to Jason before I do anything hasty. He's like my anchor."

He's more than that to you, darling, Moana thought. They sat in silence for a few moments, Moana's hands clasped over her belly. Kate settled back against the pillows.

"I never thought I could find her so quickly, you know? I guess once I was ready, Creator knew and showed me the path."

"Kate, you've been incredibly brave doing this work, and I think it's wise of you to take your time with this decision."

"Thank you."

"I have a question."

"When haven't you had a question?" Kate asked, laughing.

"Now that your research is done, what will you do with yourself while you're waiting for Jason and Lonnie to come?"

"Gosh, that's a really good question. You know me. I can't just sit around journaling or even go hiking every day. When I think about the future, my mind just swirls in circles. So I don't want to just sit and reflect for two weeks. Actually, I'd like to do something to earn my keep. You wouldn't accept my check for this extra time, and I'd like to give something back for your generosity in letting me stay after the retreat was over."

"Well, Kate, you know we have many programs here. Programs for healing, physical and spiritual, programs for youth..."

Before she could finish, Kate said, "Yes!"

"Yes, what?"

"Yes, I'd love to be of service in a youth program. I found out how much I love working with kids when I went undercover in Toronto, and met Lonnie. I seem to have a, um, sixth sense with them. But whatever you need, I'd love to help."

"That's a grand offer, Kate. I'm not surprised you're offering to be of service. Okay, let me speak with Tamanu, who heads up the Youth Education and Service program."

"Say, that's the same acronym as the one my mom and her husband work with -- 'The YES Project'.

"Yes!" said Moana, holding out a hand for a high five, her whole body rolling with chuckles.

The next day, Kate decided to breakfast at the Lodge instead of a quick bite in her bungalow. A handsome Polynesian man who looked about her age approached her table and said, "Kate, I'm Tamanu -- Tam. May I sit down?"

"Yes, of course," Kate said, holding out her hand. They shook hands, and he said, "I'm Tam Mathews, team leader for the youth program here at the center. And you're Kate Mackenzie."

"Yes," she said, smiling. "And I'm sure Moana told you I'd like to help."

"Well, we can always use help. Have you had experience working with kids before?"

"Oh, just survival skills," she laughed. "What do you need?"

"Well, Moana tells me you have a spiritual practice, and we're a little lean in that area at the moment. As you know, this is a holistic place, and we strive to meet the physical, mental, emotional, social and spiritual needs of our kids. They all come here broken or damaged and gradually find themselves."

Kate said, "Well, let me think about it, and I'll give you a proposal," she said.

"That would be great. No letterhead or business plan needed though. Just a wee sketch, Mackenzie."

Kate went back to her bungalow smiling.

The next morning, as she sat on her deck gazing at the dawn sky illuminated with pink and gold, she wrote a prayer in her journal, "Creator, thank You for guiding me so faithfully. I give thanks that a good idea comes swiftly through your wisdom. How can I serve these young ones?"

She closed her eyes and waited. Then a picture formed in her mind. She saw them sitting in a circle. She recorded the answer she heard, "Teach them to pray." She waited, then heard, "Teach them to meditate. Help them to know Me and to know themselves."

On a fresh sheet of paper, she drew a sketch of herself sitting in circle with several youth, and beneath it wrote a title, "Honoring Your Spirit: the Courage Circle" There were three bullet points. "1. Know yourself. Know your story; 2. Paths to prayer; 3. The Journey of Meditation.

She found Tam in his office at the lodge and said. "Tam, I started thinking. The kids I know seem to be natural mystics. They're searching for meaning. They're trying to find out who they are, so I believe I have some tools to share." She handed him the single sheet. "Here's my proposal, with a wee sketch as you requested."

"Say, this looks good! I'd like to be in a circle like this myself."

Tam told her she would need to sign a confidentiality form, and that this would be a trial run. "Oh, I know. It's really only for two weeks anyway."

He raised his eyebrows at that, but didn't question her further. "Moana advised me to skip the usual police screening. You must have some mysterious top level clearance around here." Kate just blinked.

They talked about how many she would want in the circle. "I'd like to work with, say, seven to twelve kids, whatever number you think best, and a mix of boys and girls."

He nodded and asked her, "What resources do you need?"

"Well I need a very private place for the circle, because we're going to make some noise, a journal and pen each, drawing supplies, and a way to play some music. And, do you have any drums? Or big pillows for the floor?"

"Yes, we can manage all that. I'll consult my team about the kids who would be up for something like this, and then brief you tomorrow, give you some background on each one."

"Is that absolutely necessary?" she asked.

"Hmm, why do you ask?"

"Well, I trust you and your team to choose the kids, but I would rather not know anything about them ahead of time. I want to meet them without any preconceived ideas, and just see them with fresh eyes."

Tamanu stroked his chin and smiled. "I think you might have something there, Miss Kate."

Two days later, Kate awoke feeling both excited and nervous. She prepared herself with prayer in the medicine wheel in front of her bungalow. This mattered, working with kids on spirituality, especially wounded kids. She thought of an expression she had read once: "the wounded healer". Did she have what it would take to mentor them? How would they react to what she had to offer? Thinking about Lonnie, remembering the trust that had grown between them, and the love, gave her a shot of confidence.

A half hour before her first session was scheduled to begin, Kate walked across the campus to the youth lodge, where Tam had reserved a private room for the circle.

Kate entered a high ceilinged, wood paneled room, with windows open to the breeze. On the walls were colorful paintings of Hawaiians planting, eating fruit together, and playing on a beach.

Within a few minutes, Tam walked in. "Morning, Miss Kate. Let me help you set up. I brought along the drums. You look great by the way." Kate had pulled her long hair into a high pony tail, with a white and yellow frangipani tucked into it, and was wearing a hip length bright purple and white orchid blouse, the staff uniform for the day, skinny white pants and flip flops. "You look like a local," he said.

They moved the chairs into a circle, and Kate tossed some oversized pillows on the floor as well. She placed a small table which she covered with a yellow cloth, and stacked small journals and pens on the table along with a bowl of fresh flowers. She put the drums and art supplies on a long table in the back of the room for later. She also had an I-pod set up with small Bose speakers, on loan from the supply hut.

Tam said, "So, are you all set? I'd be glad to introduce you to the kids."

"That would be helpful," Kate said.

"By the way, there are nine of them, ages thirteen to seventeen. Here is the attendance sheet with their names. Please check them off at each session, since we need to know if they are attending or not." Kate nodded.

She brought out some diamond shaped nametags and colored markers from her bag and placed those on the center table too. She took a deep breath and waited. At a few minutes to ten, the first ones arrived. Tam welcomed them at the door, and asked them to take a seat. Kate smiled and introduced herself to each one, "Hi, I'm Kate. And you are?" She checked each name on the sheet.

At ten sharp, all but one of the nine were present. Tam stood and said, "This is Kate. She's a new volunteer on our staff, and offered to work with you. She could have been assigned to raking the beach, but she decided this would be better." Some kids rolled their eyes and a couple of the girls giggled. "Kate will tell you more about herself. We're lucky to have her. Kate, I'll leave you to it."

Kate said, "Thanks for being reliable and coming on time. Seems that things around here start exactly on time, not island time."

A pretty, dark-skinned girl nodded and said, "You got that right." The kids were a human rainbow: Asian, American Indian, Caucasian and African-American.

Suddenly, a small disheveled boy raced into the room and took a seat. "Sorry, Miss. Sorry I'm late."

"Welcome. Have a seat. My name is Kate, and you are?"

"Charlie, Miss."

Kate said, "Today we'll get to know each other a bit, I'll explain the program we'll be sharing for the next two weeks, and what to expect. First, I'd like to invite each of you to write your names on a nametag on the table, including your first name printed nice and clear, and a symbol of who you are." The kids got busy doing as she asked.

A girl named Yen who looked Chinese said in a crisp American accent, "What do you mean, a symbol?"

"Something that you like, either something real or a design. For example, the Bald Eagle is meaningful for me so I'm going to try to draw one. Not promising anything though!" she laughed.

Yen smiled and nodded. She drew a profile of Diamond Head in the center of her tag, then taped it on her blouse. "Just take another minute to finish up," said Kate. "They're called 'gem tags' to help you remember you are a gem of great value."

"Now, we'll have a short prayer, and then I'm going to play you a song. Please stand with me."

"Creator God, thank you for bringing each of us to this healing place, for blessing us with second chances, for opening us to change, and giving us the gifts of forgiveness, courage and strength to make new beginnings. Help us in this circle to trust one another and ourselves. All my relations."

She said, "Please sit down. This is a song I think you'll all recognize. It's a song about the human spirit." She played "Man in the Mirror" by Michael Jackson.

"I'm gonna make a change,

For once in my life

It's gonna feel real good

Gonna make a difference

Gonna make it right..."

The youth listened, some of them mouthing the words.

Kate said, "What Michael was singing is what this circle is about. This is a Courage Circle. It's about having the courage to look at ourselves and share our stories truthfully, to take an honest look at ourselves -- like Michael says, 'the man (or woman) in the mirror'. We're all here to find a path forward, to change our lives for the better. We're going to do some sharing, a lot of listening, some art and other activities. Here are the boundaries."

She held up a sign: The ART of boundaries: Assertiveness, Respect, and Trust.

"We call on Assertiveness to speak our truth to ourselves and each other about our own experience. I will not expect you to do something you really don't want to do, so speak up if you want to pass. We'll show respect by listening fully, without interrupting, teasing or comparing. We'll practice trust by keeping everything that is said here confidential -- just between us. What we say here stays here. Can you all commit to that? Please show a yes by raising your hand." She looked purposefully around the circle, making eye contact with each one. "Good, then you can all stay." A couple of them laughed.

"So, we're going to start with this list of questions, to get to know one another a bit today." She pointed to a poster taped to the wall with:

My name

Where I'm from

My favorite color

In this circle I hope we do…

In this circle I hope we don't…

I came to Ho'o ponopono because

A virtue I bring to this gathering

"We'll listen to each person, then when he or she is finished, we'll all say, "Welcome, and their name.""

Kate said, "I'll start with myself. My name is Kate. I'm from Canada. My favorite color is purple. In this circle, I hope we will build trust and learn about ourselves. I hope we will have the courage to dive deep. I hope we won't hold back. I came to Ho'oponopono because I needed healing. I just finished a healing retreat, as a participant. And I had nowhere else to go." She noticed their gazes becoming more intense. Pointing to the virtues poster on another wall, she said, "A virtue I bring to this gathering is Hope." She paused.

Keesha, the black girl, said, "Welcome, Kate" and the others followed suit. Kate sat back and smiled, and waved her hand to the boy next to her.

Kate was surprised by the candor with which each of them shared why they had come to the Center. "I had no place to go" was a common one. "I needed to get off the street."

"It was the only option other than suicide," said Keesha.

When each one had shared, Kate said, "What was helpful about that exercise?"

Keesha raised her hand. "Well," she said, "you were a surprise. You look so…so normal and sort of perfect. I thought you were part of the staff, not someone who needed help like us. It made me want to share."

"Thank you for your honesty, Keesha. Anyone else, what was helpful or meaningful?" She unabashedly borrowed this closure and integration question from her experience with Marianna.

Louis, a tall gangly boy with acne scars on his face raised his hand. "It was sort of a 'misery loves company' thing. Kind of comforting to know others had thoughts like mine, like offing myself."

Whoa, Kate thought. *They're getting right to it.* "How many of us have had that thought sometime in our lives?" she asked. Gradually every hand went up, including hers. "So, what kept you going? What kept you alive?" she asked. "Let's go around the circle one by one and listen with compassion and detachment. Do you know what that means?" Several shook their heads.

"Okay, I want you to put your hand on your heart as if you are putting on a strong shield. These two virtues can protect you. You can listen compassionately to each other, yet detachment – the ability to step back – keeps us from taking on each other's feelings."

"Does anyone want to start?" she asked. No one answered. She said, "Well, you know now I'm doing this with you, not to you. So I'm willing to go first. Now, put on those shields. When each of us finishes, others will give that person a virtues acknowledgment, such as my saying to Keesha I saw her honesty. You can say, 'I appreciate' or 'I see your' or 'I honor you for your virtue of…' You can refer to the list on the poster."

Kate spoke of her mother's alcoholism, the abuses she suffered as a child. She ended with, "The worst memory for me was the cold, the freezing cold." And she shivered. "I guess what made me keep going was love, my Da's love, my Gran's. They made me feel like I was worth something, even though my mother was too sick to do that. Okay, that's enough for now." As she looked around the circle, she saw empathy in their eyes.

A Hispanic boy named Alfredo spoke. "Kate, I see your, um, resilience, to survive all that pain and cold. Plus you're a sharp dresser." The laughter splintered the tension.

Another boy said, "I see your wisdom to come to Hawaii, where it's warm!"

More seriously, Keesha said, "You had determination, or you wouldn't be here, determination to keep on keepin' on."

"Thank you for your excellent companioning, including the virtues. Now, would someone write those virtues on my gem tag so I can remember what you said? Who's next?"

As they shared their stories of survival, Kate felt deep respect for each of them. The virtues acknowledgments to each other were accurate and meaningful. They listened with rapt attention. She looked up at the clock on the opposite wall and realized their time was nearly up.

"Thank you all for your openness today. Tomorrow we're going to experience one way to honor the spirit. We'll do some drumming, which is a form of prayer my people practice." She heard murmurs of "Cool!"

"Now let's stand together and have a gratitude circle. Say just one word or phrase of a gift you're taking from our first session." They said things like, "Awesome." "Grateful for you helping us." "I'm not alone."

"Would anyone like to offer a prayer to close?" Keesha raised her hand and nodded to Charlie. Together they sang in gospel style, "Man in the Mirror." Kate thought, *Oh, God, I love them.* She said, "I'll be starting right on time at 10 AM tomorrow. So please be reliable. I'd love to have you with me." She smiled as they nodded and then left.

Charlie stayed behind. "Miss Kate, I really was sorry to be late. I was finishing my chores at the farm."

"Thanks for telling me, Charlie. Sounds like you were being responsible. Is there a way you can be reliable about coming on time tomorrow?"

"Getting up the first time the bell rings. I don't wanna miss any of this!" He grinned hugely and raced off.

Kate thought, *I've never been so in love.*

43

Between planning the sessions and facilitating them, Kate found the days passing quickly. She had little time to yearn for Jason or to obsess about whether he shared her feelings. Suddenly two weeks had gone by. That very night, Jason and Lonnie would be flying into Kauai. She found herself blushing repeatedly as she brushed her hair and dressed for the day in capris and flowered shirt, the staff uniform for the day. *Be the calm in the wind, Katy,* she said to herself, imitating Gran.

At the session that morning, Kate decided to be open with the kids. "I know this is our last session for the moment," she said. "I want to be truthful with you. I'm not sure what my plans are for the next while, but I will let you know when I know. So, this isn't goodbye. As far as I'm concerned, we're family. I love each one of you, and I'm so proud of you for so willingly exploring your spirituality.

"Now, each one of you has committed to one or more spiritual practices -- doing daily kindnesses, regular meditation, and prayer of different kinds. I'm going to take a little time to sort my plans out, but I promise you we will gather again in the next week. And I have a request. Please pray for my discernment, will you?" They nodded.

"Now, let's do a gratitude circle and each share a gift you're taking and a commitment you're making."

Several of them said "I know how to give myself a better life, with Creator's help." Others named the practices they had already created as daily routines. Of course, Keesha led a song that touched them all, "Hero" by Mariah Carey. The words illumined the hope each one of them had found.

"It's a long road
When you face the world alone
No one reaches out a hand
For you to hold
You can find love
If you search within yourself
And the emptiness you felt
Will disappear."

Kate was surprised when the boys came up to give her quick, hard hugs and then received long soft ones from the girls.

She was trembling as she dressed before going to the airport with Moana. She took extra time to shower and wash her hair. She smoothed a light rose-scented coconut oil on her body and in her hair, which was gleaming by the time she finished. She left it flowing loose down her back. She put on a violet and white sarong and a white cotton shawl around her shoulders, and plucked a gardenia for her hair. She went to dinner, but avoided sitting right next to Moana, hoping she wouldn't notice how acutely anxious

Kate felt. Moana looked at her briefly and thought, *Oh, Lord, Jason is a goner! She's gorgeous.* She smiled, and busied herself with her own plate of food, respecting Kate's space, but hoping she would manage to get a few bites into her before they left for the airport after dinner.

Moana and Kate stood in the waiting area at the tiny Kauai airport with fifteen year old Laurel, a "veteran" of the youth program, who would be Annie's mentor, and a boys' counselor named José. Kate was noticeably pale beneath her glowing bronze complexion. As the plane carrying Jason and the three children landed, Kate instinctively moved behind Moana.

"Oh, no you don't," Moana said, chuckling and pulling her out. "You've got to face him sometime. Might as well be now."

"God help me," Kate whispered. Moments later, as Jason and his little band of scared looking children crossed the tarmac, Lonnie suddenly spotted Kate and came barreling toward her. "Janie! Janie!" he screamed, and threw his arms around her waist.

"Oh, Lonnie, my boy."

She hugged him back, then held him at arm's length. "Gosh! You've grown some." He grinned and then grabbed her again. She looked over his head, into Jason's eyes. He looked at her with such hunger and love, that her doubts were well and truly shaken.

As everyone was introduced around, Kate slipped up beside him and took his hand. They looked into each other's eyes, and Kate said, "I'll never be able to thank you enough for bringing him back to me." Before she could think about it, she had wound her arms around his neck, and he held her close.

"Hey, you guys, get a room!" yelled Lonnie. In the van on the way back, Lonnie jumped into the seat beside Kate, and she said, "Lonnie, there's something I need to tell you. Janie was my undercover name. My real name is Kate."

He blinked and then said, "Oookay. I can handle that, I guess. You're still you," and he grabbed her hand.

"We've got a lot of catching up to do, don't we, Lon?"

"Oh, yeah," he said. "So," he whispered. "Is this guy for real?" pointing a thumb at Jason in the front seat. "What about this place? And what the heck are you doing here?"

Kate laughed, seeing her own relentless curiosity mirrored in Lonnie. "We'll have time for all that soon, Lonnie, but I'll tell you this. Yes, Jason's very much for real -- a really good guy you can trust. And the rest is a long story. What I can tell you now is that you couldn't be in a better place. You'll see. We'll talk later. Now look out the window. You don't want to miss the scenery."

"Holy sh--, I mean Holee," said Jason as they rounded a curve, and the ocean view stretched out below the road, shimmering with reflected rose tints of the setting sun.

Once they arrived at the center, the kids were led off to their various dorms, and several staff came up to greet Jason.

Kate said, "Jason, I know you'll be busy getting settled, so I'll leave you to it. We'll catch up later."

He grabbed her hand. "Kate, I need to talk to you tonight. Once I spend a bit of time with the staff, may I come to your bungalow? It won't be long."

"Of course" she said, smiling at him "I'm in Serenity Hale." He couldn't take his eyes off her as she walked off down the gravel path.

Moana looked at him and shook her head, laughing.

"What?" said Jason.

"You are in so deep," she said.

"True."

Kate waited on the deck, watching for Jason. She sipped green tea, and tried to relax, but felt a current running through her body. It was all she could do not to lift off with excitement. The hour seemed to go on forever, and as dusk fell, she saw him round the bend in the path.

Before she knew what she was doing, she was running to meet him. He held his arms out to her, and held her tight, his rapid heartbeat matching her own. He breathed in the fragrance of her hair, then cupped her chin in his hand and gently kissed her. She responded by melting against him and deepening the kiss. He devoured her with his mouth. He could feel tears dampening their cheeks, but didn't know whether they were hers or his own. He nuzzled her soft neck and moaned.

"We have to stop meeting like this," he said, laughing softly, as he gently pried himself away from her, put an arm around her waist, and walked to the bungalow. "We'd better stay out here," he said. Kate just smiled and cried, and held onto his hand.

"Kate, I have something to tell you, I mean ask, er...I mean…" and he visibly reddened in the light spilling from the window.

"Doctor, I've never seen you tongue-tied before," she said coyly. "Let me help you out." He nodded.

"I love you, Jason. I have no idea what the future holds, but if you feel the same, I want to be with you."

He nodded again, as tears coursed down his face. "Oh, Kate, of course I feel the same. I've loved you since we met in Telegraph Creek, maybe even before, and I fought it for a long time. Now I know that Creator wants us to be together. We'll sort out the future – together. A'ole pilikia – no worries! Now come and kiss me, Kate. Oh, I like the sound of that." Kate curled into his lap and he put his hands in her hair and drew her mouth to his. They kissed with blissful desperation, their bodies molding to each other.

"Kate," Jason said, breathlessly. "I love you. And I need to go. The kids are having their orientation, and I promised I'd be there."

"I'll come too, and I love you, Jason."

Lonnie, Annie and Carlos were being oriented in the youth common room. Until Kate and Jason arrived, the three were restless and distracted. Jason knew that the young ones needed to feel grounded by their presence. The kids jumped up from their seats when they saw Jason and Kate walk in, both glowing with happiness. All three started talking at once. Kate and Jason laughed, and hugged them.

"Carry on, José. We're not going anywhere, kids." Jason said.

They added two chairs, bringing Jason and Kate into the circle, and José continued, "I want to talk to you about boundaries. There are only a few, but each one is important, so we ask that you learn them now. Here's a sheet to tell you what they are. They're a promise about how we want to treat each other here -- about respecting each other, using clean language, telling the truth, working things out peacefully, and sharing service. We all have chores to do, and you get to say which of the ones on the list suit you best. Any questions?"

Lonnie, as always the leader of the pack, asked, "So who's paying for this, and whatta we gotta do to pay it back?" José said, "Maybe Jason can explain that one."

Jason said, "Lonnie, I appreciate your assertiveness to ask a hard question. This place is fully funded by various corporations that want to be good citizens – and get tax breaks too -- and by some foundations as well, like United Way.

"The basic philosophy of Ho'o pono pono is that every one of us has the power to make the world a better place, by using our lives as Creator intended, by learning what our gifts are and using them in service. So, our goal is to help you heal what needs to be healed, support you to dream your dreams, and educate you, body, mind and spirit to make them a reality."

"Are you f…, are you kidding me? Is this for real?"

"Good self-discipline there, Lonnie. I can see you're already using clean language." Jason smiled at him. "Yes, there are good people and caring organizations in the world that want to give kids a real chance at life. This isn't the only place like this. We started ours about ten years ago."

"So, like I said, whatta we gotta do?"

"We do ask that everyone who comes here respect the boundaries and give their best effort. The chores that José mentioned could be anything from cooking to farm work, and include keeping your own place clean and tidy."

"Cooking?" said Lonnie, his eyes gleaming. "Janie, er, Kate, remember I told you I wanted to be a chef someday? Could I sign up for cooking?"

Jason said, "I'm sure you can. The chores on the list are the ones that really need helpers so I'm sure the chef would welcome you into his kitchen."

"It's a guy? Cool!" said Lonnie.

"Any other questions?" José said. "You can ask anytime but tonight we want to answer whatever is on your minds now."

"Do we have to go to church?" Carlos asked in a small voice. He had been recruited for a program with some urban missionaries, and had found it humiliating and boring.

"There's no rule about that, but you can get transport to attend services on the Sabbath. We have many diverse Faith communities on Kauai: Jewish, Catholic, Unitarian, Congregational, Baha'i, Mormon, and Buddhist. We have a chapel here for private prayer, and there's a Catholic garden with the Stations of the Cross."

Carlos said, "Really? My mum was Catholic. My whole family was…is."

When the orientation meeting was over, Jason and Kate said goodnight to the kids and walked back to her bungalow, their fingers entwined. Kate felt pulses of light moving up her arm into her body. Touch had always been enmeshed with memories of pain and fear, yet Jason's touch was pure and magnetic. Its sweet power amazed her. She knew she would have to use every ounce of her strength to keep the promise she made to Gran that she would save herself for marriage. And she had no idea if Jason had marriage in mind.

"Let's sit for a little while, Kate, then I'm going to go." Kate felt a mixture of relief and regret.

"There's so much for us to talk about, Jason. I have so many decisions to make. I've been waiting to tell you what's been happening because I wanted to talk it all over with you."

"I'm listening."

321

She took a deep breath. "Well, it feels as if I've been following a path and now it has ended, literally, at a cliff. I cannot imagine the life I am meant to live, the work I should do. My career as a journalist is at a dead end, at least for now. It's just too dangerous. And after being here, Toronto doesn't feel like home, not that it ever did. And there's so much I need to tell you about my mother…"

"Katy, how about tomorrow, you share what has happened during your retreat and we'll start there. And there's 'us' to talk about too."

"Oh, Jason, that would be perfect. So much has changed for me. This place is really magic! And honestly, I can hardly take it in, what we've said tonight."

"And Katy, about something you said earlier…I cannot imagine a future without you. I want you in my life more than I can ever say."

Kate leaned her head back and just took it in. "Yes," she whispered. "Yes, yes."

"I want to say something else, and then I'm going to go and let you think about it. Number one, I want you to be safe. So, maybe you ought to change your name one more time…to Red Deer. I would love for you to be my wife."

As they stood and embraced, Kate whispered, "Yes, with all my heart. And soon, my love, let's make it soon."

44

The next evening, Jason invited Kate to dinner at his home, so that they could consult together about the future. He had asked one of the staff to drive her over. The car climbed a long driveway through a grove of coconut palms to a high bluff overlooking the sea. The car pulled up to a large contemporary two-story house, made of wood, stone and glass. Jason opened the wide polished teak door before Kate could knock. Her smile was so bright, he felt washed in light. He waved at the driver and pulled her inside, then drew her into his arms and buried his face in her neck. "Let me just hold you for a minute."

"Oh, I don't think a minute is quite long enough," she said as she melted against him, putting her arms around his waist and her lips to the base of his throat. Her soft curves molded perfectly to his body.

Jason pulled away and cleared his throat. "Katy, welcome home, I mean, to my home. Oh!" He paused, as if just realizing it would soon be theirs. He smiled into her eyes. "I hope you like it. Anyway, I thought it would be good if we had some privacy tonight to talk about everything that's been on your mind. So, it's only the two of us. And I'm cooking something special for you."

"I've already sampled your cabin cuisine. You really like cooking?"

"Yeah, it's a hobby for me. Why don't you take a look around? There's a glass of fresh lemonade in the front room, and I'll show you more of the house later. Dinner will be ready in a few minutes," he said, as he led her into a sprawling living room, wood floors gleaming, with area rugs in muted colors.

The high ceilinged room was decorated with indigenous carvings, a large rattan sofa covered with white and silver flowered island fabric, and wide matching chairs. Other chairs and side tables were casually arranged around the room. A slice of polished mahogany cut from a huge tree served as a coffee table, featuring pink and coral hibiscus blossoms floating in a crystal bowl. The interior wall was made of smooth, rounded stones, and a stairway of wide wooden steps led to a second floor. On the other side of the stairs, a dining room with a long table set for two at one end paralleled the living room. Kate could smell tantalizing aromas of garlic and onions frying in the kitchen she glimpsed beyond the dining area.

Holee, she thought, gazing out the two-story living room window at the panoramic view of the sea. French doors opened onto a flagstone lanai bordered by a garden of lush flowering plants. There was a barbecue pit, a rope hammock strung between two coconut trees, and several lounge chairs and couches facing the ocean. Kate sat down outside and took in the sunset.

As the sun slowly sank, its reflection left a shimmering path of gold on the sea. She tried to calm her beating heart. *Is this the life I'm meant to live?* she wondered. She grinned like a cat that had found the cream. She was in awe of the profound magnetism between her and Jason. *I never thought it could be like this* she thought, and forced her mind back to the promise she had made to Gran before she died.

"When you meet your true life partner, Kate, I have one request. Marry him and keep the marriage bed sacred. Don't fall into the easy coupling that young people do nowadays. When you make love, your souls connect too. Believe me, it will be worth the wait."

At the time, Kate couldn't imagine coupling with anyone, but she said, "All right, Gran. I promise." Gran went on to give Kate the closest thing to a lecture she had ever made, talking about her course at McGill on gender equality, and what psychologist Rollo May had said -- that in modern times, sex has become trivialized: "The fig leaf has shifted from the genitals to the face."

She went on, "People nowadays act like love doesn't matter, Kate. They hardly *know* each other when they jump into bed. They don't make love, they have sex. I hope to God you will save yourself for your soul-mate, one that Creator chooses for you, one who already knows you and will cherish you as you cherish him." Kate remembered Gran starting to cough, leaning back, drained and pale. She had put her arms around her and whispered, "I promise you, Gran. I promise."

Dinner did not disappoint. "Jason, this is fabulous!" she said, savoring the tender Mahi Mahi steaks covered with sautéed mushrooms, onions and garlic, with mashed breadfruit, corn on the cob, and salad of butter lettuce, thinly sliced cabbage, avocados, sweet tomatoes and yellow star fruit with a piquant lemon tahini dressing. After dinner, needing to keep her hands busy, she insisted on helping to clean up the kitchen, and put the dishes in the dishwasher. She didn't trust herself not to slide her hands over Jason's broad shoulders or into his long hair, pulled back with a thong. Jason was using every ounce of his own self-restraint not to do the same.

Once they were settled in the living room with coffee and a bowl of chocolate covered macadamia nuts and crisp shortbread cookies, Jason said, "Kate, it's all I can do to keep my hands off you, but I really think we should talk."

She nodded and said, "I know, believe me. Which brings up something important I need to tell you." She revealed the promise she had made to Gran, and said, "I honestly never thought it would be a problem, but I've never felt this way before, ever. What can we do, Jason?"

326

"Well, I intend to help you keep that promise, so I promise too. That means we'd better figure it all out pretty quick." They smiled into each other's eyes. "Let's talk about what's been on your mind now. How about I get my laptop and write what we come up with? And I'll sit over here," he said, moving to a straight backed chair.

"Great idea," said Kate, laughing.

Jason listened with rapt attention as Kate told him all about the retreat and the insights she had had. At times she read excerpts from her journal. "I've made a decision. I want my mother in my life. I need her. And she needs to know I've forgiven her."

"Let's make that a goal, Katy. I'll help you any way I can." For the first time, he began to type.

"I've been asking myself where I would live and what I would do. It's so strange to have come to a different world and to feel so at home. And now you're here, and..." She paused and blushed deeply.

"I know, Katy. Our love changes everything."

"Yes," Kate said. "To be honest, I've always buried myself in work. I've been a total workaholic until I came here. It's been an awakening in so many ways -- to beauty, to unstructured time, to reflection, and more than anything to loving you, Jason. I adore you. And my God, what's happening to my body! So much for the untouchable ice queen! It reminds me of a joke Mae West wrote: 'I used to be Snow White, but I drifted.'"

"Stop, Katy, I can't stand it," Jason said, laughing. He suddenly looked more serious. "Okay, I'm going to suggest something. It's taken years for us to find each other. Creator took his time. I don't think we need to wait to get married. Let's do it soon. We need to be together."

She hesitated, "I know. It's just that…"

"What, love?"

"Well, there's one thing that worries me. It haunts me, really. What if that assassin comes after me again? I couldn't bear it if anything happened to you, and I don't want to put you in danger. Just because Sabatano is in prison doesn't mean he has any less power. I want to talk to you about ideas for the future, but last night, I realized we can't trust the future. God forgive me, but that's how I feel."

"Kate, I know you want to protect me as much as I want to protect you. What's your worst fear?"

"That he'll track us down here and do some horrible damage to this dream you've built, and that he'll come after both of us."

Jason was quiet for a long minute. Then he said, "Okay. Here's what I think. Creator didn't bring us this far to leave us now. There must be a way. Let's pray about it and come up with a plan. You know, the Indian tom-tom is always available. I think it's the not knowing that is so terrifying. If we had any information on this guy, we'd have something to go on."

Kate nodded. Then she said, "The other thing that makes me wonder if we can go ahead and marry soon is my people -- I know my family would feel terribly disappointed if they couldn't come to my wedding, and now, I want my mama to be there too. And I've always had a kind of picture in my mind of how it would be."

"Tell me," he said.

Forty five minutes later, they had a plan. They had brainstormed a storybook Hawaiian wedding, even started a guest list of Kate's relatives in Canada. They decided to make contacting Charlene their first priority, and Jason suggested they bring Moana into planning the wedding. "She knows all the local talent – dress designers, florists, musicians, even Keali'i Reichel, who's her cozzie bro."

"So I heard," Kate laughed. "Bubba says he's related to him too."

"Kate, I'm glad we're talking about the tough issues too -- your safety, your career, and how the two go together. I will do everything in my power to track down this bad guy and figure something out. Are you willing to leave that to me?"

"Yes," she whispered.

"Also, I know Creator has a calling for you, and I'll do everything I can to support you, once you've had time to think about what you want to do. Then we can sort it all out. I know we can find a way that both of us can pursue our purpose and also be together."

"I know we will, Jason. And as for my work, I have some ideas, now that I've been doing something entirely different for the Center."

"I can't wait to hear!" he said, "Now let me get you home to your bungalow before people start to talk."

"Too late for that, honey!"

45

The next morning as Kate sat on her deck waking up with a cup of Kona coffee, she realized she had no idea how to approach her mother – write her a letter? Email her at the ranch? Or just fly to Utah and surprise her? *I need to ask for guidance*, she thought. She took out her cell phone and texted Jason, "Please pray for me, Jason. I'm asking Creator for wisdom, for the best way to contact my mother."

He immediately texted back, though it was only six AM. "Of course! Praying now. I love you."

She stood in the medicine wheel and chanted the familiar prayer to the four directions. Suddenly she found herself facing East, where the spirit of Eagle brought wisdom and spiritual insight. "Grandfather, thank you for all you have done for me, your love, your protection and guidance, and now I ask of you, please grant me the wisdom to know how to reach out to my mother."

She waited, eyes closed, her arms raised, and suddenly, a thought came clearly. *Trust me. Trust Jason.* She breathed in that promise.

Then she heard, *Go to your mother, but not without warning. She needs time to prepare.* Kate breathed deeply and murmured, "Thank you, Grandfather. All my relations."

By 7 AM, Kate was sitting in Jason' office at his computer. He was sitting across from his desk. Her eyes were bright, and her face glowed. "Here goes," she said.

She went to the YES website, found Charlene's email and typed, "This is Kate, Mama. I need to see you. It's time we connected. I'd like your permission to come and see you, as soon as possible. Love, Kate." She read it aloud to Jason, and he just nodded. Before she could hesitate or change her mind, she pushed "send," and breathed out a huge sigh. "I'm trusting in God about this Jason. I can only do my part. My mother will do hers. Now, how is your time, today?"

"I have a long staff meeting after breakfast, and then some time in the clinic, but I'm free later this afternoon for a couple of hours. Shall we meet with Moana and share the news? I can tell you right now she'll start planning the wedding before we even invite her to!"

"Yes, let's do it!" Kate said. "I'm going over to have breakfast with Lonnie and the other kids this morning. See you later, gorgeous." She gave him a quick, light kiss, then walked across the gravel trail to the youth area, feeling light and free. A soft breeze ruffled her hair, and she breathed in the delicate scent of frangipani warming in the morning sun. Never in her life, other than summers at the cabin with Gran as a child, had she felt so safe and so loved, despite lingering fears of the one who had hunted her. And never had she felt such radiant joy. The profound passion she felt for Jason was incredible to her. And to her surprise, as she thought about her mother, none of the familiar feelings of fear and rejection arose, only love and hope.

When she walked into the youth dining room, heads swiveled, and half a dozen children and teens rushed to hug her. She laughed and allowed herself to be engulfed in a group hug. "Hey! I knew her first!" Lonnie said in his low husky voice, pushing closer.

Once the other kids ran off to fill their plates, Kate put her arm around Lonnie. "How are you doing, buddy? Do you believe it's for real yet?"

"Yeah, and today I get to help in the kitchen!" he grinned.

"Oh, Lonnie, thank Creator we found you."

"I know," he said. "I do thank him." He smiled up at Kate.

"Come on," she said, "Let's get some breakfast."

The food was laid out buffet style. There were platters of fresh sliced pineapple, mangoes and papayas, as well as yogurt, peanut butter and an assortment of rolls, breads and jams. The next table held covered silver serving dishes warmed over burners, keeping the bacon, sausages, scrambled eggs, and pancakes hot. "Can you believe this, Janie, I mean Kate? Shoot! I'll get it right. Anyway, it's like the Royal bloomin' York."

Kate laughed, "I see you're really cleaning up your language, Lon! Good on you!"

After they ate, Kate checked with José, then asked Lonnie, Carlos, and Annie to stay behind to talk to her. "I want to talk to all of you." Once they settled, she asked, "How was your first couple of nights? What is this like for you so far?"

Annie, usually quiet and withdrawn, was the first to answer. "This is like a dream. Laurel is so nice to me, and it's warm. And the food…"

"You're really feeling grateful, aren't you, Annie?"

She smiled and nodded shyly.

Kate waited. Lonnie spoke up after clearing his throat. "I think this might work. I didn't know there were people like this, except for you, but I'm starting to think it might be for real."

"Sounds like you're beginning to trust," Kate said.

"I guess."

"And what about you, Carlos?"

The small, emaciated ten-year-old said, "It's like they said. It's good. But I'm worried."

"About?"

"This is so far away, we had to get on a big plane and fly across the ocean. How will my Mom ever find me if she ever, um, wanted to?"

"Carlos, you're brave to talk about this. There may be something we can do to try to find her."

"Yeah, but only if she's...um, not on the stuff."

"She's an addict, Carlos?"

"Yeah, she's got it bad. Heroine. And she's in jail, I think. I haven't seen her for a long time, since I was a child."

Kate's face betrayed little of what she was feeling, and remembering. "So, sometimes you wonder what it would be like if she got clean and sober, and came to look for you?" She remembered her own early fantasies that Charlene would appear one day, smiling and healthy, to take her into her arms.

Lonnie said, "Hey Carlos, I've got a news flash. You're still a child." He stopped at a warning look from Kate. "Sorry."

Carlos looked so pitiful, Kate wanted to scoop him up into her arms. *Maybe I will another time*, she thought. She wondered for the first time, how group living would be for a child this young, rather than having a home with parents. She knew the foster care system wasn't an answer, either, but made a note to speak to Jason about it later.

"Carlos, how about we say a prayer for your mom, and ask Jesus to watch over her?"

"Can we do that here?" he said, looking around guiltily. "I was in a foster home once, and they weren't Catholic. They didn't even go to church."

"Of course, we can. Let's do it right now."

46

That afternoon, Kate and Jason sat at arm's length on his lanai so they could talk through some of the issues confronting them -- Kate's next step in reaching out to Charlene, her career options, and also the wedding plans. Kate had also been thinking about Jason's long period as a single man, free to go and do anything anytime. How would marriage impact his mission to follow Creator's will without restrictions?

"Okay, love, come and give me a quick hug, and I do mean quick. We have a lot to talk about, and Moana is joining us later. I think she might suspect what we have to tell her." Kate took advantage of the moment and gave Jason a long, hungry kiss before gently pushing him away. "Okay, now we can talk."

He shook his head, grinning.

"Well, let's talk about our agenda," said Kate. "First, my mother, second, careers, and third, the wedding. Can you think of anything else?" Jason looked a bit puzzled at the use of the plural in careers, but shook his head, and waited. Kate had ordered her own laptop and no longer needed to use Jason's. She quickly typed in the topics for their consultation.

"Okay, let's talk about my mother," Kate said.

"Have you had an answer from her yet?"

"No, not yet," Kate said. "So, what I need to decide is what to do even if I don't hear from her. Creator just said to give her warning, give her a chance to prepare, and I've done that."

"What are you hoping for, Kate?"

"Well, the main thing is, I want to open the door I've kept locked all this time. I have forgiven her, and I believe I even understand her a bit, and I'd like to tell her that. If she's willing, I want her in my life. Most of all, at the moment, I want her at our wedding! Oh, I can't believe I'm saying that word!"

Jason laughed. "So, let's consider next steps."

"You know what? I just want to go. I feel Creator has us in a swift current right now, and I want to go with it."

Jason said, "Say, I have family in Swift Current. Seriously, though, I agree we're in the flow of guidance. Do you want me to come with you?"

"Thanks, Jason, no. This is something I need to do by myself. Just keep praying for me."

"Oh, I will, Katy."

"Okay, I'm going to go at the end of this week. That gives her a few days to respond, but also I want to spend more time with Lonnie and the other kids before I go. Speaking of which, let's talk about careers."

"Yes, let's." Jason had a strange expression on his face. He sat forward, his elbows on his knees.

"So, you know all the preparation I did to become a journalist. The thing is, as I said before, I really have no way to know if Sabatano still has a contract out on me. So it isn't really safe to be in the public eye. Besides, something's changed." She looked pensive.

Jason waited, then said, "What's changed?"

"Well, you know that I offered to help with the youth program, and Moana took me up on it. I loved it, Jason! I used some tools I've experienced in some of my courses and here at the retreat, as well. And the kids were so open and trusting. I fell in love with them."

"I get the impression it's more than mutual," Jason said, smiling.

Kate went on. "Jason, I think what you and your team are doing here is amazing. I can hardly believe the difference it's made in my own life. And I think that even if we weren't getting married, I'd want to be part of it."

Jason said, "Kate, this is fantastic. You fit right into Ho'o pono pono. As you've already discovered, this is a caring community. We work hard to keep our own relationships clean and healthy, which gives us the right to offer healing to people around the world. But don't get me started. Tell me what attracts you to this work."

"Well, I've given it a lot of thought. Even if my career as an investigative journalist weren't at a standstill, I think that I've discovered a different talent working with children and youth, helping them find themselves. It came out of the blue when I was underground in Toronto and met Lonnie. Somehow I knew what to do! It was like riding a raft down a river, effortlessly going with the flow. I've felt that way a few times when I write, but this was every moment. It felt so natural. I want to be part of this life-changing work, to pass the gift on to others, especially Lonnie. And I have a feeling writing will come into it later. Maybe a book…"

"Kate, you're more than welcome to be part of this. You have so much love, experience, and compassion to give. What you're describing reminds me of what Rumi said: 'Let the beauty we love be what we do. There are hundreds of ways to kneel and kiss the ground.' I'm just in awe at the surprises you keep coming up with. When you mentioned careers, is this what you meant?"

"No, Jason, it isn't. This isn't all about me. I've been wondering how our being together will affect your work, your mission, the freedom you're used to. I don't ever want to be the reason you hold back if you're called to serve in some way. I don't ever want to interfere…"

"Oh, my Kate," Jason said as he moved closer and took her in his arms. "Has it occurred to you that together Creator will allow us to do more than I could ever do alone?"

"Oh, Jason. I do love you so."

"Sit down again, Katy. I need a computer or something between us. And we need to follow your agenda and talk about the wedding."

"I thought men didn't like to talk about things like that."

"Well, I enjoy putting on fund-raising shows for the community from time to time. It's a good diversion for me and we have excellent staff with experience in event planning."

"Okay, let's talk about the basics and see how we feel, and then Moana can help us get it all together."

Kate pulled out her journal and opened it to the back pages, where she had sketches and lists. "I haven't computerized this yet. I wanted to talk to you first."

Jason caught a glimpse of a sketch of a form fitting, strapless mermaid dress before Kate quickly turned the page. "You're not supposed to see that before the wedding!"

"Katy, I don't think I could take seeing you in a dress like that until the day we're married. It's perfect for you."

Kate listed the music she'd thought of, the people she wanted to invite, and even a simple ceremony with them writing their own vows. "Do you think if we design our own wedding, we could ask a minister or Justice of the Peace to marry us? Or is it important to you to have a church wedding?"

Jason laughed and said, "I don't how you came up with all of this so quickly, Kate, but anything is possible. And you know that the earth is my church. I'd rather include several spiritual traditions to tell you the truth."

Kate wriggled with excitement at Jason's enthusiasm for her ideas. "So, how do you think Moana will take to this?" They both turned as Moana entered the room.

"Take to what, my darlings?" She looked at Kate's glowing face, then at a beaming Jason, and said, "Don't keep me in suspense, you two." *As if I don't know*, she thought.

Jason put his arm around Kate and said, "Moana, we're getting married!"

"Oh, thank God! Come over here, children, and give your Aunt Moana a hug."

She sat and fanned herself. "I'm so happy for you both. You were made for each other. This is wonderful. How can I help?"

"Well," said Kate. "I've always had this dream..." Moana practically rubbed her hands together, thinking *Oh, yeah, that's what I'm talkin' 'bout!*

"Kate, I would love to help you. As Jason may have told you, I have my own dream team, including an event planner named Naomi we work with for our fund-raising shows. She's a genius with the local vendors."

Jason added, "I told Kate, whatever we need, Moana, you know someone or you have a relative who's an expert in it."

"True!" laughed Moana. "So, when is this event to be?"

Jason and Kate looked at each other. Jason said, "How soon can we get it together, do you think?"

"Hmm. Well, there's a break in the retreat schedule coming up in three weeks, which is Thanksgiving week. That's probably not what you had in mind…"

"Yes!" they shouted in unison.

"It's perfect," Kate said.

"Oh, my, we *are* in a hurry," she grinned.

"Moana, I have to leave for a little while. I've decided to see my mother, and I want her to be here for the wedding."

Moana nodded and smiled. "Katy girl, you have really come a far piece."

"I'm sorry to leave so much on your plate…"

"Have you noticed how I like to pile my plate? No worries at all!"

"Oh, Moana, you're an angel. I need to get in touch with the rest of my family to give them some notice. I'd better do that today. And you too, Jason."

Then Moana did rub her hands together. "Ooh, I love this. Let's get going!"

47

Charlene paced the large bedroom in the log house she and Phil had built. "Phil, I just don't know what to say to her after all this time."

"I don't think it matters much, love, as long as you say something. It's been three days since you got her email. And I know you've been pining for her for years."

"Oh, God, this is bringing it all back, what I did to her. I can't go there again, Phil. I just can't. We've been happy. I've been happy. I just always thought she was better off without me."

"I know, and in your own way, that was a way of loving her. Now she's asking for something new. She wants to connect."

Charlene sat on the bed and leaned into him. "This is the first time I've even thought about taking a drink in all these years."

"Well, we know you won't. What's your biggest fear, Char?"

"That she hates me."

"Did it sound like that from her email?"

She jumped up again, "I don't know! I can't tell. I don't know what she wants from me."

"Well, you've made it through plenty of tough times before. What if you just ask her?"

Charlene put her head in her hands. "Oh, God help me. Okay."

As Kate was packing for the flight to Utah, she saw an email pop up on her phone. Her heartbeat sped up.

It was two lines. "Kate, you'll never know how sorry I am. I don't know what I can ever do to make amends. What can I do for you?"

She's scared, Kate thought. She quickly typed in, "I'm coming to see you. I'd like to talk face to face. I'd like to know my mother."

For the next two days, awaiting Kate's arrival, Charlene hardly sat. She worked feverishly in her garden, spent hours grooming the horses, which had already been groomed, cleaned her house from top to bottom, and prayed. She attended two AA meetings and reconnected with her sponsor of many years, who reminded her of how strong she was.

"You can handle this, whatever happens with Kate," he said. "Call me anytime."

When the plane landed in Salt Lake City that Saturday morning, Kate was practically hyperventilating. "Are you okay?" her seat mate asked.

"Uh, I will be, God willing." When she walked out of baggage claim into the waiting area, she saw an attractive Native couple scanning the passengers, a terrified look on her mother's lovely face.

She walked up to Charlene and said, "Mama?" and burst into tears, as did Charlene.

"Oh, baby," said Charlene said, and then they held each other as Phil looked on, tears in his own eyes.

"Come on, ladies, let's go. You can talk when we get home."

They climbed into an SUV, and Charlene turned toward Kate sitting in the back seat behind Phil, who was driving. She couldn't take her eyes off her daughter. "Katy, you're so beautiful," she said, "and you have your Dad's eyes. I'd forgotten..." Then she cried again as Kate leaned forward, keeping a hand on her shoulder.

Kate said, "Look, I don't want to impose, so I've booked a motel in downtown Provo."

"Oh, no you don't," said Phil. "We'd both love to have you stay with us, that is, if you'd be comfortable."

"Mama, is that okay?"

"Of course, Sweetheart. This is our chance to get to know each other, like you said."

Kate and Charlene curled up on the ends of a brown leather sofa, scarred and soft with age, holding mugs of hot tea. Phil had lit the logs in the large stone fireplace, and left them alone, listening to the fire hiss and crackle.

Charlene was shaking. "I can't believe you're really here. It's so surreal. And I honestly don't know how to start."

"I'd like to, Mama." Kate told her how she missed Charlene from the moment Hiram had taken her away. "I knew even then that you were sick, that you didn't mean to do those hurtful things. What was hard for me, as the years went on, was never hearing from you. I thought you didn't care, that you were just moving on with your life."

Charlene started to interrupt, "But, baby, I was just…"

"Let me finish, Mom."

Charlene sat back, her hand over her heart.

"I've had a good life. Gran was wonderful to me, and I've had an excellent education. We'll talk more about all that later. What I

348

need to tell you is that your letter has been a lifeline for me. I've read it over and over during the years. Then, a few weeks ago, I went to this amazing healing retreat in Hawaii, and I read your letter with new eyes. I saw, maybe for the first time, that you stayed away because you *did* care."

Charlene put down her tea, and covered her face in her hands. Kate moved over and took her in her arms.

"I never thought you'd be able to understand," Charlene said.

"Mama, I need you to know that I forgive you for all of it. I just want you to be in my life."

Charlene looked up, her deep-set eyes full of joy and sorrow. She nodded and hugged Kate tightly. "Yes," she whispered. "Oh, yes."

Kate said, "When you're ready, I want to hear your story, what it's been like for you all this time -- whatever you want to tell me."

"Well," said Charlene, "I'll tell you one thing right now. You're one of the most courageous women I've ever known."

Over dinner, the three conversed about the YES program Phil and Charlene had created. Kate found herself getting really excited about the parallels between their program and the one she was joining at Ho'o pono pono. She said nothing about it, just savored the sound of her mother's enthusiasm as she talked about the changes equine therapy made in the lives of children for whom their program was often a last resort. "It's a kind of healing that is so intuitive and magical, it's hard to believe. The horses are incredibly gentle and playful with kids who are aggressive, and for some of the autistic kids, it's the first time they have related or spoken to another living being. The horses have a knowing, as if they connect to the souls of the damaged. And they've been a lifesaver for me, as has this handsome guy here." She squeezed Phil's hand.

Phil asked, "By the way, how long can you stay, Kate? This is our slow season, so we have plenty of time to visit."

"Well, actually, there's something I'm in the middle of back in Kauai, so I only have a few days. I'm booked to return on Thursday." She wanted to save the big news until after she and her mother had done their cup-emptying.

"Well, we're happy, really happy you came. I can't tell you..." he said, his eyes misting.

Both Kate and Charlene said, "Don't start us again!" And they all laughed.

The days flew by, as Charlene showed Kate the clean, simple youth cottages, the horses, the fields where they worked with the kids. They took a four wheel jeep up to nearby Y Mountain Slide Canyon trail, and hiked, showing Kate some of the areas where the youth experienced wilderness survival camping. She was silently taking notes the whole time in her mind.

Charlene told her, "We find that very clear boundaries are essential for these kids to feel safe. Many of them have had very rough times with alcoholic and drug addicted parents, who are totally unpredictable. Some have attachment disorders."

Suddenly she blushed, realizing what she had just said. In a low voice she said, "Maybe that's why you felt so safe with Gran. She had super clear boundaries, eh?"

"Yes, Mama," Kate smiled tenderly.

The trail opened up into a high meadow. Charlene pointed to a spot up the trail just before it met the open meadow. "Let me give you an example of our boundaries. One of our rules is that these kids, who habitually use the F-bomb in every sentence, have to clean up their language. What they don't realize is that we're teaching them a life-skill, basically a new vocabulary to help them enter society, get jobs, and so on."

Kate nodded, thinking of Lonnie.

"So, if one of the kids says a single swear word, we immediately stop and circle up. They and the whole group have to come up with ten words or phrases they could have used instead, like, 'I feel angry' or 'I'm disappointed,' or 'this is totally frustrating.'"

Suddenly, just before the crest of the trail, Charlene stopped and pointed to the ground. "During the initiation hike and wilderness camp experience, one of the kids got blisters on her heels, and kept mumbling and complaining all the way up the trail. When they got to this point, she threw down her backpack and yelled, 'Fuck this!' and plopped down on the ground.

All the other youth groaned, because it meant putting off arriving that much longer. The counselors stopped immediately and said, 'Circle up!' After about ten minutes of standing there – and they were all thirsty, hungry and exhausted – they came up with the ten other expressions. The girl finally said, 'Sorry'. The counselors then pointed to the meadow three feet in front of them and said, 'This is our campsite.' All the kids fell on the ground moaning, then they laughed. That's how clear our boundaries are."

As they sat on the grass for a picnic, Kate asked, "Mom, how did you get from driving a big rig to this?"

"Well, to tell you the truth it was the furthest thing from my mind until I opened my business."

"What business?"

"That's a long story, honey. I had this dream of a retro diner, and Katy, I did it!" Charlene described the diner down to the chrome bases of the red vinyl seats at the soda counter. "And I named it after your Gran."

"Mom, you are absolutely effing awesome! Excuse the language."

When they stopped laughing, Charlene went on to tell Kate about the kids who started drifting into the backyard of the diner, mostly First Nations teens who rifled through the scraps in the garbage.

"They were dirty and hungry, some were couch surfing at cousins' already crowded homes, others…I don't know how they made it through those cold winters. I started preparing extras, handing out meals, getting to know the kids, and I knew I had to do something more to help them, especially because…"

"I know, Mama."

"The satisfaction of owning my own business was great, but it wasn't enough. I had to give back. So I sold it in turnkey condition, for a very tidy sum. Phil was totally on board with the idea of starting a program for kids, and he had the counseling skills.

Once we had a plan on paper, we were able to get matching funds. We started in Flin Flon, but when we attended a conference on youth programs in Arizona, we heard about the ranch here in Provo. It was the horses that sealed the deal, learning how powerful equine therapy and wilderness experiences can be, even for kids who seem beyond help. When we saw the place, we fell in love with it. So, here we are."

Kate could hardly contain her excitement about the synchronicity between them, both making a radical shift in careers to work with youth. "Mama," she said, "there's so much I want to tell you, but I want to hear the rest of your story first. Do you feel ready to talk about the painful part?"

Charlene had relaxed and bloomed over those few days with her daughter. She nodded and said, "Tonight, after dinner, we'll talk." Later, as they settled onto the couch, she said, "First of all, I'm so grateful to you, and to Creator, that you've come back to me."

She then began to talk about the Women Into Healing Center, which, thanks to Kate's father Hiram, had started her healing journey, then the long haul driving, the mine work in Flin Flon, the years of AA meetings to hold onto her sobriety. They laughed together as Charlene described the tough persona she adopted to fend off the teasing and aggressive overtures of the truckers and miners she worked with, who had gradually accepted her as one of the team.

Charlene told Kate about her grief, her profound sense of loss. "I lost you, my mother, and my husband and worst of all, I packed around a huge load of guilt, because it was my own doing. Sometimes it felt unbearable. As I sobered up, I knew I needed to make contact with you so that you wouldn't think it was your fault --

any of it. That's the ninth step in AA – to make amends except when to do so would injure oneself or others. I felt it would hurt you to have direct contact with me, but a letter felt right. That's when I decided to send the letter to your Gran. I knew she'd give it to you when the time was right."

"Mama, how have you found the strength to stay off the drink?"

"Well, these days, we only hang out with Mormons!" They both roared with laughter.

They talked into the wee hours, and when Charlene seemed complete, Kate took her hand, looked into her eyes and said, "Mama, thank you for your sacrifice, for loving me so much. What awesome resilience to build a new life, and to find the courage to be happy."

Charlene's eyes were sparkling. "Thank you, my darling Katy. You understand! You really understand. Now, what have you been holding back? I can tell you have a lot to say."

"I'd like Phil to be here too. Is he still awake do you think?"

"Oh, yeah, he never sleeps until I come to bed. I'll get him."

Kate told them first about the YES program in Kauai. "Can you believe it?" Charlene just kept grinning and shaking her head in wonder, holding tight to Phil's hand.

"And now, there's another reason I had to come." She took a deep breath. "I'd like you to come to my wedding!"

"Oh, Katy! Really? Who is he? When is it? What...?" Phil patted Charlene on the back. "Whoa, Nellie, let her tell you, love."

Katy told them she had met the love of her life, and that the wedding was only two and a half weeks away. She said, "I know it's getting really late and we're all tired, so I promise to tell you more tomorrow. And yes, Mama, he's gorgeous."

"Holee," said Charlene, sounding just like Gran. "Well, honey, you'd better skedaddle and do what you have to do. We'll be there, I can tell you that. I wouldn't miss it for the world."

"Mama, you need to know, I'm inviting the family."

Charlene gulped and said, "Listen, baby girl, after what you and I have done in the past few days, I can face anything."

Kate said, "No one's ever called me that before, Mama." They smiled sleepily at each other.

"Okay, you two, time for bed. Let's have a prayer first." They bowed their heads and Phil began to chant, then said, "Creator, we thank you for bringing this family back together to walk in the sacred way. All my relations."

48

In the visitors' center of Millhaven maximum security prison in
Ontario, Sabatano sat across the table from two of his men, looking
like an enraged bull about to charge. He leaned forward, his face red,
veins standing out in his neck, and he was breathing hard. Despite
the fact that he was cuffed, and a guard stood looking on from the
back of the room, the men were nervous.

"How did it happen?" he hissed. "Answer me that. This is the second
time the 'merchandise' was lost. This new guy was guaranteed. He
lied about the 'shipment' departing -- to me. He lied to ME! You've
got to do something about the merchandise we lost on this deal. But
first, cancel the contract. He cannot be allowed to carry our line or
anyone's again. Do you get me? Do you know what's at stake for
you two if this does not happen?"

They nodded, "Yes, Boss."

"And when the contract is terminated, I want documentation --
photos. Now, go!" Sabatano had no idea this was the last order he
would ever give.

Within a few days, Hunter's dedicated client cell phone rang.

"Yes?"

"We have a job for you. It's complicated and it's soon. Are you free in the next week?"

"Yeah."

"You'll need to get to Prince Rupert. Do you know it?"

"Of course."

"You have to take a bus as part of a fishing tour from Vancouver, then get on the Spirit of the North ferry run from Port Hardy."

"Why don't you just fly me up?"

"Not this time. Draws too much attention. You need to mix in as part of a group of fishermen. You got fishing gear?"

They sent instructions to a P.O. Box he kept under an alias, along with expense money for the bus up to Port Hardy on Vancouver Island and the cruise up to Rupert. He was told he would receive further directives by one of the local people when he arrived. It was unusual, not knowing the target ahead of time, but he shrugged. The money was excellent. He smirked, thinking, *two kills in BC in one year*. He prided himself on accepting unique and challenging contracts, and thought of himself as "a true berserker" – a warrior who would fling himself into any battle.

Hunter had no suspicions. He was not into media of any kind, other than several untraceable cell phones. He kept his mind concentrated on his work, which he considered an elite skill. Strip clubs, which he frequented several times a week, were his only distraction when he was not working a contract. He had heard nothing of Kate's reappearance. As far as he was concerned, she was just another notch on his belt.

He took the ninety-minute sail on a super ferry from Horseshoe Bay north of Vancouver on the mainland, across to Nanaimo on Vancouver Island. He stood outside in the smoking area most of the time, puffing on hand-rolled cigarettes and enjoying the cool sea breeze. Trips like this were ideal for him to clear his mind before a kill. Gazing across the sun-dappled water, he felt an exultant sense of freedom. He had no one to answer to but clients who came and went, no one to control his whereabouts. After a violent childhood with his single, alcoholic father, then troubled teen years shunted from one foster home to another, he had no desire to be tied down to anyone.

After the trip from the ferry terminal in Nanaimo north to Port Hardy, the tour bus pulled up to the Glen Lyon Inn, a serviceable accommodation with its own bar and restaurant where tourists would overnight before boarding the ferry the next morning.

There was a small balcony off his room jutting over the water, where he could smoke and watch bald eagles diving for fish. The carcass of a large salmon was on the beach below and several of the large black and white birds swooped down to tear at it with their sharp beaks. He enjoyed watching for a while, and then suddenly felt a chill, as if some danger awaited *him*. He looked over his shoulder, then shrugged at the unfamiliar thrill of fear.

After an early breakfast, Hunter got in line with the other bus passengers for the seven-thirty boarding onto the ship. It was a fourteen-hour voyage up the Inland Passage to Prince Rupert, considered one of the most scenic, beautiful and pristine natural areas in the world. There were high mountains and rainforest in all directions. Humpback whales were often spotted as they migrated, and countless waterfalls plunged into the sea. The large, modern ferry moved through the heart of the Great Bear Rainforest. There had been several sightings of the white Spirit Bear in recent years.

It was a gray, rainy day, and Hunter preferred being outside on the back of the boat to watching tourists mill around between the cafeteria and gift shops or standing in a long line for the famous buffet in the lounge. He deliberately went outside during the dinner hour, which started at five pm.

It was already dark, as he stood in a light rain on deck under an overhang, puffing on a cigarette. He was alone, until two men opened the nearby door, and came out chatting about the fishing in Prince Rupert. "I've caught some big mother fuckers before, and this time of year is perfect for it," he heard one of them say. They were wearing typical tourist gear -- expensive Gore-Tex jackets and new hiking boots. He vaguely recognized them from the group on the bus.

One of the men took out a pack of cigarettes and patted his jacket, apparently looking for his lighter. "Damn," he said. "You got a light, Harry?"

"Nah, I left it in my pack. I'm trying to cut down. Just came out for some air."

The smoker turned toward Hunter, and said, "Say, buddy, can you give me a light?" As Hunter reached into his jeans pocket for his lighter, he was grabbed from behind by the non-smoker, and jabbed in the thigh with a hypodermic held by the smoker.

"Hey!" he yelled, his eyelids already fluttering closed. Between them, they swiftly tilted him over the rail, then turned him over on his back. As he dangled there, unconscious, one pulled out a smart phone and took a flash photo, making sure to get a clear focus on his face. They quickly took concrete blocks from a hiding place in the corner and tied them to his legs. More photos were taken. Then they tilted him and slipped him into the churning water.

No one heard the splash.

49

Kate and Jason sat on his veranda on the outdoor couch, backed by large overstuffed pillows facing the shimmering bay, their shoulders touching, their hands linked. As Kate shared all that had happened with Charlene, she could feel Jason's silent, captivated attention.

"Kate, you did it! That's one of the bravest things I know -- to love and forgive after so much hurt. I adore you. Let me hold you a while. Moana's coming over in about a half hour to talk about the wedding plans, so we can't get too carried away."

Kate shifted into Jason's arms and he held her against him, one hand under her head, her body curled around his. Their lips met in soft kisses that quickly deepened into passion. They consumed each other with their mouths. Kate moaned, took one of Jason's arms from behind her back, and kissed his palm, then placed it on her breast. Jason pulled back. "Don't, Katy, this is hard enough."

"Yes, I know," she cooed, "Very hard." She gazed up at him with those thick-lashed eyes of hers and a naughty smile.

Jason sat up and moved her gently beside him. "Look, Katy, you said you wanted to wait until our wedding, to make it sacred."

"I know. I know. I did mean it, at the time. I do mean it."

"Well," said Jason, "I think it's time for a walk around the garden, or something. I made you a promise and I'm going to keep it, if it kills me."

After Moana's visit, they wended their way down to a small dock beside the boat house to watch the sky turn gold with swaths of pink, and huge cumulus clouds edged with glowing crimson mirrored in the still water of the bay. Kate leaned against Jason's muscled shoulder.

"I love you so much, Jason. I never thought I would ever find you."

"I love you more, my Kate."

"We'll see," she said, sighing deeply. "If we keep this up, I'm going to burst."

"Just three more days," he said.

"And thank God, there's still lots to do, although Moana seems to have everything well in hand. I'm getting really excited."

"So, I noticed."

"Oh, don't start me again, Jason." She hit him on the arm.

Moana was waiting for Kate the next morning at breakfast, with a strange, knowing smile on her face. She motioned to her to sit beside her. Kate grabbed a coffee and sat, smiling back at her. "What is it Moana? You look particularly righteous or something, this morning."

Moana sat back and said, "My dear, I have a special wedding present for you and Jason. I've asked him to join us because I'm not going to show it twice. Eat up because we have to go to my office for this present."

Kate looked around and spotted Jason at the breakfast buffet. He sensed her and turned. Their faces lit up. Moana chuckled and shook her head. "You two really are something."

Kate jumped up and made her way to the buffet line. She took small amounts of one or two hot dishes, and a good helping of papaya and mango with yogurt. Jason was eating by the time she got back to the table. Kate had trouble keeping her body out of Jason's gravitational field now, so she sat across from him. She said, "Auntie has something for us."

"I know. She has some highly secret gift. Guess we'll hear all about it soon."

Moana just kept eating and grinning.

Once she closed the door to her office, she said, "I believe this will be one of your more noteworthy wedding gifts, dear ones." She turned the screen of her computer toward them and brought up two articles side by side. "Look at this!"

There was a New York Times article about a huge sting operation across Italy in which one hundred and sixty three members of the 'Ndrangheta mafia gang were arrested, including forty kingpins in Calabria alone, headquarters for the notorious crime syndicate, now one of Italy's biggest. It said that over the last twenty years, it had grown to become the biggest supplier of cocaine in Europe. "Officers also seized 1300 pounds of drugs and a codebook with lists of names and locations…"

Kate said, "Oh my stars! It's happening!"

Beside it was an article in the Toronto Globe and Mail: "Mafia Don Dies of Shock in Prison". Anthony Sabatano, imprisoned as a result of Kate's exposé, was dead. Apparently, the news had triggered a massive heart attack.

Moana said, "Kate, do you know what this means? If there has been a vendetta putting you in danger, it's over. They have enough to worry about, and besides you know how they operate. Sabatano was just one boss. The others could care less about settling any scores for him. I think you can do whatever you want now."

"Oh, Moana, I've already planned to do just that." Kate grabbed her in a huge hug. "Thank you! It's a wonderful present!" Jason was already murmuring a prayer of gratitude.

50

As family members arrived from frozen climes across Canada, they blinked in the golden light, stunned by the beauty of the island. They happily stripped off jackets and sweaters, delighting in the tropical warmth, still in the upper 70's and low 80's in late November. Attractive young staff in bright flowered uniforms escorted them to their bungalows on the Ho'o pono pono property.

On the day of the wedding, Moana's assistant Naomi and her team scurried around efficiently, erecting the flowered arch where Kate and Jason would recite their vows, arranging a sea of flowers everywhere, accented by purple, white and lavender orchids, checking with caterers, setting up the table rounds and chairs in a massive tent erected near a long, white sand beach.

Moana, dressed in a lavender flowered muumuu with a huge fluffy flower ei on her head, perched on the couch in the bridal suite where Kate and Jason would spend their first night together, watching Kate turn in front of the mirror to adjust the sheer veil falling from the back of her simple gardenia tiara, the only adornment on her long, shining hair. She looked as if she were poured into the strapless dress, made of white satin with traces of lace and tiny seed pearls, which clung to her curves from bust to just above her knees, from which layers of chiffon and lace flared out. She wore tiny pearl earrings, and a simple strand of pearls, wedding gifts from Jason. She and Jason had decided to go barefoot, wanting to feel grounded on Mother Earth. Moana sighed in wonder at the unselfconscious beauty of this exquisite woman, the ideal partner for Jason. *I never knew this day would come,* she thought.

"Moana, show me the program again, please," Kate said.

"Katy, all you have to do is watch the celebrant. She'll lead you through the ceremony. She's lovely by the way. I didn't even know Buddhists had nuns. Are you ready with your vows?"

"I hope so. I've been memorizing them for days."

There was a knock on the door, startling Kate. Charlene poked her head in and said, "May I come in?"

"Of course, Mama."

She took Charlene's hand and said, "I can't tell you what it means to me that you're here. And you look beautiful!"

Charlene was wearing a silver sheath, with a sheer, flowing jacket of purple and lavender, to complement the colors chosen for the wedding. Her hair was up in a French braid studded with flowers, and she wore silver earrings with a Haida design of raven, her totem animal, etched on them. "And you look like a princess, my daughter, a beautiful princess."

"Okay, love," said Moana, "here comes your Uncle Willy. It's time."

Willy knocked on the door, and poked his head in. "Ready, Katy girl? Oh, wow."

Charlene quickly slipped out to take her place, standing at the wedding arch across from Jason and his best man Tam. He had chosen a special groomsman to carry the rings in the processional.

Kate said, "Uncle, you look gob-smacked!"

"Well, you're the loveliest thing I've ever seen. Beautiful doesn't really say it…"

"Thank you, Uncle, now please don't let me keel over."

Moana gently handed Kate her bouquet of frangipani and white lilies, and said, "I'll be right ahead of you, darlin'." Kate had asked her to be her Matron of Honor along with Aunt Esther, also clad in lavender. Kate could hear the lone piper start the processional, playing "Highland Wedding", a traditional Scottish call to ceremony. As he finished playing, Keali'i Reichel stepped up beside the wedding arch and blew the conch shell, a tradition in Hawaiian weddings. Then he sang the Hawaiian Wedding Song, Ke Kali Nei Au, acapella, in his smooth, rich voice.

Moana and Esther slowly made their way down the aisle followed by Lonnie, who walked with his shoulders back and his thin chest puffed out, wearing a white suit and white flip flops, his usually wild hair slicked back, proudly carrying a small cushion holding the wedding rings. Annie had agreed to overcome her shyness and began tossing multi-colored rose petals just ahead of Kate and Willy, as they stepped onto the long white cloth spread over the grassy area just off the beach where Jason stood with Tam and the celebrant, Kimiko.

Kate and Willy made their way past smiling family members and friends who rose from their seats when Kate appeared. She looked up and locked eyes with Jason, who was wearing a loose, white on white, flowered collarless silk shirt over grey pants, a lei around his neck. He looked awe-struck, as if Kate was an angel floating toward him down the aisle. Kate took Charlene's outstretched hand and handed her the bouquet. Moana and Esther moved behind Charlene and remained standing as witnesses. Kate and Jason stepped forward under the arch, clasped hands and faced one another.

Kimiko, in a purple silk kimono faced them and the guests. She said, "Aloha, aloha, welcome to you all. We come together on this beautiful day to witness a sacred event. Kate and Jason are blessed by your presence as they commit to one another and their marriage with all their hearts and souls. They have chosen for this wedding and for the life they will share, the theme of unity, of oneness, while honoring diversity. Thank you Mr. McBride for the pipes which honored Kate's Scottish heritage from her father Hiram, and Keali'i for blessing us with a traditional Hawaiian song. We will now hear a Metis prayer chanted by Phil Pelletier, of the bride's family."

"This prayer was handed down to me by my grandfather. It is a privilege to offer it here as a small gift to Kate and Jason." He held a round drum and carved drumstick and began to drum, then chant in a deep voice, which rose higher and higher, into a wail. Then he softly brought his prayer song to a close and continued drumming softly for a few seconds.

"All my relations" said, Kimiko. "This is an indigenous 'amen' that means we are all related to everything under the sun, all that Creator has made. Kate and Jason have asked that you, who are their most cherished relations, participate in their marriage. We will now pass around their rings for you to hold and to bless silently with a prayer or a word of love and support. As we do this, Keali'i, a Kahuna and one of Hawaii's treasures, will sing 'The Road that Never Ends'."

Keali'i began to sing:

"Here we are, in this holy place together,

bearing witness as the two of you become man and wife.

Love...is the circle that surrounds you.

You can find it on the faces of your family & friends.

Love...let it wrap its arms around you and guide you on your journey down the road that never ends."

Kate and Jason smiled radiantly, fingers laced together, basking in the waves of love they felt from this circle of friends and family as people reverently touched and passed the rings.

Kimiko thanked the guests for blessing the rings Kate and Jason would wear throughout their lives, and nodded to Lonnie who was standing very erect. He stepped forward to once again to take the small cushion holding the rings, as it came around to the front.

"Father McCreary, please come forward to bless this marriage."

Kate and Jason knelt before the sandy haired young priest, who placed a hand on each of their heads and recited the Catholic wedding prayer. "O God, who in creating the human race willed that man and wife should be one, join, we pray, in a bond of inseparable love these your servants who are to be united in the covenant of Marriage, so that, as you make their love fruitful, they may become, by your grace, witnesses to charity itself. Through our Lord Jesus Christ, your Son, who lives and reigns with you in the unity of the Holy Spirit, one God, for ever and ever."

Charlene thought to herself, *this is all about healing. Kate has thought of everything.*

Kimiko said, "Thank you, father. I am of the Buddhist tradition, and I would like to share this Buddhist blessing, which I feel really speaks of Kate and Jason's intentions. It was written by Lama Thubten Yeshe:

'Today we promise to dedicate ourselves completely to each other, with body, speech, and mind. In this life, in every situation, in wealth or poverty, in health or sickness, in happiness or difficulty, we will work to help each other perfectly. The purpose of our relationship will be to attain enlightenment by perfecting our kindness and compassion toward all sentient beings.'"

To Kate's surprise, Keesha from her youth group then walked up, wearing a long pink gown, her hair braided into an elaborate crown. She was trembling, but she looked at Kate and smiled. Her voice rose and soared through "Hero." Moana, who had arranged for Keesha to sing, couldn't have known what it would mean to Charlene to hear the song that had helped her climb out of the darkest part of her life.

Marianna came forward, opened a small book. "This is a Baha'i marriage tablet: 'The bond that unites hearts most perfectly is loyalty. True lovers once united must show forth the utmost faithfulness one to another. You must dedicate your knowledge, your talents, your fortunes, your titles, your bodies and your spirits to God and to each other. Let your hearts be spacious, as spacious as the universe of God! No mortal can conceive the union and harmony which God has designed for man and wife. Nourish continually the tree of your union with love and affection, so that it will remain ever green and verdant throughout all seasons and bring forth luscious fruits for the healing of the nations.'"

Kimiko looked out at the crowd then faced Jason and Kate: "Jason Norman Red Deer, Katherine Johns Mackenzie, it's time for your vows and the exchange of rings."

She then nodded to Lonnie, who solemnly held out the pillow with the rings -- simple matching bands of silver with a Haida design of Humming Bird, a symbol of eternal joy and love.

Jason picked up Kate's ring, took her hand in his and slipped it on, saying, "Kate, I love you with all my heart and soul. You are the answer to a question I didn't know I had. I honor you for your brave heart, your compassionate soul, your wise and brilliant mind, your sweet humor, your strength to go through all your fires, your abiding faith, and your passion for service. God willing, together, we will help the people heal. I thank Creator for bringing us together. I will cherish and protect you all the days of my life, and I will love you through all the worlds of God."

Kate placed the ring on Jason's finger and holding his hands in hers, said, "Jason, you are the love of my life, my soul mate, the other half of my being. You have awakened me to healing, wonder and beauty I have never known. Your selfless service and the sacrifices you have made fill me with hope for the world. Your generous spirit, your incredible dedication inspire me to walk beside you, to love and support you always. You are a gift from Creator and I am thankful beyond measure. May we love and serve and grow together forever."

Kate turned to her mother and said, "Mama?" Charlene handed Kate a large book. Kate turned toward the crowd and said, "I dedicate this day to my beloved grandmother, Elvira Johns. This is our family Bible, which Jason and I will sign. Gran, I love you. We love you."

At that moment, a hummingbird darted straight toward Kate and Jason, hovered for a moment and disappeared. There was a hush, and then Kimiko said, "Well, I'd say this marriage is well and truly blessed! On this Thanksgiving day, we truly give thanks that Spirit has brought you two together. Congratulations, Dr. and Mrs. Jason and Kate Mackenzie Red Deer". Everyone applauded as Jason and Kate moved together in a long kiss, then walked swiftly down the aisle, as the photographer snapped picture after picture of the recessional. Bubba and a few other locals played "All You Need is Love" on their ukuleles.

As guests made their way to the reception tent, Kate and Jason and the wedding party walked onto the beach just beyond the flowered arch for more photos. The couple kept gazing into each other's eyes, as if neither could quite believe what had just happened. Finally they were seated at the head table, and took a moment to look around at what was on offer.

There were signs above various serving stations, each with a chef wearing a tall white hat and immaculate chef's jacket. One had a sign, "Luau Buffet" on a long table, bountifully laden with silver chafing dishes and an enormous suckling pig with the traditional apple in its mouth, along with huge dishes of poi and other traditional luau fare.

Another table held a golden brown turkey with every Thanksgiving dish imaginable -- stuffing, yams with marshmallows, green bean and crisp onion casserole. Another smaller table had a sign saying, "Spamalot", with several varieties of spam dishes, a traditional favorite of Hawaiians and Native Canadians. A third station contained fresh lobsters flown in from Nova Scotia live that morning, as well as a beautifully presented whole salmon from British Columbia, and caribou steaks from the Yukon.

There were two "bars", one with champagne and a variety of spirits, the other which read "Virgins Only" which had non-alcoholic Margueritas, "slow grin fizz" shooters, sparkling ciders and non-alcoholic wines, both white and rosé. Servers were taking drink orders and making sure that everyone was served, as a string band played lilting Hawaiian tunes in the background.

Then, tapping glasses with a spoon, Tamanu and Moana stood at the microphone. Moana said, "Raise your glasses to our loving couple, Kate and Jason, two halves of a very beautiful whole."

Tam stepped up and said, "Let us pray. Father mother God, we are all so very thankful to you for blessing us this day with this holy alliance, for all your many gifts, and for this beautiful food. This is a true Thanksgiving for all of us. Amen and all my relations! Please everyone, help yourselves."

Young women in purple, white and silver sarongs began to serve salads, and some came around with baskets of popovers, croissants, and bannock. Kate grabbed a bannock and started laughing. "Moana you've thought of everything!"

Jason said, "Auntie Moana, you are a wonder. Now I know you're going to hit the spam station first, am I right?"

"Of course! Gotta have me some spam," she said.

Jason kept stroking Kate's arm and she said, "Jason, if you don't stop that, I will not even make it through this meal before I…"

"I know, Katy, okay. Let's go grab a bite."

"There you go doing that double entendre thing. Are you aware of how often you do that?"

"Actually, yes" he laughed.

Kate and Jason tried to enjoy their meal, especially the roast pork with crisp crackling, which Kate was eating with her fingers. At one point Jason put her hand to his mouth and started sucking off the grease from each finger.

"Jason," Kate said, as her eyes closed and she fought off a groan, "You're impossible." She dipped her fingers in a finger bowl and dried them.

Suddenly they heard someone at the end of the head table tapping a spoon against a glass. "Oh, here come the speeches," Jason said.

Lonnie stood at the microphone, looking terrified but determined. He had a piece of paper in his hand. He cleared his throat and said, "First, congratulations to Jason and Kate. You deserve each other. You're both so, so, swell! I just wanted to say you're welcome. After all, I'm the one who helped you get together, right?" Kate and Jason nodded.

After speeches from a couple of others, Uncle Willy got up and said, "Time for the first dance." Jason and Kate rose and walked to the dance floor, hand in hand. She put her arms around his neck and he held her waist. The musicians switched to band instruments and played Etta James' "At last". Then, a lovely African American singer stood at the mike and soulfully sang the words:

"At last my love has come along.

My lonely days are over, and life is like a song..."

Kate and Jason moved closer, and he kissed her. The band struck up Michael Bublé's "Everything," and Jason beckoned others to join them. He danced with Moana, and Uncle Willy took Kate into a jerky fox trot. The guests all seemed to be having a grand time.

A chef beckoned to Moana and she steered Kate and Jason toward the small table where the tiered wedding cake stood in its glory, smooth lavender icing adorned with cascading white butter cream roses. On the top tier under a little flowered arch stood the dark-haired bride and groom with tiny leis around their necks. Surrounding them was a circle of children.

~~~

Jason picked Kate up and carried her into the pristine bridal suite. He shut and locked the door. "Come to me," she whispered. They stood together, their hands moving over each other, Jason covering her neck her shoulders her throat with kisses, her head thrown back. Her hands went under his shirt and stroked his muscled chest. They both moaned, and she turned for him to unzip her dress. As it fell to the floor, he scooped it up and laid it on a chair, then turned to see that under the dress, Kate was wearing nothing at all.

As they clung together, Jason said, "Katy, I will be very gentle. I know that I am your first…"

"My last and my always," Kate whispered. "I'm longing for you, Jason."

Their kisses deepened as their hands stroked and explored. "You're so beautiful," Jason whispered. "Oh, my God, Katy, you're ready for me."

Soon, Kate cried out, "HOLEE!" as a shattering release took them both.

They lay back and started laughing. "Yes it was, my love, yes, it certainly was."

51

The next morning after a hearty breakfast served on the lanai outside the wedding bungalow, Kate and Jason drove to a small airstrip where a helicopter waited, with their bags already stowed. "Where are we going, Jason?" Kate asked.

"I told you, Katy, it's a surprise. It's Moana's other gift to us."

The chopper swung up and lifted them over the turquoise bay and the deep navy sea toward a small, private island, which allowed access only to Native Hawaiians. "This means she's adopting us," Jason explained later as they settled into their beach front cottage with a panoramic view of Kauai, with its green mountains and white beaches.

"Is this Heaven?" Kate said, leaning back on the double chaise, her arms above her head.

"Oh, Kate, it is Heaven, because you're with me."

When they weren't making love in the surf, on the veranda, or in the large four poster bed in their bungalow, they ate, swam, walked, and talked.

"Kate, your creativity knows no bounds," Jason said, over fruit and crepes one morning.

"You mean now that I've broken the ice barrier?" she said, wiggling her eyebrows.

"Well, yes, you wild thing. But that isn't what I meant. I was remembering the look on your mom's face when you brought her up to the gifts table, and handed her that check."

All the wedding guests, except for Charlene and Phil, had been informed that in lieu of gifts to the couple, who were very well off and really didn't need household goods, they could contribute to the YES equine therapy program in Provo. A staff member counted the money before the ceremony, and at Kate's instruction made out a check to Charlene Mackenzie Pelletier, earmarked for the program. Charlene looked flabbergasted as she accepted the check for $500,000, which had been "rounded up" substantially by a contribution from Kate's trust.

Kate said, "Mama, you and Phil are giving all you have to these kids. Our family and friends know that this gift is blessed, as you pay it forward for the sake of the kids you serve." The two women threw their arms around each other as the guests erupted in a huge cheer. The wedding photographer captured the moment.

"You know, love," Jason said, "I've been thinking."

"When have you had time to think?" Kate laughed.

"Never mind," he grinned. "I've been thinking about your gift with kids. And Lonnie and I had a man to man chat before the wedding."

Kate drew her legs up, hugging them with her arms. "I'm listening."

"You know the other kids that were in that squat with Lonnie?"

"Yes, it broke my heart to leave them there," Kate said.

"I know. And I keep seeing the face of Kevin, "piano boy", when I had to say goodbye." He cleared his throat. "Well, I have an idea. When Lonnie, Carlos and Annie have found their feet and had some time in the program, what do you say, we all go back…"

Kate jumped up and threw her arms around him, "Oh, Jason. I love you so much! That's a fabulous idea. We could have a rescue team -- kids helping kids. It's probably the only way the others would trust anyone to help them."

That evening, as the setting sun laid out a path of gold in the dappled waves, Kate and Jason stood within a medicine wheel made of shells from the beach. As they faced the four directions, their chants of gratitude echoed across the water -- a pure, sweet song, carrying a promise to the waiting children.

The End

AUTHOR'S NOTES

This is my sixth book, and my first novel. I never considered myself a writer until my mid-forties, when my husband Dan, brother John and I founded The Virtues Project in British Columbia, Canada. We wanted to do something to end the violence, especially murder and suicide among children and youth. To do that, a book was called for, to give parents strategies for raising kind and confident kids who know their own worth and purpose. So, out of necessity, I became a writer. It has become my passion.

My husband Dan, a pediatric clinical psychologist and scholar of the world's sacred texts, did the research, my brother John, a former Walt Disney Imagineer, designed, and I wrote *The Family Virtues Guide*, which became an international best seller, and led me to the Oprah show and our own television series in Canada: "Virtues: A Family Affair". Over the next twenty-five years, as the project grew into a global grass roots movement, other books on virtues followed. Gradually, I have come to know that I am a writer. I never conceived, until recently, that I could also be a novelist.

The idea for this book came out of the virtues-based healing retreats and workshops I have been privileged to facilitate with First Nations across North America, particularly in Canada, as well as in the South Pacific. The stories of "the stolen generation" of children, forced from their villages into religious residential schools are based on the real lives of indigenous Canadians and other native peoples across the world.

The retreats were meant to help them heal the internalized shame and oppression which they continued to carry long after being released from the schools, and to retrieve a sense of their own worth. The virtues approach supported them to honor the values of their traditional culture, and to give them tools for rebuilding their parenting practices.

The residential schools committed many sins against these children, largely because they existed on a premise of unconscious racism, and a sense of superiority of belief and culture -- a belief that they were "saving the savages". The sexual and physical abuses in these schools are legendary, but to me, possibly the greatest abuse was spiritual – the destruction of their pride in themselves and their heritage -- as Kate says to Jason, "true identity theft".

Also, having lost the role models in their families, there was a gap of parenting skills over several generations. The residual grief, even decades after their release from the schools, is profound. This has led to an epidemic of addictions to chemicals and alcohol as self-medication, lateral violence and tragically high rates of suicide.

The Indian residential schools were a network of boarding schools funded by the Canadian and American governments' Indian Affairs departments. In Canada they were administered predominantly by the Roman Catholic Church and Anglican Church of Canada for the purpose of ethnic assimilation in order to "Christianize" and "civilize" more than 150,000 Canadian First Nations children in the late 1800's and mid-1900's. About 70,000 Native Americans in the

U.S. were placed in boarding schools during that same period. Rife with abuse, the schools attempted to "kill the Indian in the child." Some of them were put through a sterilization program. At least six thousand children died while in the custody of the Canadian residential schools, many placed in unmarked graves. The last residential school in Canada, located in Saskatchewan, was closed in 1996.

On June 11, 2008 the consensus that there had been severe damage to these children came to a head with a public apology from Stephen Harper, Prime Minister of Canada. The Indian Residential Schools Settlement Agreement, a Canadian federal court-approved settlement, announced on 8 May 2006, recognized the damage inflicted by the Indian residential schools, and established a $2 billion compensation package for the approximately 86,000 people still living who were forced to attend these schools. It was the largest class action settlement in Canadian history.

As recently as April 2016, after two First Nations communities in Canada declared a state of emergency in the midst of an epidemic of suicides, an article in *The Guardian* linked them to the legacy of the residential school abuses. They wrote that the crisis has turned a spotlight on this long ignored issue. Across the country, suicides and self-inflicted injuries rank as the leading cause of death for First Nations people younger than 44. For First Nations youth, statistics are even bleaker: suicide rates for young First Nation males are ten times higher than for non-indigenous male youths. For young First

Nations women, the suicide rate climbs to a staggering 21 times that of their non-indigenous counterparts. To quote the article in *The Guardian*:

> "We're crying out for help," said Attawapiskat chief Bruce Shisheesh. 'Just about every night there is a suicide attempt.' There is no single reason for the toll. In Attawapiskat, Shisheesh pointed to overcrowded houses riddled with mould, drug abuse and the lack of a recreation centre that could give youth something to do. But mostly, he said, these children have fallen victim to the deeply rooted systemic issues facing Canada's First Nations.
>
> Chief among those is the lingering impact of the country's residential school system, where for decades, more than 150,000 Aboriginal children were carted off in an attempt to forcibly assimilate them into Canadian society.

In Maclean's magazine, author Joseph Boyden wrote: "You can't attempt cultural genocide for 140 years, for seven generations – the last of these schools closing their doors in 1996 – and not expect some very real fallout from that."

While the stories of abuse, escape and generational aftermath in this novel are genuine, I only touched the surface of this catastrophic phenomenon, for good reason. Dan and I drove up to the Yukon to revisit people I had spent time with in virtues healing retreats, some over twenty years earlier, to ask permission to share their stories.

They all said yes. Yet, I particularly hoped for the blessing of a chief who had called on my services and applied The Virtues Project in her community for many years. Originally, this was to be a serious, historical novel focused entirely on the residential school story, but that changed after the chief and I met. Not only did she refuse her blessing, but with righteous anger, she said it was a story that should be told only by a survivor, not by me. I promised to respect her view, and offered to mentor her to write the story if she felt called to do so. This hasn't happened yet, but the offer stands.

I left that meeting feeling an emptiness in my gut, because I honestly felt she would welcome the idea of the story being told. It soon dawned on me that she had granted me a new freedom -- to write whatever I chose, to blend adventure, crime, and romance with the reality of the stories I had been privileged to witness.

Although names and many details have been changed to protect peoples' privacy, the stories of residential school are all based on genuine life experiences of First Nations people I have worked with, including the more positive story of Gran's experience. The healing aspects of our work with First Nations over more than two decades involved deep grief work on the multi-generational losses of self, family and culture, and their redemption through recognizing traditional virtues of unity, generosity, reverence, and honor, and offering virtues-based life-skills for re-parenting themselves and parenting their children.

There are other aspects of the novel that are also real. I spent ten summers at the Canadian wilderness cabin with my "gran", a Scottish elder friend who, in many ways, resembled Kate's Tahltan Tlingit grandmother, Elvira. The description of the cabin where Jason helped Kate to heal is as accurate as my summer memories allow.

The character of Jason is based on a young medicine man I was blessed to know intimately, as a spiritual mentor and abiding friend. The mystical experiences of Kate's vision quest, the message of the fox, and her and Jason's out of body experience together are events I have personally experienced.

Women Into Healing is an actual treatment center outside of Vancouver, BC, and the Virtues Cards and picks are used in healing facilities, hospices, schools and counseling centers across Canada and the world. The retreat in Hawaii and all its exercises are based on similar retreats I have conducted across North America, Europe, Asia, and the South Pacific.

The Forgiveness Fire was created for a Virtues Project retreat on the south island of New Zealand, attended by indigenous Maori, among others. I hope that psychotherapists, healers and Virtues Project facilitators will find these practices useful.

My research on crime syndicates in Canada revealed the elusive 'Ndrangheta as the dominant mafia organization in Toronto and in the cocaine trade internationally. On the very day I was attempting to discern an ending to that aspect of the novel, an amazing synchronicity occurred. A news item appeared in the New York Times that a raid had occurred in Italy virtually dismantling the 'Ndrangheta organization. This, of course, triggered the idea of Sabatano's death in prison.

I began this novel in the Yukon Territory of Canada, and completed it on Aitutaki, our home in the Cook Islands, a tiny comma in the South Pacific. Through the wonders of technology, it is possible, and it is my hope, that Kate and Jason's story will touch and, in a small way, help to heal many hearts.

ACKNOWLEDGMENTS

First of all, I want to thank Boo, my Scottish elder, who built the wilderness cabin on Atlin Lake, where I took refuge and revived over many summers. Her wisdom, charm and humor are reflected in the character of Gran. As my muses, I called on the spirits of three authors I have loved and found inspiring in their own genres. Gene Stratton Porter, who celebrated idealism, a love for nature's gifts, and the triumph of the human spirit in books such as *Freckles* and *Girl of the Limberlost* -- sources of great inspiration during my childhood; Anne Morrow Lindbergh, whose writings reflect the delicacy of contained emotion with such grace. Her personal resilience and endurance were among Anne's core virtues as the wife of Charles Lindbergh, the famous American aviator, a man under relentless public scrutiny for his unpopular isolationist views during World War II. Anne and Charles also experienced the devastating loss of their kidnapped child. I am particularly grateful for her classic book, *Gift from the Sea*, which soothed my soul during my years as a young mother; and Agatha Christie, a creative genius with plot, who I like to believe helped me with the twists and surprises as my book unfolded. Thank you for your inspiring help with this debut novel.

Frances Dick, a First Nations artist who served as Education Director for the Tsawateineuk First Nation in Kingcome Inlet, for inviting me and Dan to give the first ever Virtues Project workshop. Kingcome Inlet is the village named in *I Heard the Owl Call My*

Name by Margaret Craven. Dan and I were invited back twenty years later to discover The Virtues Project still in use, and a well-used virtues poster still adorning the school wall.

Diana Gray Eyes, Director of SOARS (Society of Addiction Recovery Services) applied The Virtues Project broadly, and took me to Ottawa where a government minister said The Virtues Project had been taken to heart within First Nations cultures across Canada more than any other program, because of its respect for traditional culture. Gratitude to the Aboriginal Healing Foundation for funding much of our work across Canada.

A special nod to Charlotte Johns Hadden, Bobby Smith, Rose Caesar, Teddy (moose hunter extraordinaire) and his wife Mary, and Robert Greenway for all they shared. Sadie Greenaway, long time director of Kaakawis and Kaackamin Family Development Centres for creating a culture of virtues for staff and client families over two decades. The people of Liard First Nation especially Chief Anne Maje, for being a keeper of hope for her people, and for opening her community and many others across the north, to the virtues healing strategies.

I am grateful for the contributions to what I consider soulful psychology from Virginia Satir, author of *Peoplemaking,* and the prolific author and retreat leader, Bill Plotkin, author of *Soulcraft*: Crossing into the Mysteries of Nature and Psyche; for the inspiring works of His Holiness, The Dalai Lama; Jesuit mystic, Anthony De Mellow (particularly his book, *Wellsprings*); Vietnamese monk,

Thich Nhat Han (*Peace is Every Step* et al); the luminous poetry of Sufi mystic Jalal'u'din Rumi; and poet Pablo Neruda; the Holy Bible, and many sacred texts including the Writings of the Baha'i Faith (www.bahai.org)

My first readers were enormously helpful. The "She-bears" -- friends who have been gathering at a river or lake for a week each summer for twenty years: Betsy Lydle Smith, Cheryll Simmons, Pat Johnson, Terrie Ward, Kara Hunnicutt, Barbara Rosencranz, and Pamela Auffray. With utter vulnerability and a combination of hope and dread, I read my virginal first chapter aloud to them. There was a moment of silence, followed by a loud collective scream. That scream gave me a great boost of confidence that I could indeed write a novel, especially when they begged me to continue reading other chapters, which I did at bedtime. She-Bears Kate Marsh and Brigitte Aiff were unable to attend that summer, but have still cheered me on. Pat Johnson and Terrie Ward gave invaluable feedback to the early version.

Another friend who encouraged me was 98 year old Eleitino Paddy Walker, my Samoan guardian angel on a visit to her beachfront home, "Happiness House", in Rarotonga, Cook Islands. When I expressed doubts about writing a novel, she said, in her inimitable way, "Don't be ridiculous, Linda, it won't come from you, but through you, like everything else you've done."

I was blessed to have, as another first reader and astute critic, my beloved brother, Tommy Kavelin, an avid reader and an eloquent man of words. He visited us in Aitutaki while the book was still gestational, and laughed and cried as I read aloud.

I am thankful to my island sister, Paula Maoate on Aitutaki for her enthusiasm and encouragement over many months of hearing details of the unfolding story, both of my writing process and the content of the book.

Many thanks to the exquisitely honest Julie Brooks, an American artist residing in Aitutaki, who read the first draft with acumen and an eagle eye.

I appreciate the willing permission of artist, Judy Currelly, Boo's daughter, for me to mention Boo by name in these notes and to use a photo I took of the cabin on my website.

Thanks to my friend, David Hadden, for his positive comments after reading part of an early version of the book. I value his opinion greatly. David was a dear friend of Boo's and helped her to construct her wilderness cabin on Atlin Lake in northern British Columbia.

My cherished sister friend, Evelyn Eiras Belzer, with whom I have been close since we met amidst the frightening masses milling about on the first day of high school in Manhasset, Long Island, was my final "first" reader. I treasure her incisive and intelligent insights, as a dedicated reader of many novels as well as non-fiction.

Finally, to the love of my life, my husband, Dr. Dan Popov, now known as Papa Dan, the island sunset photographer, for his companionship as we made the long drive to the Yukon several years ago to reconnect with survivors I had known. He summoned incredible patience and encouragement when I plunged into the writing, talking endlessly and often tearfully about the characters as they grew and evolved and even populated my dreams. Dan also helped to conceive of the death of Hunter. Finally, he has generously provided his artistic sense to the lay-out and cover of the book, which is a photo of the Northern Lights Kate (and I) saw from the window of the cabin.

All my relations, Linda

Subscribe free to Linda's blog at www.gracefulendings.net, www.lindakavelinpopov.com or on Facebook.